THE YEAR OF THE BEAR

ENDORSEMENTS

"Bears can move and climb surprisingly quickly; so, too, does this fast-paced and highly satisfying debut novel set in rural Maine, richly evoked. *The Year of the Bear* tells a coming-of-age story, its action seamlessly interwoven with moments of indigenous wisdom, personal discovery, and universal truth. If the immediate experience is cinematic, its aftereffect is inspirational. A compelling and uplifting work."

Scott Mason
Author of *The Wonder Code: Discover the Way of Haiku and See the World with New Eyes*

"Fans of classic, enthralling adventure (and I'm one) are in for a rare treat."

Josh Lieb
New York Times best-selling and Emmy Award-winning author of *I am a Genius of Unspeakable Evil* and *I Want to Be Your Class President*

"*The Year of the Bear* is a wonderful coming-of-age story. Jason, our young protagonist, faces a series of challenges, both physical and emotional, and comes out as a better young man as a result. The adventurous story draws you in, and the development of the characters keeps you reading. Congratulations on a wonderful story."

Robert Ford, Jr.
2014 Footlocker Co-National Coach of the Year

"A Newbery award contender, for sure!"

Katie Cruice Smith
Senior editor and author of *Why Did You Choose Me?*

"This is truly a powerful coming-of-age story which connects the expanse of nature and human emotion at a level of intensity that carries the reader deep into the lives of its characters. A rich and engaging read!"

Rev. Dr. Cheryl L. Tatham
Minister, North Chevy Chase Christian Church, Chevy Chase, MD

"*The Year of the Bear* is an exciting and exhilarating novel that will keep both students and adults on the edge of their seats. Mr. Lanzo does a fantastic job of bringing the characters to life and allowing young adults to make real world connections to the subject matter and the characters in his work. *The Year of the Bear* is an engaging and compelling read."

Gregory D. Pacific, PhD
Board of Directors/Faculty
Akamai University
Durham, North Carolina

"As a child my grade school teachers read the Laura Ingalls Wilder books to us after lunch. Her descriptions were so clear that it seemed like I was transported into their lives. The time was different, but the place was nearby. Reading *The Year of the Bear* gives me that same feeling. The detailed descriptions of the land, lakes, rivers, with their plants and animals have described a place I have never seen, but I feel like I now know and am walking with Jason and his whole "family." And the personalities of each of the characters are different, and yet they understand and love each other."

Pastor Roger Berner
Current pastor of Lutheran Church of Our Savior, Port Washington, New York
Former Pastor for 28 Years of Trinity Lutheran Church in Rockville, Maryland

DOUGLAS J. LANZO

THE YEAR OF THE BEAR

A NOVEL

AMBASSADOR INTERNATIONAL
GREENVILLE, SOUTH CAROLINA & BELFAST, NORTHERN IRELAND

www.ambassador-international.com

THE YEAR OF THE BEAR

Hardcover ISBN: 978-1-64960-468-2
Paperback ISBN: 978-1-64960-210-7
eISBN: 978-1-64960-318-0
Library of Congress Control Number: 2022944232

Editing by Daphne Self and Katie Cruice Smith
Cover design by Hannah Linder Designs
Interior typesetting by Dentelle Design

AMBASSADOR INTERNATIONAL
Emerald House
411 University Ridge, Suite B14
Greenville, SC 29601
United States
www.ambassador-international.com

AMBASSADOR BOOKS
The Mount
2 Woodstock Link
Belfast, BT6 8DD
Northern Ireland, United Kingdom
www.ambassadormedia.co.uk

The colophon is a trademark of Ambassador, a Christian publishing company.

To my identical twin sons, Gregory and Alexander, who brighten each day and inspire much of my creative writing.

In the words of my "Lighting up Life's Sky" poem published in Time of Singing's *Spring 2021 Issue:*

Pollux and Castor
Gemini twin stars of spring
brighten my night sky
commemorating the birth
of my precious lights—twin boys.

They loved The Year of the Bear *and strongly encouraged me to publish it. The rest is history . . .*

AUTHOR'S NOTE

The Year of the Bear is a novel of inspiration steeped in the remarkable coming-of-age story of Jason Wilson, a larger-than-life tale of a seemingly ordinary teenager confronted by extraordinary events which transform his heart, mind, and spirit. While fictional and legendary in nature and more exciting than most teenage lives, the novel was inspired by a confluence of passions, influences, and experiences.

Haunted by the life and death connections between humans and black bears in *Legends of the Fall,* I searched my mind for the genesis of the incredibly close connection I have felt to nature since childhood. Memories flashed to my earliest days as a Connecticut toddler tentatively touching a lobster with taped claws on our kitchen floor to mornings chasing our bacon-stealing Chihuahua into his thieving, under-bed den to afternoons launching our talkative Myna into circular flights around our living room. Recollections proceeded to kindergarten days catching a yellow ring-necked snake by the back of its neck while picking up our mail and tossing apple slices to red squirrels encamped on our back porch. This made-to-order red squirrel feast followed on the heels of a record blizzard that converted our steep, rural street into a carless course for sledding.

adults typically weighing between 125 pounds for females and five hundred pounds for males. By the completion of a black bear cub's first year in the wild nursed and mentored by its mother, it normally weighs eighty pounds and has learned many skills necessary for its survival, including to varying degrees, how to forage, fish, hunt, scale trees, and avoid male black bears.

This is vitally important, as male black bears other than their father will, upon encountering a mother with her cubs, sometimes kill the cubs in order to induce the female to go into heat earlier than she otherwise would. Absent such an abhorrent occurrence, the mother black bear spends sixteen to seventeen months with her cubs, nursing them, snuggling with them, and closely bonding with them prior to their abrupt parting of ways during the breeding season of their second spring together.

Given that bears in general boast the highest brain-to-body bass of all carnivores in the world, it is unsurprising that black bears are exceptionally inquisitive creatures. In fact, they demonstrate effective planning and adaptation that enables them to thrive across a range of habitats and environments spanning from Mexico to Alaska. Significant populations of black bears inhabit the northernmost ranges of the Appalachian Trail, with an estimated population of between twenty-four thousand and thirty-six thousand black bears found in Maine.

An admirer of Native Americans and their respectful co-existence with nature since my childhood days, I decided to research more fully the ties of Native Americans to black bears. In doing so, I became engrossed with the history and culture of Penobscot Indians and their legendary ties to black bears.

According to Penobscot legend, a Penobscot boy traveling with his family to a great council in Canada became lost in the wilderness. Unbeknownst to his distraught family, the boy became adopted and lovingly cared for by a black bear family. A Penobscot, who was disrespected among his tribe for laziness, searched for the boy. Unfortunately, as the story goes, he slaughtered the entire black bear family by their den, despite each bear's displaying a trademark birchbark canoe of the Penobscot people. His black bear family needlessly slain, the "orphaned" boy huddled in a dark corner of a cave weeping for them. Returned to his human family by the Penobscot, the boy began to grow bear bristles. Though he ultimately grew up to be a Penobscot, the grown man and his lineage have ever since been called Bears by the entire Penobscot people, marking the legendary founding of the revered Bear Clan. These ties between black bears and the Penobscots, passed down from generation to generation, powerfully manifest themselves within *The Year of the Bear.*

Sasquot, his daughter, Autumn, and his wife, Zephyr are each prominent figures in *The Year of the Bear* and members of the Bear Clan of the Penobscot tribe. The Penobscots traditionally were Abenaki-speaking members of the Wabanaki Confederacy. This Confederacy spanned portions of New York, Maine, New Hampshire, and Vermont and united a number of adjoining tribes, namely the Passamaquoddy, Penobscot, Malecite, Mi'kmaq, Cowasuck, and Sokoki nations. The alliance formed in the late 1600s as a defensive counter to increasingly brazen raids by enemy Iroquois and decimating battles against English-allied forces. In *The Year of the Bear,* terminology is used regarding the

Native Americans that is historically accurate but no longer in use today.

Tribes of the Wabanaki Confederacy, including the Penobscots, traditionally have called themselves "People of the Dawnland," and the very name Wabanaki translates as "Dawnland." This is an especially fitting appellation for the Penobscots, who inhabited the environs of Mount Katahdin in addition to other territories along the Penobscot River Basin. This peak stands as the northernmost terminus of the Appalachian Trail and one of the first points of sunlight in the United States each day. The Penobscots named this majestic peak, the highest in all of Maine, Mount Katahdin, which translates as "The Greatest Peak." They revered it as a sacred mountain inhabited and protected by a feared god of thunder and saw the mountain as a symbol of birth and spiritual enlightenment.

Unsuccessfully attempted to be summitted by Henry David Thoreau and then successfully scaled by Teddy Roosevelt before he became president, Katahdin's significance was readily recognized by all those who had the privilege of gazing at its beauty, let alone those fortunate and hardy enough to climb it. Mount Katahdin was established within Baxter State Park by the great Maine governor and philanthropist, Percival Baxter, who, opposed by timber companies and hunters alike, could not persuade Maine's legislature to purchase it. Refusing to give up given how deeply Governor Baxter felt the need to preserve the magnificent tract of land, he personally purchased the tract and then donated it to the public, thereby founding Baxter State Park. In the engraved words of a plaque on a boulder by Katahdin Stream that encapsulates the governor's spirit and is sometimes even directly attributed to him: "Man is born to die. His works are short-lived. Buildings crumble, monuments decay, and wealth vanishes, but Katahdin in all its glory forever shall remain the mountain of the people of Maine."

The novel primarily takes place within the pristine mountain-lake environs of Moosehead Lake in Maine, comprising ancestral lands of the Penobscot people. Indeed, the Penobscots' very name derives from a rocky portion of the mighty Penobscot River. The Penobscots traditionally were a peaceful tribe of hunters, fishermen, traders, and—to a lesser extent—farmers, whose homeland spanned the entire length of the Penobscot River.

To this day, as the second longest river in Maine, the Penobscot River flows with mighty schools of spawning salmon, shad, and alewife, together with brook trout, white perch, and chain pickerel. The picturesque river features rocky stretches of whitewater rapids navigated for centuries by Penobscots paddling birchbark canoes. Penobscot legend holds that their namesake river formed from the piercing of a greedy frog destructively gorging itself on the regions' waters by a tree wielded by Gluskabe, a legendary hero whose name translates as "Man [created] only from speech."

Another influence on *The Year of the Bear* has been my love of cross-country ever since my high school and college years running cross-country across New England, New York, and New Jersey. Protagonist Jason Wilson experiences epic cross-country battles, challenging him in unexpected and personally transforming ways both on and off the course. With Footlocker National Coaches of the Year Robert Ford, Junior and Senior, as coaches and mentors during high school, a love of running and quest to be the best runner I could be for both team and personal fulfillment became a significant part of my life. Running a rare sixteen-hundred-meter, thirty-two-hundred-meter, and five-thousand-meter combination during each high school track meet, I set Fairfield Prep's five-thousand-meter and cross-country course records and became an All-State Cross-Country and Track Athlete and Fairfield Prep's Scholar-Athlete. I was, likewise, honored to be able to run as a Division One walk-on at Harvard, becoming a varsity runner named as the Scholar-Athlete of the Mens' Cross-Country Team.

The main inspiration for the timing of releasing *The Year of the Bear* has been the COVID-19 pandemic. Although I had written a handful of poems every year since my twin sons' toddler years, I did not seriously market any of these poems in national or international literary journals until the onset of the pandemic. At that time, I prayed that God would bless my poetry and use it to inspire and offer hope, glorifying Him in the process.

Beyond my wildest expectations, my poetry has exploded nationally and internationally ever since, with over 240 poems subsequently having been published in over fifty literary journals to date and five anthologies across ten countries on five continents. This prolific explosion has led to my poetry being featured in numerous literary journals and garnering an award in my first haiku competition. Similar to my yearning to share poems with readers around the world, during the summer of 2021, I felt led to share this powerful and inspirational novel through publishing it with a well-established and reputable publisher with an international reach. Within weeks of submission, God blessed my novel with a publication contract with Ambassador International, a distinguished international publisher of high ethics and integrity.

None of this would have been possible were it not for God's inspiration and the encouragement and support of countless others. These include dear friends, family, colleagues, ministers, fellow lovers of nature and the rich history of Maine and of Native Americans, former teammates and coaches, the entire team at Ambassador International, readers of my poetry and my twin sons' poetry, and fans around the globe captivated by *The Year of the Bear*'s story. I hope that *The Year of the Bear* will likewise immerse you in its exhilarating journey.

Welcome to the great adventure, which lies within . . .

CHAPTER 1

Summer, 1985

A pained, bloodcurdling sound pierced the quiet of the cool, cloudless night. Startled and roused from his slumber, Jason sat upright and strained to hear what had awakened him. He saw the floodlights of the main house suddenly illuminate the front porch and heard the husky voice of his father summoning the dogs. Like a soldier called into battle, Jason leaped from his bed, descended the farmhouse ladder, and grabbed his pellet gun. The family canines flung the front door wide open as soon as Jason had opened it a foot. Mitch, an aggressive German shepherd—lean, young, and muscular—burst out first, followed by Max, an immense but good-natured Newfoundland. Quick on their heels, lanky, thirteen-year-old Jason, dressed in flannel pajamas, sprang out into the night.

"Son, this way!" his dad shouted from the vicinity of the sheep pen, half a football field to his right.

Max waited for Jason to get his bearings, then contentedly bounded beside him as Jason ran at full speed toward the pen. Mitch, meanwhile, streaked yards ahead of them barking loudly, ears perked and tilted forward in anticipation.

Jason could see sleek, dog-like shadows darting for the woods beyond the farm gate. He counted four shadows in close succession making good time out of harm's way. A fifth labored to the edge of the woods, with the rump of a limp lamb hanging from its blood-soaked mouth. She measured two-and-a-half feet tall and almost four feet long, a beautiful specimen of the gray wolf and the alpha female of her pack. She instinctively understood that the dogs posed a mortal danger to her and did not respect the hierarchy of her wolf pack. Jason, for his part, realized that a chase to the death had just begun.

Both dogs sharply adjusted course and rushed for the she-wolf. Alarmed, the wolf dropped her meal and snarled as she turned from her enemy and then bounded into a forest path in pursuit of her departed pack. Jason's dad took aim and fired his rifle at the fleeing predator. The shot glanced off the wolf's tail, causing a yelp of fearful surprise.

"Blasted sight!" his father mouthed, adjusting his rifle on the run.

Having nearly caught up to his dad, Jason entered into the bowels of the foreboding Maine forest. An abundance of wildlife hid, hunted, and lurked close to the forest trail he followed toward the blue-gray mountains looming to the east of Moosehead Lake. The air was crisp and clear. Even from this distance, Jason could see the moon's ghostly sheen shimmering upon the lake's restless surface. The full moon bathed the lake in a tremulous luster of pale white.

Gazing back at the trail, Jason witnessed Mitch and Max disappear around an upcoming bend. Cloaked in the darkness of the dense underbrush, the dogs relentlessly pressed on in pursuit of their prey.

"Remind me to set more wire along that pen," his dad instructed as they continued yet deeper into the forest. "We won't see the last of this pack of wolves until we take a couple down. They're smart enough that'll scare them away for a while until their hunger drives them back."

"I've never hunted a wolf before," Jason observed shyly.

He had seen and shot eastern coyotes, which thrived in these Maine woodlands on snowshoe hare, porcupine, and white-tailed deer. Wolves were a far superior predator, capable of bringing down a full-grown moose. Their power and hunting prowess commanded Jason's respect.

"You'll kill your first one tonight then, son. Mitch had a good jump on her, and it won't be long now before they scrap. I'll hand you my rifle when we close in."

Excited barks could now be heard not more than a quarter mile ahead. Then, just as quickly as they arose, the barks ceased. Jason and his dad sprinted for the next bend and rounded it expectantly. Vicious snarling arose from a furious tumbling ball of furry forms before them. Eyes wide open, Jason was nearly knocked off his feet by the powerful combatants. Mitch snapped his jaws at the she-wolf's haunches while Max struggled to get a jaw-lock on her neck. With a Newfoundland's bite strength, one jaw-lock could be deadly.

"Jason, put down your pellet gun and take my rifle!" his father instructed, moments later deftly tossing Jason his rifle.

But his dad immediately realized the problem. There was no way Jason could get a clear shot at the wolf in the midst of the dogs' attack. "Down, Mitch! Down, Max!" he commanded at the top of his lungs.

Mitch obediently retreated from the she-wolf, but Max remained engrossed in a life-and-death struggle with his haggard opponent. His father had no choice but to attempt ripping the 150-pound dog free of his quarry. Pulling with nearly all of his might, his father's muscular arms rippled with tension as he finally managed to separate the outmatched wolf from her would-be slayer.

Having nervously watched the action, Jason now gripped his dad's rifle, cocked it, and took deliberate aim. His trigger finger trembled backward, but before he could fire, a bellowing roar froze his body in fear.

Jason's father shouted, "No, dear Lord, please! Jason! Turn around, now!"

Jason turned his head to see a full-sized black bear on its hind legs, claws menacingly swiping through the air. Survival instinct assumed control. Jason instantly dropped to the ground, rolled away from the bear, and fired at the blurred attacking form.

The shot must have hit flashed through Jason's mind as the bear roared in anguish.

Apprehending the grave danger to their masters, Mitch and Max abandoned their she-wolf prey and cagily barked threats at the wounded titan. The bear's eyes flashed with the deadliest mixture of fury and terror. Jason lay on the ground only a few feet away, mouth agape, hands trembling with fear.

His father fired the pellet gun at the bear's eyes, blinding it in one eye and causing it to swipe at nearby forest saplings in disoriented rage. Swiftly, the dogs moved in for the kill. In a coordinated attack, Mitch and Max lunged at the bear's trunk-like legs, only to have Mitch shaken loose with one powerful kick. Max, the stronger of the two canines, struggled to maintain his viselike grip on the brawny, shifting quadriceps of the towering creature. The bear's razor-sharp front claws swiped at Max, drawing blood that spurted out onto Max's thick coat along his back. Shocked, Max fell sideways to the forest floor. Mitch cowered back, barking but overpowered with fear. Jason reached for his dad's rifle but felt nothing, his mouth wide-open in speechless disbelief. He flung himself face down in desperation.

Protect the head! Protect the head! Jason's survival instinct commanded.

He placed both hands over his head, fearing the worst.

A bullet whizzed overhead, shearing the tense forest air. The bear let out a roar of excruciating pain. Then the bear bellowed in pain and fell on its fours, then its side, writhing in agony.

From his prone position, Jason saw his father's eyes flare with intensity as he cocked back his rifle and took aim at the grievously wounded creature. A sure shot, his dad fired again. The bear's head abruptly dropped, ending its misery.

The shot reverberated throughout the forest, echoing eerily into the quieted night. Jason mustered the courage to lift his head from the forest floor and surveyed the scene. His amazed eyes stared, riveted to the listless body of his fallen foe. His mind felt as though it were emerging from a state of suspended animation. Then, in one wrenching moment, it snapped back to reality and recalled Max's plight.

Jason swiftly turned to Max, his first dog and fiercely loyal companion. Max appeared to be seriously injured. His blood flow had to be arrested within minutes, if not sooner, or else he would fall into shock. His dad tore off his shirt and tightly wrapped it around Max's back to staunch the blood flow.

"Son, help me lift Max and carry him to the farmhouse. We're going to have to tranquilize him and stitch this wound as soon as possible. Come on, boy, you can make it," Jason's father almost pleaded to their dog.

Head crestfallen, Mitch followed the anxious train back up the forest trail toward the farmhouse. The excitement of the chase had abruptly dissipated for Mitch and his masters. Jason and his father barely even noticed that the she-wolf had managed to lumber away in pursuit of her pack with relatively minor injuries. Her battle scars would mainly be psychological. Once contact with her hunting companions was restored, she, the pack's dominant female, would have to endure the humiliation of licking her wounds before her hunting companions.

Meanwhile, the black bear, Maine's king of the forest, fearing man and man alone, lay motionless in a bed of saplings that had snapped under its prodigious weight. It would not rise again. Its entrance ironically had saved the wolf from imminent death at the cost of its own life.

Why had the bear attacked? Jason silently questioned. This was the first black bear attack he had heard of occurring in Piscataquis County in two years.

"What should we do with the bear?" Jason innocently asked his father.

"Leave it to rot. I hope that carcass is picked over three times by the time I lay sight on it again."

Jason shuddered, recalling the bear's bellowing roar and flashing black eyes—eyes from which Jason had cowered in fear. But strangely to him, he did not hate the fallen bear. He only asked himself what had provoked the bear to attack them, without arriving at an easy answer.

Jason would question Sasquot, his father's wise, old farmhand, as to why this had occurred when Sasquot arrived in the morning. Sasquot would explain what spirit had guided the bear to act so violently—whether fear, anger or revenge. This unassuming man observed the ways of the wild, speaking few words but saying much when he did. He possessed an uncanny ability to predict nature: which stags would clash for mating rights and which would prevail; whether a moose would charge an intruder or, unphased, continue to feed on water lilies; and when an eagle would make its final swoop for unwary prey. Growing up, Jason had watched what seemed to him nature's savagery and beauty through Sasquot's knowing eyes. But never had he seen this.

Jason and his dad labored to carry Max from the forest trail past the agitated pen to the farmhouse. His dad had tended to injured livestock and cattle for years. Thus, the farmhouse held a store of medicines for treating sheep, cattle, and other animals, whether sick, injured, or in heat. The first floor of the farmhouse functioned primarily as a toolshed for his dad's carpentry work and the second floor as Jason's summer loft and getaway.

Not long ago, this same farmhouse had stabled four prized horses of Jason's grandfather. The last had died only last year, a trophy-winning chestnut stallion with a passion for hunting, riding, and jumping. Jason had ridden Untamed Heart since he was four.

As they hurriedly carried Max into the farmhouse, Jason noticed that Max's body was unnaturally cold to the touch. He seemed either unconscious or in shock, his chest registering rapid, shallow breaths.

Jason's eyes welled up with tears. "He's not going to make it," he sobbed softly.

"He's a fighter. Let's lay him down right here, son," his father indicated. His father pointed to a worktable covered with cloth and immediately began to go to work after they had gently laid him on the table. He scrubbed his hands and forearms up to his elbows in a large, metal sink and signaled Jason to get the medical kit. Jason pulled the heavy, metal kit down from some oak shelving and placed it on the makeshift operating table beside Max. In a matter of less than a minute, his father had removed a syringe, a dose of Novocain, the tranquilizer alprazolam, a bottle of hydrogen peroxide, an electric razor, a pair of latex gloves, a stitching needle, and Ethilon sutures.

"We're going to have to hold his legs up as much as possible to increase blood flow to the heart and keep his blood pressure up," Jason's father explained as he pulled the clear latex gloves on snugly.

Jason nodded, gently grabbing hold of Max's two hind legs while allowing Max's two front legs to rest against his chest. He watched intently as his father readied the tranquilizer and injected a carefully measured dose into the right side of Max's hip. Max let out a pained whimper in instant reaction to the injection.

"Easy, boy," his dad coached soothingly.

Jason prayed that Max would react well to the injection and not fall into a state of shock. He knew his father had little choice but to risk the potentially precipitous fall in Max's blood pressure, given the need to immediately clean, stitch up, and dress the wound.

His dad gently untied the shirt he had wrapped around Max's injury minutes earlier. Fortunately, the blood had clotted sufficiently to proceed with the stitching. Jason's father plugged in the electric razor and began shaving off Max's fur around the wound, revealing three long, razor-like cuts caused by the fierce swipe of the bear's claw. Jason readied the hydrogen peroxide and assisted his father in cleaning Max's lower back in preparation for the stitching. Max jerked his body away from them and had to be held down as the sting of the peroxide flared through the exposed area and temporarily overwhelmed the relaxing effect of the tranquilizer.

"Okay, now for the hard part. Try your best to calm Max as I stitch him up," he instructed.

Jason stroked Max's head and neck and whispered soothingly that he would be okay. Max was only four-and-a-half years old in human years—in the prime of his life—and he had many adventures awaiting him if he could only pull through this ordeal.

After fifteen long minutes of suturing, the longest of the tears, a nasty-looking twelve-inch gash, had been completely stitched up. Max's skin color, which had begun to turn a pale shade of blue, now appeared ruddier. His father diligently completed stitching three more minor cuts along Max's back.

"Let's wrap him up in a blanket and carry him into the house," his father said.

Jason climbed up the farmhouse ladder and, soon afterward, climbed back down bearing a blanket from his bed. His dad gingerly lifted Max up while Jason loosely wrapped him in the warm, wool blanket. Once Max had been comfortably wrapped up, Jason helped hoist Max off the carpentry worktable without subjecting the freshly stitched wounds to any contact. Mitch, who had watched the stitching in agitated silence, whimpered plaintively as he followed his masters back to the house and into the den. By the time his father had stoked the fire and rested Max within the radius of its rekindling warmth, Jason was fast asleep on the couch dreaming of chasing wolves into the forest.

CHAPTER 2

The bright sunlight of a late August morning filtered through the windows and slanted into Jason's eyes, disturbing a deep sleep that had passed into an agitated one. Jason's dream had mirrored the reality of the previous night, except that he had found himself transformed from the hunter into the hunted. In his dream, Jason had stood alone in the center of a slowly but steadily constricting circle of bears stalking their prey, not for hunger but for revenge. He had killed one of their own, and Jason could discern from the intense fire that burned in their eyes that they had sentenced him to death. Jason shuddered for an instant in the nether world between sleep and consciousness and then gratefully found himself in the waking world.

Jason's first thought was for the welfare of his loyal dog, who had nearly sacrificed his own life in defense of his threatened master. Max lay fast asleep, wrapped in his blanket with a half-eaten bowl of dog food beside him. Jason took this as an auspicious sign, recognizing that, beyond the sustenance it brought, feeding evidenced a psychological will to live. For Sasquot had ingrained in Jason an appreciation of the power of a being's spirit to overcome adversity and even death, telling Jason from childhood,

"Spirit inside is the fire of man. So long as the fire burns, death will have no power to steal the body away."

Jason smiled with appreciation as he prepared a breakfast of cereal covered with slices of freshly picked apples. Max had weathered four Maine winters, a scrap with a Great Dane, and two raccoon bites. Max had not cowered from the bear in fear, but rather had pounced on it to protect his young master.

What a spirit! Jason beamed with admiration. *If only I could act so bravely in the heat of such danger.*

Engrossed in thought, Jason made his way from the main house to the sheep pasture where Sasquot would be grazing the sheep, absent one unfortunate lamb. Jason's reflections centered on his family stock and whether he could ever measure up to their bravery.

Jason's great-grandfather, James Wilson, had been the pioneer of the family. He had journeyed to America in 1897, bearing only a one-way coach class ticket and a few worthless possessions on a steamer out of London. James was a strapping, young mustached man who later came to be a great admirer of Teddy Roosevelt and his larger-than-life way of living. Tired of the urban squalor of newly industrialized London, James had soon reveled in the freedom of farm life in Maine. He had lived in a rugged log cabin for his first three years in America, until he had saved just enough from clearing land for wealthy Mainers to buy a farm of his own. Over the years, he had continued to purchase and clear land, chopping down trees and burning underbrush to accommodate a grand thirty-acre cattle and sheep farm with three grazing pastures. He had married the prettiest daughter of a local trapper and trader and started the Wilson family lineage in Greenville, Maine.

Jason only knew James through pictures and stories, many of them told through the eyes of his late grandfather, Stephen. Thinking of Grandpa evoked fond memories of hunting foxes on his grandfather's steeds, fishing trout and salmon out of Moosehead Lake, and trekking to the lake in snowshoes alongside Grandpa to ice-skate or go ice fishing. Stephen had instilled in Jason a zest for life, and Jason felt as though he and Grandpa could do anything humanly possible together and perhaps a bit more.

Jason's faith in his ability to surmount any challenge or obstacle in life had been shattered the winter before last. That terrible winter would forever be etched in Jason's memory. That was the winter Stephen had broken his hip in a freak riding accident. Grandpa had never fully recovered from the injury, developing an alarming cough that only worsened as the winter days grew colder and darker.

Never one to admit pain, Grandpa had refused, despite family protests, to deviate from his daily routine of chopping wood, feeding and grooming Untamed Heart, and telling Jason tales, all of which simply took longer to do. This continued until one February day, when, in the small hours of the morning and the midst of an especially bitter nor'easter, Grandpa left his bed to attend to his prized show-horse. Grandpa must have been concerned that Untamed Heart would fall sick from the cold because he had lumbered to the stable with extra blankets and sugar-coated apples, the horse's favorite treat. Untamed Heart weathered that storm, but Grandpa had not. He perished in a snowdrift within twenty yards of the sleeping household. Jason's father, Kyle, found him at sunrise, frozen to death.

Sasquot once told Jason that his father had not forgiven himself nor nature for its hand in his father's death.

When Jason came to the edge of the main pasture, his gaze focused upon the figure of a Penobscot Indian, his face worn and tested like weathered leather, his eyes deep and dark, storing great mysteries within. The fifty-year old Penobscot appeared stern and distant, but as Jason approached, Sasquot turned toward Jason, his countenance radiating paternalistic concern and affection.

"Young friend, I have heard of your exploits," Sasquot announced in the tone of a father speaking to his son. "This morning, I spoke with your father about the bear. My heart overflows with joy that you are safe and without harm."

Jason smiled sheepishly and turned away, presuming that Sasquot had little respect for how he had acted in the face of danger—covering his head, frozen in fear.

"I, too, once faced an angry bear, Jason. To soothe its anger, I spoke to it like a father to a baby and retreated from its path. The bear sensed I was not a threat and soon went on its way."

"Sasquot, why do you think the bear was so bent on attacking us?" Jason asked, eager to gain the benefit of Sasquot's intuition. "It rose to its feet, ready to tear me apart."

"To understand why a bear attacks, one must first understand the spirit of the bear. Unless a bear has gone mad, it needs a reason to attack, whether the reason is founded or not," Sasquot answered firmly. "Jason, show me the bear. I will try to place myself in its mind at the moment of attack to discern its reason. Autumn, please keep watch over the sheep and do not let them wander near the woods," Sasquot called to his daughter, who was busy shooing a wandering lamb back to the herd. "I will return before the midday sun."

"Yes, Father," she dutifully replied, looking up at Jason and smiling. Slender and lithe, Autumn had liquid brown eyes and long, flowing, black hair.

Jason ignored her. He was thirteen, and girls were not important to him now. Proving his manhood was all that consumed him. "Come on, Sasquot. I'll show you the bear. I'm sure it's the biggest and meanest beast you've ever seen."

Sasquot shot a skeptical glance at Jason, and Jason immediately became half-defensive, half-apologetic. "I mean . . . wait until you see it, Sasquot. Then you'll understand why we had to kill it."

"Let us go, Little Hawk. You waste many words with little action," Sasquot gently instructed and gestured toward the main forest trail.

"Little Hawk" was the affectionate nickname Sasquot had given Jason two years earlier when Jason had successfully brought down his first game, a wild turkey. In so naming him, Sasquot had presented the young hunter with a handsome headdress made of feathers of the red-tailed hawk. Though proud of this recognition, Jason looked forward to being named after a more fearsome predator, like the eagle, wolf, or bear.

Jason and Sasquot presently passed into a thick forest flush with color and life. Ghostly blue spruce, red-tinged maples, birch peeling in paper-thin sheaths of silver-white, and soft moss carpets of hunter green passed them by, weaving together a tapestry of hues while the sunlight flickered and sprayed candle-colored rays throughout the forest in playful movement. A black-backed woodpecker flew to a diseased fir tree and, with vigorous sideways movements of its bill, scaled off bits of bark to feast upon beetle larvae underneath. To their right, a gray jay, known as the "Camp Robber" for its penchant to steal food from campers, scolded away a brown boreal chickadee to claim some conifer seeds scattered along the forest floor. In a red maple ahead, a yellow-bellied sapsucker drank the sweet sap of the maple tree and picked at insects that had crawled into a sticky hole. Everywhere Jason turned, he saw life, movement, and color.

Sasquot signaled Jason to stop and pointed to a large pine tree off to their right. At first, Jason could not make out anything. Then his eyes tracked some movement up the tree. He saw a sleek, blond-brown pine marten streak up the pine in hot pursuit of its favorite red squirrel prey. The red squirrel jerkily scurried higher into the tree. The pine marten steadily closed in on the squirrel, fast approaching within striking distance. Sensing imminent death, the squirrel darted onto a branch nearly interlocked with a neighboring tree and jumped to safety. The pine marten lifted its head in disappointment, revealing a striking orange throat patch.

"Wow, what a handsome animal!" Jason exclaimed.

"Trappers almost killed off the pine marten in these parts, Jason. Then laws were passed to protect them. Today, they grow in large numbers."

"Why was it trapped, Sasquot?"

"The modern reason for many things, young friend: money. Its pelt fetches many dollars. Do you know, Little Hawk, that the law also protects wolves?" Sasquot asked, alluding to the fact that the Federal Endangered Species Act protected the gray wolf from being hunted.

"But wolves kill livestock, Sasquot. They should be hunted," Jason opined.

"Wolves do not often kill livestock, my friend. Wolves more often make nature stronger by weeding out the weak and sick. Only when man and wolf claim the same land to hunt and live do wolves eat healthy and strong animals. We should build fences higher rather than killing innocent creatures for our mistake in judgment. Killing any animal should be our last resort, not our first resort, Jason—only allowed when truly necessary to save lives or protect from injury."

"Father gave me his rifle to try to kill my first wolf yesterday."

"Your father is a good man, Jason, but his heart is not right with nature. He sees nature as the enemy. Nature is not our enemy and not our friend. In nature, creatures must live together in their natural roles, for every creature has natural predators and prey, except for man. No creature lives to prey on man, but man preys on many creatures. We sometimes kill animals that are not needed for food, protection, or for the good of the animal population. This, I firmly believe, violates nature and is wrong."

Jason listened carefully, trying to understand and store every sage word of Sasquot in his memory. Not long thereafter, they approached the final bend leading up to the scene of last night's confrontation.

"It's right around the corner, Sasquot," Jason said, trying hard to fortify himself so as not to exhibit any fear upon seeing the bear's carcass.

As they rounded the bend, two coyotes that had been feeding on the decaying bear quickly scampered away into the shadows of the thick woods. The stench of the carcass filled the air but was not yet overpowering. Jason grimaced at the smell.

"This smell is like mountain mint compared to the stench of rotting beached whale, young warrior," Sasquot said with a knowing smile.

Sasquot walked around the bear's body slowly and carefully, visually inspecting it. The bear was lying on its back, with evidence of a rifle-shot to the chest and a pair of ribs exposed by the coyotes and other scavengers that had already begun to feast upon its carcass. Jason was surprised at how much smaller the lifeless bear now appeared to be, compared to yesterday, when it had seemed to be a towering beast.

"This is a fully grown female, Little Hawk. She weighs about two hundred pounds."

Sasquot carefully crouched down beside the bear and gazed intently into her glassy, brown eyes, as if communing with the fallen beast.

"This bear was not crazy," he pronounced at last, rising to his feet. "She protected her cub from the danger on all fronts—from a wolf, from hunting dogs, and—I am sad to say—from you and from your father, who slayed her."

"Cubs? We didn't see or hear any cubs, Sasquot," Jason said, puzzled at Sasquot's conclusion.

Sasquot began to walk further into the forest. "What time did the attack happen?" Sasquot asked Jason from over his shoulder.

"I guess it was sometime between eleven and midnight," Jason said. "Because when we brought Max back to rest after stitching him up, it was a quarter past twelve."

"Bears like to feed during twilight hours. I am curious why the bear was not asleep deep in the forest growth so late at night."

Jason now followed Sasquot into the famously lush forest underbrush of the Maine woods. He witnessed rich ferns thrusting up from the well-watered forest floor, clumps of red sumac clothed in bright red foliage and covered with red berries and clusters of white flowers, and black berrylike fruit growing on Elder trees.

Sasquot motioned for Jason to come to him. "This is bearberry shrub," Sasquot said, pointing to a ground-hugging, two-foot-long shrub with glossy evergreen leaves and white, waxy flowers that were giving way to spiky, reddish berries. "Bearberries are a favorite fall food of black bears. My tribe makes tea from its leaves, which have many good minerals and can cure some infections."

Jason nodded and asked, "Can you safely eat the berries?"

"Yes, humans can eat bearberries without getting sick. People of the Dawnland to this day use them to make jelly. Some even use bearberries to make wine."

Jason's thoughts fell back to the history he had learned. People of the Dawnland or "Eastern" was an Algonquin translation for the members of the northern New England and southern Canadian tribes comprising the Abenaki Confederacy. Forged out of necessity from constant warring with the fierce Iroquois and land-seeking English colonists, the Confederacy generally allied with the French during the seventeenth and eighteenth centuries. The main tribes of the Confederacy, including the Penobscots, fought alongside the Americans and the French in the Revolutionary War. The Abenakis who managed to endure and survive this tragic period of New World colonization did so at a terrible cost to their culture and heritage. The decimation of their people from battle and disease was an immeasurable casualty of colonization. Autumn, Zephyr, and Sasquot descended from the Penobscots, the principal tribe of the Abenaki Confederacy and, sadly, the only Abenaki tribe to retain its name, territory, and identity to this time. Jason was brought to the present by sudden movement beside him.

Sasquot cupped his hand to his ear. "I hear the whimpering of a cub not far past the brush ahead."

Sasquot and Jason quickly made their way through the summer brush. They whisked by delicate clusters of Queen Anne's Lace and starflowers with an air of urgency. Their eyes presently widened as they came upon an agitated black bear cub. The poor cub cried out as it desperately struggled to disengage its right front paw from the closed jaws of a steel bear trap. Fortunately for the health of the cub, only three of its five claws, rather than the flesh of its paw, were caught in the trap. If not ultimately freed, however, it would die of starvation.

Sasquot rushed to the bear and spoke soothingly to it as he dexterously worked to disengage the trap. In a matter of moments, the cub was free, and it immediately raced away in the direction of its fallen mother.

"That's her cub," Sasquot said. "The mother bear was just trying to protect her cub from all of you last night."

"How does it know where its mother is? I can't see her at all from here."

"A bear's smell is as keen as the sight of an eagle or the hearing of a deer, Little Hawk. Come, let us see our freed friend." Without pausing even for a moment, Sasquot retraced the path they had just traversed to the trap and came to the forest path at the exact point where the cub's mother lay. Jason scrambled behind Sasquot, who was the most fleet of foot fifty-year old whom Jason had ever encountered.

The cub whimpered and pressed its nose against its fallen mother, visibly unsure of what to do. Jason felt a sudden sense of sadness and sympathy for the cub, and his former fear of its mother completely dissipated. No longer did he worry that he would embarrass himself by involuntarily shuddering in front of his Indian mentor.

Sasquot and Jason peered at the cub from behind a maple tree by the edge of the path. "What will happen to the cub?" Jason whispered to Sasquot with concern.

"Chances are that the cub will not survive the winter," Sasquot said softly. "You see, cubs this age still depend on their mothers. Mother bears wean cubs into the early fall. A cub this age still needs to learn how to forage and hunt on its own."

Jason looked at Sasquot and then stared at the cub, which was gently tugging at its mother's paw, not accepting or even understanding that she was dead. A sense of sadness swept over him.

"Bears are sacred animals to my people. I feel responsible for this brother of my people," Sasquot suddenly said. "Man destroyed its chances to survive on its own in the wild, so man has a duty to help it survive."

"Can we raise it, Sasquot?" Jason asked with excited expectancy.

Sasquot looked directly at Jason with penetrating eyes. "A bear is not a toy, or a cat, or even a dog, my friend. It is a wild animal and demands much more attention and care than a pet. If we raise a cub, we will need to teach it how to hunt, fish, and forage. Boys of your years do not want such a heavy responsibility."

"I want this responsibility, Sasquot. I want to be a man, not a boy."

Sasquot nodded and silently considered Jason's words. Finally, he answered, "I will raise this cub from my home, but the cub will be your responsibility until it learns enough to survive on its own. Once this happens, we must set the cub free."

"Okay, okay," Jason said at once thrilled at the prospect of raising a bear cub and disappointed that they could not keep the bear for good. "But do we have to release it so soon?"

"Wild animals belong in nature. Once the cub learns how to survive in nature, our sacred duty is to set it free. Do you understand and agree?"

"Yes, Sasquot," Jason answered in a somewhat deflated tone of voice.

Before Jason had even considered how to capture the cub, Sasquot had removed his shirt, stealthily crept up behind it, and scooped up the unsuspecting cub from beside its mother. Sasquot wrapped up the claws of the startled cub in his shirt and tied a knot tight enough to prevent the cub from swiping at them. Then, like a father cradling a baby, he carried the cub along the forest path to a clearing, from which he headed for his home, followed by an extremely excited Little Hawk.

CHAPTER 3

That night, Kyle returned home from a long day purchasing lumber and negotiating the sale of furniture pieces he had recently completed to small stores in the center of town. Mitch greeted him enthusiastically at the door, while Max sauntered over quietly, much more subdued than usual.

"Jason! Jason, did you feed the dogs?" Kyle called out to an empty house. "Can't give him any responsibility," Kyle mumbled to himself.

He stroked Max's head and delicately inspected Max's stitches. The stitches had held, and the wound was healing. Kyle applied some antibiotic cream and vitamin E gel along the stitches in order to keep the wound free of harmful bacteria and facilitate the healing process.

Max will make it through this. Kyle was heartened by the realization.

He strode out to the farmhouse and, on his way, spotted Autumn bringing the sheep back to their pen. The farm currently maintained a flock of twenty-one Katahdin sheep—a hardy, adaptable breed raised for its tender, mild-flavored meat. They were ideal for Maine's harsh climate, as they grew extremely thick winter coats that were shed during the spring. Kyle prized them not only for their succulent meat but also for their low maintenance, as they did not produce a fleece and thus did not need to be sheared.

"Where are Jason and Sasquot?" Kyle demanded of Autumn without so much as a perfunctory greeting.

"They went into the woods this morning and have not yet come home, Mr. Wilson," she answered respectfully.

"Great, just great," Kyle murmured half to himself.

"They took the main forest path," Autumn added, trying to be helpful.

"Autumn, finish corralling the sheep back into the pen. I'll meet you out here in five minutes with my rifle."

Kyle jogged back to the house and decided to give Sasquot's home a quick call. Zephyr, Sasquot's wife, answered the phone. "Hello, Mr. Wilson. Yes, they are safe. They are in the woods doing a ceremony for the bear. They both should be back shortly. Sasquot and I invite you to join us here for supper. We would be honored for you to be our guest."

Kyle half-heartedly accepted the invitation, relieved that they were safe. *But what was this nonsense about a bear ceremony?*

He walked out to the pen and offered Autumn a ride back to Sasquot's cabin along Moosehead Lake.

"My father's canoe lies by the edge of the lake. It is big enough for four people and would be faster," Autumn offered in response.

This pleasantly surprised Kyle, who had assumed that the canoe was moored down by Sasquot's lakefront cabin. Kyle loved canoeing out onto Moosehead Lake at dusk, when the land and waters were bathed in the serene colors of sunset. Instantly, his demeanor toward Autumn softened.

"In that case, let's go," he said and followed Autumn down a narrow trail to the southeast shore of the lake.

Coming to the edge of the lake, each of them was struck by the golden reflection of the sun's orb melting into the lake's placid waters.

No matter how many times I gaze upon the lake's sunset, it is breathtaking, Kyle thought. He watched as the sun splashed magenta and orange rays upon the shimmering surface of the lake.

As the two paddled along in the agile birchbark canoe, Kyle could not help but be enthralled by the pristine beauty of the lake meeting the sky. Continuing to gaze toward the west, he spotted a black-crowned night heron foraging along the shore. Interrupted in its twilight feeding, it barked a loud squawk before briefly alighting to a safer lakeside haven. Heard before seen, a flock of Canadian geese flew in a V-formation several hundred feet overhead, honking unabashedly as they navigated past the canoe and disappeared in alignment over the darkening treeline.

Covering 117 square miles and featuring over four hundred miles of shoreline, Moosehead Lake was an immense glacier lake that prided itself upon being Maine's largest and, arguably, most beautiful lake. The first time Kyle had paddled these parts, he had been astounded by the breadth of what Sasquot called "our Inland Sea." When a gale-force wind or tempest arose upon the lake, the agitated waves would approach those of the rocky Maine shore. This evening, though, the waves were mild, gently lapping up against the canoe as it swiftly cut through the water.

Kyle paddled robustly from the bow of the canoe. Autumn, though slight of build, possessed far superior handling skills. Thus, it was Autumn, rather than Kyle, who sat in the stern, deftly steering the craft with her six-foot maple paddle. So natural and effortless was canoeing to Autumn that she could raise the blade of her paddle into the air and catch the drip of water running down the handle while barely pausing in her strokes.

»«»«»«

Of this invention, I am most proud of my people, Autumn happily mused as the canoe sliced through the water, leaving little wake.

Several years ago, her father had painstakingly shaped, fitted, sewn together, and waterproofed the canoe, employing the same methods and techniques as countless generations of Penobscots before him. Under the welcome shade of a maple situated by the lake, he had deftly worked his craft while supervising his less experienced helpers: Mr. Wilson, eight-year-old Jason, and Autumn. Together, they had labored for four consecutive summer weekends to construct the handsome sixteen-foot craft.

Armed with little more than an axe, a wooden mallet, a crooked knife, and an awl, the team had taken pieces of nature and woven them into a thing of beauty. In an incredible transformation, sheets of birchbark became the frame, birch rails the gunwales, curved cedar the bow and stern, thwarts of ash the seats and cross bars, cedar strips the lining, and forty cedar pieces—each placed an inch apart—the ribs of the canoe. To make the canoe watertight and elastic, they had applied pitch from a fir tree mixed with a little animal fat to its body. Sasquot had even decorated the oval pieces of bark that fit on either end of the canoe, reinforcing the bow and stern, with etchings of a black bear, a moose, and a Penobscot medicine man. In this way, they had recreated the renowned birchbark canoe, the Penobscots' principal mode of transportation of centuries past.

Her father had instilled in Autumn a deep respect for the cultural significance of the birchbark and spruce bark canoe, comparing it in importance to the invention of the wheel in transforming the lives of their ancestors. He had taught her in particular to admire the light weight, quiet movement, and durability of her canoe, qualities which he cited as the main reasons that the People of the Dawnland had for centuries carried them to and from Maine's numerous rivers, lakes, and other waterways to transport themselves, hunt, and approach enemy camps by stealth.

"The very name of our tribe means 'it forks on white rocks,'" her father had taught her. "Our history is rooted in the water routes of this land, which flow in our veins as part of us."

While she was still young, he had also taught her the legends of their people, making clear that they were fictitious stories, yet at the same time important to understanding the history of their people. Among these legends was that of Klose-kur-beh, the fabled first man to inhabit the land of the Penobscots. According to this fable, Klose-kur-beh formed himself from the dust of creation. Wielding special powers, he watched with great concern as a life-threatening drought took hold across the land. Legend held that Klose-kur-beh discovered the source of the drought to be a giant frog that had greedily gorged itself upon the Penobscots' fast-depleting water supply. To save the Penobscots, Klose-kur-beh had burst open the frog with a towering pine, creating a deep depression from which the mighty Penobscot River had sprung forth.

As she effortlessly stroked toward the cabin, able to hear the sound of each paddle gently dipping into the dark blue waters, the fluid depths of the river seemed to whisper these stories. Fondly recounting them, Autumn felt connected to her family, tribe, and their rich cultural heritage that preceded her for many generations spanning to the origins of their recorded history. Gazing at the colored peaks of Mount Katahdin rising majestically to the east of the lake, Autumn sighed contentedly. *I am truly a living part of the history of my people, a daughter of the Dawnland plying through its rivers in the same manner as my ancestors.*

CHAPTER 4

Jason watched, mesmerized, as the flames swelled and fanned around the body of the fallen mother bear. Pained at witnessing the once noble creature being scavenged by coyotes and ravens, Sasquot had decided to cremate the sow. He felt this would be more honorable in such circumstances than following the usual Penobscot custom of making use of nearly every part of a slain animal for food, clothing, medicine, and ornament.

Sasquot's tribe traditionally revered the black bear both in legend and in real life, viewing it as a "brother" or "cousin" of their people and sometimes referring to tribal members as "Old Bear," "Little Bear," or "Woman Bear." Organized into loosely knit hunting families, the Penobscots gave the appellation Bear Family to one of their most highly ranked family units. The Bear Family was esteemed by the rest of the tribe for its dignity, good repute, and legendary kinship with actual bears.

According to tribal legend, an ancestor of the Bear Family was abducted by black bears and treated as one of their cubs. Following the boy's "rescue" by a Penobscot who needlessly slayed his bear family, the boy exhibited physical and behavioral characteristics of the fallen bears. Ultimately, however, the boy grew up into a full-blown Penobscot Indian who married and fathered Penobscot children. Legend held that this man became the founder of the Bear Family, an extended family that revered black bears as pseudo-supernatural kin. Members of the Bear Family often depicted themselves as bears in carvings on powder horns, pieces of birch bark, and other possessions. They also refrained from killing or harming their bear relatives in any manner.

Sasquot's distinguished lineage traced itself to this legendary founder of the Bear Family, and among his ancestors were great shamans of the Penobscot people. Sasquot's great-grandfather, whose name translated as Diviner of the Winds, was reputed to have powers to summon the wind, the clouds, and the rain to envelope an enemy camp in mist and to invoke terrifying "white-outs" upon enemy scouts. Though Sasquot afforded such stories the same level of credibility as he did the legends of his people, Sasquot took great pride in his family history. In particular, he held his late father in the highest regard and paid tribute to his memory by regularly visiting his grave.

Sasquot's father had combined the miracles of modern medicine with traditional tribal herbs and remedies to cure many illnesses among his tribesmen, championing a more holistic concept of healing which focused equally on body, mind, and spirit. Though Sasquot had not shared his experience with anyone but his immediate family, his father's untimely death had both shaken him to his core and transformed his life. It was a shocking irony that his father, the great medicine man and a man renowned among his people for curing the most intractable illnesses, had himself helplessly wasted away from cancer, but his death had also given Sasquot new life.

After his father's death, Sasquot found a prayer journal lying in his father's nightstand. The journal chronicled his father's prayers to a personal God Who had died in human form for his sins. It had amazed Sasquot that his father's prayers were filled with thanksgiving to God for having created him, for having so loved him that He had died in human form to forgive his sins, and for sending His Holy Spirit to bestow peace of mind and spirit upon him during his devastating illness. The prayers his father had recorded focused little on himself, instead asking God for unity, love, and peace for his family and, most especially, for his wife and son. This had greatly moved Sasquot and, after deep reflection and many soul-searching talks with the minister of the local Methodist church, Sasquot had accepted Jesus Christ as his personal Savior. Sasquot had made this commitment only after being convinced that he could be both a Christian and a devoted member of his tribe. To this end, Pastor Roberts had persuasively pointed to the examples of Penobscots who centuries ago had been converted to Christianity by Jesuit missionaries or Protestant ministers but whose descendants nevertheless remained active and respected members of the tribe to the present day.

So it was that Sasquot felt a sacred duty to dispose of the mother bear's body with the honor and respect fitting for the creatures of God's creation. He felt an ancestral kinship to the noble creature and great sadness for its tragic death. Before disposing of her body, Sasquot removed each of the front claws from the sow. He did this in remembrance of an-age old Penobscot tradition: that of preserving and wearing the claws of a bear that had been slain.

As Sasquot had been taught by his father as a boy, wearing a necklace of bear claws and red beads indicated high rank and was an honor accorded to men who had demonstrated great courage in battle or the hunt. His father had gone on to tell the spellbound child that wearing bear claws could protect him from great danger if he were worthy of wearing them. Although Sasquot could not in good conscience wear the bear claws of this slain bear himself, he planned to save them to be worn by Jason when he had proven himself worthy of them.

"Once you are tested to your core and show the courage that burns inside, then and only then will you have earned the high privilege of wearing these noble bear claws," Sasquot intoned with the weightiness of a proven man to an uncertain boy. "You will bring great honor to your family once you achieve this."

As the flames enveloped the prone creature, Sasquot gripped a root club engraved with the bust of a warrior and decorated with the face of a snarling bear that had been carved into its side. In rich, deep, guttural sounds, Sasquot sang, his eyes closed, his fingers clenched, his head periodically bowed, then gently raised, his unseeing eyes facing the fallen bear. Sasquot's anguish at the bear's death poured through his entire being, a death he felt at different levels had paradoxically been necessary and unnecessary at the same time. He saw it as necessary in order to save Jason's life once the bear, feeling threatened, attacked. At the same time, he saw it as unnecessary since the confrontation had been precipitated by the rash pursuit of a wolf that posed no continuing danger to man or livestock.

Would the sad beauty of this mourning song pass down to the next generation? Sasquot wondered.

He feared that even among full-blooded tribal members, too few were sufficiently versed in Abenaki to pass the language to their English-speaking children. Indeed, Sasquot considered it his solemn duty to retain the Abenaki language and pass it on to Autumn. He yearned for her to speak the flowing language as fluently as his father and grandfather had spoken it before him, lest an important part of his tribe's identity perish forever.

Dressed in his most dignified ceremonial dress—a long, square-cut, sleeved coat of moose-skin decorated with black painted designs of a bear figure around the collar, the shoulder seams, the cuffs, the front opening, and the lower skirt—Sasquot displayed the nobility of his Bear Family. His head bore his most regal coronet: a headband with hawk and eagle feathers fastened stiffly upright. A ceremonial cape-collar adorned his neck while wristbands with embroidered bear decorations covered his wrists.

Sasquot's rhythmic chants now became cries—cries of pain, agitation, and tension—while Jason watched in reverent silence. Then Sasquot's cries ceased, and he crouched down to the ground and held up his hands toward the fire.

After what seemed like a great while, the flames died down, revealing only the remains of the bear's skeleton surrounded by smoldering fragments of muscle and fur. Sasquot motioned for Jason to pour two buckets of water, which they had carried from Moosehead Lake, upon the remains. Soon the last wisp of gray smoke had dissipated into the early evening sky. Jason shuddered, suddenly cold.

"It is time," Sasquot pronounced.

In a silence respectful of the solemn occasion, Jason and Sasquot proceeded northwesterly along a forest path for several miles. The path gradually narrowed into a trail which forked into a dirt road. This road soon brought them to a humble but well-kept cabin along the eastern shore of the lake.

CHAPTER 5

As Jason and Sasquot approached the wooden steps of the log cabin's front porch, they saw the figures of Autumn and Jason's father tying the canoe to a tree by the shore.

"Sasquot, what will my dad think of keeping the bear?" Jason asked apprehensively.

"You will be the true master of the cub, Jason, but I will house it in my shed while we teach it how to survive," Sasquot replied.

Indeed, earlier that afternoon, Jason had accompanied Sasquot, with cradled cub in tow, to Sasquot's spacious oak shed, leaving it to dine on husked corncobs, early season acorns, bearberries, hickory nuts, and plenty of plant roots. On their way, Sasquot had explained to Jason that black bears—and especially black bear cubs preparing for winter "hibernation"—had insatiable appetites.

Jason had witnessed this firsthand in his first experience feeding the cub at the shed. As soon as he had deposited three honey sticks and backed away a sufficient distance, it had seized the first stick in its claws, lowered its head, and eagerly licked it clean of a mini-colony of honey-covered ants. Jason had gathered the sticks by the edge of the forest near Sasquot's shed, covered them with wild honey Sasquot had procured from a nearby hive, and gingerly inserted them down several black ant holes per Sasquot's instructions. Agitated ant warriors had attacked each intruding stick, only to find themselves clinging helplessly to its honey.

"Together, we will need to teach the cub how to hunt and forage so that the cub can survive the winter," Sasquot stated. "I will ask your father's permission for you to do this. Hopefully, he will understand this solemn responsibility, since his actions have orphaned the bear cub, and it will otherwise die of starvation."

"Yes, Sasquot, I understand. I'm sure he will approve of that. And don't worry at all; I will come and feed the bear every day after school."

"No, Little Hawk. The bear cub must learn how to hunt and forage for food in its natural environment. We can only feed the cub in my shed for a couple of weeks until we have gained its trust. Then, we must take the cub to streams to catch salmon and to the woods to eat berries, fruits, acorns, and roots and to hunt squirrels and groundhogs."

"That sounds like great fun!"

"Yes, great fun and a lot of work at the same time, my young friend," Sasquot said, grinning in amusement at Jason's bubbling enthusiasm. "As the age-old proverb says, 'If you give a man a fish, you feed him for a day. If you teach a man to fish, you feed him for a lifetime.' God designed man to toil and live off of the fruits of his labor. Similarly, beasts of nature need to hunt and forage in order to survive."

As Jason and Sasquot were conversing, Jason's father and Autumn approached from the forest path and hailed them with a hearty greeting. Jason's dad patted both Sasquot and Jason on their shoulders and said, "I can't believe how strong Autumn has grown. She hardly needed my help to pull our weight all the way here. Pretty soon, she'll be teaching Jason how to fight and fend for himself at school."

Jason's father enjoyed ribbing him about his strength and about his problems with the Stiller twins at school. The twin bullies, Matthew and Glen, had called Jason a sissy last spring and challenged him to a fight after school, a fight that Jason had so far managed to avoid. While his father viewed the whole scenario as healthy, or, at worst, harmless, play for boys growing up, Jason understood the ugly origins of the Stillers' animus. He knew that Matthew and Glen resented him for associating with Sasquot and his family and were searching for an opportunity to teach him a lesson for cavorting with *Injuns*.

"I'm getting stronger, Dad," Jason said defensively. "I don't need a girl teaching me anything."

Jason's father laughed and handed Sasquot four ears of freshly picked corn and a couple of eggplants from his garden.

"Thanks, Kyle. Zephyr has big feast ready for us. Come in, please."

The cabin was fairly small but clean and comfortable in a spartan way. It featured a bedroom for Sasquot and Zephyr and a smaller bedroom for Autumn off either side of the main room, which served as a living and dining room. The kitchen was at the back of the main room, with open entrances at either side to the main room and a large window-like opening so that the cook could see into the main quarters. There was no dishwasher, garbage disposal, washer, or dryer. Zephyr was a full-time housekeeper in the traditional sense of the word. The home did have simple amenities: among them, a stone fireplace, a black and white television, a radio, and a telephone.

"Welcome," Zephyr said and motioned for them to sit at a sturdy oak table.

Jason's father had built this table for Sasquot years ago as a token of his appreciation for Sasquot's help to Jason's late grandfather. Sasquot had been invaluable in breaking in and training Grandfather's horses to be ridden and, eventually, to be shown at competitions throughout Maine and the rest of New England. Sasquot had never used brute force upon the wild horses he had helped Jason's grandfather select from the mid-western horse dealers. He had used only surprisingly effective Indian techniques to communicate with the horses: "listening" to their body movements and "speaking" to them in body language and with variations in his tone of voice. He had not failed to break in even the most defiant of these hand-picked steeds through the painstaking earning of its trust. The name Jason's grandfather had bestowed upon this most proud and striking steed was Untamed Heart.

"Please, everyone, eat and enjoy," Zephyr said, motioning to steaming plates of fresh salmon and brook trout, garden-picked corn on the cob and squash, a heaping bowl of salad tossed with tomatoes, onion, and cucumber, and apple cider from the local cider mill to drink.

"Thank you kindly, ma'am. Well, this looks like a mighty meal for some grateful and hungry travelers," Jason's father said, sitting down to the feast with eager eyes.

Sasquot nodded and bowed his head to bless the meal. "Thank you, God, for abundant food and for our guests and good friends. Please bless this food, our family, and these friends. Amen."

As Jason's father began to help himself to a generous piece of land-locked salmon, Sasquot commented, "Ah, the big one . . . Little Hawk caught that one."

"Little Hawk?" Jason's father mumbled and almost laughed down a sip of apple cider. "Please, Sasquot, Jason is more like 'Little Sparrow.' He's got a lot to learn about fishing, hunting, farming, and just about everything else you've got to know in these parts."

"Jason has learned a good deal about fishing," Sasquot said with a twinkle in his eye. "A good teacher makes a good student."

Jason smiled. Sasquot had taught him how to catch fish with nearly everything imaginable: grasshoppers, worms, crayfish, lures, fly tackle, small frogs, and even his bare hands. By cupping his hands together and holding them still against the bank of a stream, Sasquot could attract curious trout into the dark cavity and catch them by quickly closing his hands. He had even taught Jason an emergency Indian survival technique: how to narcotize fish in a still pool by dropping the crushed leaves and stalks of mullein, a flowering weed, into the pool, temporarily causing the dazed fish to float to the surface.

"Jason, my boy, he's all right, but he has a ways to go to be like his old man," Jason's father said, as much of a compliment to Jason as could be expected from him these days.

Jason expected little in the way of emotional support from his father, especially since his mother's abrupt departure from their life last autumn. Jason could see that his father was having a tough time adjusting to raising him alone without help. His mother had left to jump-start her career as an architect in Boston. Though she had always been more of a "city woman" than a country one, her pre-Thanksgiving announcement that she could no longer endure the rugged Maine country life had shocked Jason and devastated his father.

Over the past couple of years, Jason had not seen his mother reciprocate his father's love. Neither did Jason understand why his father continued to harbor hope that she ever would. He had woken up late one night to secretly witness his father pleading with his mother to stay with them in Maine so that the two of them could continue to raise him as one family. Jason had overheard his mother refuse, telling his dad that she needed to embark on a new career and life in Boston. The most she had promised his father was to call it a separation and not seek a divorce so that the door would be left open if she later felt differently about things. Unlike his father, Jason held out scant hope that his mother would ever return and make their family whole once again.

"Jason has a good heart. That is the most important thing in a boy," Sasquot stated. "Autumn also has a good heart, but she unfortunately suffers the misfortune of having classmates who do not accept her. At her school each day, she is treated like an outcast by the students and by some of her teachers whenever she displays a different way of thinking. No matter what they say, she is smart and understands many things. She is wise in the traditions of my people, in important ways that they do not know or understand."

Sasquot's eyes flashed with the righteous indignation of a father for his beloved daughter. Like Jason, Autumn was about to enter eighth grade at Greenville Consolidated School. But unlike Jason, she had been placed in a special class for slow learning students because she was too shy to read in front of classmates. These were the same classmates who ridiculed her for being a "dumb *Injun*" or a "*casino Indian*," appellations borne of ignorance as well as resentment stemming from a substantial tribal land claims settlement in Maine and two bingo halls the Penobscots had opened.

"I'm sorry to hear that, Sasquot," Jason's father said, referring to Autumn's treatment. "Autumn has learned everything I've taught her around the farm without any problem. Don't listen to those kids, Autumn. You're smarter than them, anyhow."

Jason had rarely seen his father try to comfort someone like this since the separation. Although Jason could not point to the precise reason for it, he felt greatly encouraged by this expression of empathy and concern.

"Especially smarter than the Stiller twins," Jason chimed in.

"Yes, that's for sure," Jason's father said, chuckling at the reference. "If the Stiller boys were navigating, I'd still be wandering out in the middle of Moosehead Lake, dodging bats and mosquitoes."

"They should be in remedial classes rather than Autumn," Jason opined. "Matt couldn't even point to North America on a map. He pointed to Africa."

"Yeah, and Glen thought Maine was Madagascar," Autumn said.

"I always get those confused," Jason's father said with a sarcastic laugh. "Well, now, son, how does it feel now that you've gotten in your first shot at a bear?"

"Well...I don't know," Jason said, more than a little embarrassed that he had frozen in fear before the second shot.

"Jason is training for this," Sasquot announced, producing the bear claws from a rabbit skin pouch.

"What in the world?" Jason's father stammered.

"Jason and I performed an ancient ceremony for the slain mother bear. Before burning the body of the mother bear, I cut off these claws," Sasquot explained, holding the claws up once again. "I have pledged to give them to Jason once he has proven great courage."

"I see. And how do you know it was a mother bear?" Jason's father inquired.

"I examined the bear with my trained eye. Also, she was smaller than a male bear. We found the cub trapped near her. I released the cub from the bear trap, and the cub ran to the fallen mother bear right away. Black bear cubs are raised only by their mothers. A father bear takes no interest in raising them."

"Wow. I killed a mother bear. Unbelievable!" Jason's father said, visibly disappointed that he had not killed the more "fearsome" male black bear.

"We're keeping the cub, Pa. He's in Sasquot's shed," Jason excitedly added, hoping his father would be just as excited.

"What did you say?" his father demanded in an incredulous voice.

"Jason speaks the truth, Kyle. The bear cub will die without our help; but do not worry. I am responsible, not Jason, for caring for the cub," Sasquot responded.

"Sasquot, I appreciate your concern for animals, but this is going too far. A bear is a wild beast, meant for hunting, not for being raised in a shed," Jason's father stated.

"A cub this age without its mother will not survive the winter. It will starve to death without our intervention. You have a sacred duty now that you have slain the mother bear to save her cub from this terrible fate," Sasquot said solemnly.

Jason's father hesitated, realizing Sasquot would not back down easily from his position and appreciative of the tremendous respect the Penobscots had for nature. "I didn't set that trap, Sasquot. I had no idea why the bear attacked. Well, it tried to kill my son, and it nearly killed Max," he blurted out in an attempt to justify his actions.

Sasquot gazed into his father's eyes with a penetrating stare which Jason had never seen anyone match. "I will assume your solemn duty to raise the cub." Then Sasquot gestured toward the food and, turning to his family and to Jason, implored, "Please, finish eating. Cold fish and cold vegetables waste the freshness of this good food."

And so, the issue was settled. From that day forth, Jason's father never seriously questioned Sasquot's determination to keep the bear cub for the winter. And Sasquot, for his part, made it clear to his father that he would release the cub the following spring.

After dinner, Sasquot motioned for all of them to gather round the fireplace, with the adults seated on wooden chairs while Jason and Autumn comfortably sprawled out upon a colorful hand-woven rug. Sasquot started a fire by striking a piece of flint with the back of a hunting knife. Once the flames leaped up, dancing among the aromatic and crackling red cedar logs, Sasquot began to tell an old Penobscot legend. Fittingly, it was the legend of the bear family. Jason was captivated by the story of the Penobscot boy being raised by a family of bears, who were needlessly slain by a village Indian in order to "rescue" the adopted boy, but sleep got the best of Jason's over-adventured body.

When Jason wakened for but a few groggy moments, he found himself in a makeshift seat in the back of Sasquot's pickup on the way back home. When Jason next wakened to the sound of barking, he was curled up in his summer loft, and Max was tenderly pacing the farmhouse floor.

CHAPTER 6

The next couple of days, Jason's schedule was consumed by farm chores and with getting prepared to go back to school. Classes were scheduled to begin the Tuesday following the upcoming Labor Day weekend. Sasquot had told Jason not to visit the cub until Friday so that Sasquot could gradually introduce the cub to human contact and begin to earn its trust. In addition, Sasquot knew that Friday, September the first, signified the first day of the fall season for fishing Atlantic salmon from Maine's waterways.

Sasquot instructed Jason to meet him early Friday morning at an area of the mighty Penobscot River known as Bear Point to introduce the cub to the art of salmon fishing. Each year, Atlantic salmon returned from the ocean to their spawning grounds in the fresh-water rivers of Maine. Sasquot had explained to the incredulous boy that salmon and lobster had once been so plentiful in Maine's coastal and inland waterways that farmers had caught them and scattered them in their fields to use as fertilizer. Neither was nearly as abundant as in the past, but salmon still comprised a tasty part of a black bear's diet.

Friday, at the earliest morning light, Jason awakened and quickly changed into rag-tag clothing and sneakers. Without even pausing to eat breakfast at the main house, he entered the garage;

grabbed a fishing pole, bucket, and tackle box; and began to walk at a brisk pace toward Bear Point. Jason followed an old, rocky forest path westward for several miles before coming to a grassy plain adjacent to the Penobscot River shore.

As Jason approached the shore, he spied Sasquot wading out into the churning river with the cub adeptly swimming close behind him.

"He's a natural!" Jason shouted to Sasquot above the roar of the river.

"Yes, Little Hawk! We're not teaching the cub to swim. Instead, we will take a swimming lesson from the cub," Sasquot joked in his rich, guttural voice while continuing to wade into the river. He continued until he reached a pool of water which had formed from the natural damming of rocks, branches, and leaves a few meters upstream. "Come, Little Hawk, join us in search for breakfast!" Sasquot beckoned for Jason to join them in the cold but invigorating river.

The bear cub turned curiously toward Jason and kept his eyes fixed upon Jason as he waded out into the water toward them. As Sasquot soon explained, bears naturally focus their eyes in that manner upon nearby creatures in an entirely innocent behavior.

"Bear cubs hunt fish, not boys," Sasquot reassured him.

Jason relaxed and approached the cub, who appeared to be thoroughly enjoying himself. "Hi, Coda! How are you today?" Jason asked the bear cub, who understandably ignored the question and gazed down into the pool at a group of salmon.

"So, I see you already have named the cub. What if I were to tell you that this cub is a she?"

Jason looked up at Sasquot in unmasked disappointment.

Sasquot chuckled and said, "Just a touch of humor, my young friend. You are right to assume that the cub is a he, and Coda he shall be called."

Sasquot now peered down into the water, ready to try his patented trout-catching technique on the unfortunate school of salmon below. When one of the smaller salmon crept into his hand-made cave thinking it some sort of passage, Sasquot deftly closed his hands together and clasped the struggling fish.

"Bring that bucket over here, Jason. Fill it just a little bit so that the fish does not jump out."

Jason waded back to the shore, partially filled the bucket, and then returned and handed it to Sasquot. Sasquot dropped the nine-inch salmon into the bucket. "That is breakfast for one, Little Hawk."

Coda had watched Sasquot with great curiosity. Now he decided it was his turn to try his hand. The bear suddenly struck the water pawing for a fish. The salmon darted away without even being touched.

Jason smiled. "We have a lot to teach him, Sasquot."

"Yes, Little Hawk, but remember, black bears are not expert fishermen. And cubs are much worse than adult bears at fishing," Sasquot explained. "Adult black bears catch maybe three fish in ten tries—a cub, not even that. Grizzlies fish much better than black bears due to their longer and sharper claws."

Jason nodded, once again watching the cub. This time, Coda plunged his whole body into the pool and, while still underwater, rushed at the salmon with open jaws. A couple of startled fish leaped into the air in fright, but none were caught.

"When a bear holds its breath underwater and chases the fish with jaws, this is called snorkeling. Coda needs to learn much more about this technique," Sasquot stated with a wry smile.

Coda shook his head vigorously as soon as he surfaced.

"Why does he shake his head like that, Sasquot?" Jason asked.

"Bears do not like to get their ears wet. When they come up from snorkeling, they shake their heads to clear their ears. This is because hearing is vital to their survival. Bears need a keen sense of smell and hearing in order to find food and avoid danger."

"Coda needs more than just good smell and hearing to catch these tricky fish. Looks like he might just go hungry this morning," Jason stated.

"I will catch most of our breakfast today," Sasquot responded. "But come, Little Hawk, try the cave technique."

Jason had tried to catch trout this way before but had succeeded only once. The difficulty was in the timing. Prematurely closing his hands had enabled trout to dart away from the cave's edge, while clasping his hands too late had enabled them to realize there was no passage and escape.

Jason concentrated on getting his hands close to a fish, then forming the cave and keeping them absolutely motionless. A salmon darted past but did not venture in. Then a brook trout approached and edged toward the cave, curious to explore. Just then, Coda pawed for the trout and missed by a foot, causing the scared trout to leap away.

"Coda!" Jason cried out disapprovingly.

Sasquot was bent over laughing on a nearby rock. "Good teacher, good teacher, Little Hawk."

Jason blushed and looked away. He turned toward the sound of thrashing water, only to see Coda hurriedly scamper out of the water in the opposite direction.

I must have frightened the poor cub with my loud, disapproving voice, he thought.

"I'm sorry, Coda. Come here, boy," Jason called.

Meanwhile, Coda's attention was fixated upon the bucket that Sasquot was holding, his gaze intently tracking the shadow of the salmon as it circled its plastic exterior.

"As a reward for all his efforts, Coda gets to eat the first fish this morning," Sasquot pronounced and tossed the salmon safely onto the shore.

Coda hurried to the flopping fish, pinned it to the ground with his paws, and tore its head off with one bite.

"Hey, I didn't eat breakfast yet," Jason protested.

"Bears eat many times the amount that we eat, Jason. Use the cave technique I taught you to catch another fish. Coda is a safe distance away this time," Sasquot observed with laughing eyes.

Without interference from the preoccupied cub, Jason's next attempt was successful. He caught a ten-inch brook trout and proudly brought it to the bucket.

"Here, Coda," Sasquot called.

Coda clearly didn't recognize his name but nonetheless he followed Sasquot as he waded back into the pool, eager to find more breakfast. Sasquot effortlessly caught another salmon, but instead of tossing it into the bucket, he slapped it with modest force against an outcropped rock. Once the fish was temporarily stunned, Sasquot tossed it back into the water in front of Coda. Coda quickly swiped the injured fish, marking his first successful catch.

"All right, Coda!" Jason cried out. "Good job, boy!"

Coda once again lumbered ashore and unceremoniously ripped off the fish's head with his teeth.

"I guess bears would love sushi," Jason speculated innocently.

"You have been to the city too much, Little Hawk," Sasquot ribbed. "Here, I will catch two more, and then we can start the fire and pan-fry them."

Once Sasquot had secured a large salmon and a good-sized trout using his ingenious technique, he found a clear, sandy area on the shore. Guided by Sasquot, Jason gathered some rocks to make a fireproof wall for the fire. He and Sasquot then found some dry birchbark and twigs and arranged them within the circle of rocks. Sasquot removed a piece of flint from his pocket and rubbed the back of his hunting knife against one of the rocks to strike a spark. Sparks readily formed, and one caught a piece of birchbark, initiating the fire. Soon, a good-sized fire had flared up.

"Why don't you and Coda play in the river?" Sasquot suggested. "I will call you once the fire dies down enough to cook the fish at its proper temperature."

"Cool. He's safe to play with, right?"

"Bear cubs won't injure humans. Just keep your tone of voice gentle and friendly," Sasquot instructed.

Jason decided the best way to befriend Coda was to follow Sasquot's example of catching and stunning salmon for the cub. This seemed to work. After slapping a cave-caught salmon on a nearby granite rock, Jason gently tossed it into the stream a few feet away from the hungry cub. Coda pounced on the helpless fish, clutched it in its paws, and brought the tasty morsel ashore. Once devoured, Coda ventured back into the pool beside his newfound friend, ready to retrieve more.

Encouraged by Coda's reaction, Jason decided to play a game of hide-and-seek with the cub. He caught a trout and then hid behind some large rocks along the riverbank. Equipped with a sense of smell many times more powerful than that of a dog, Coda instantly smelled out Jason's position. The excited cub plunged into the cool river in pursuit. Jason darted from behind the rocks and ran full speed down the sandbar, testing whether Coda could catch him. Coda bounded down the shore, quickly overtaking both Jason and the trout.

Impressed, Jason tossed the trout to Coda, who pounced on it with his claws. His black paws then brought it to his mouth to tear its head off.

"Wow, can that cub run or what?" Jason remarked, panting for breath.

"Yes, Little Hawk. Bears can run as fast as thirty miles per hour. If you make Coda angry, do not run away," Sasquot said only half-jokingly.

"How dangerous are black bears, Sasquot?"

"Bears are mostly shy creatures. They prefer to run from danger rather than to stand and fight, Little Hawk. History has taught bears to flee from predators when necessary to survive. Many, many moons ago, black bears had to escape vicious predators, such as saber-toothed tigers and packs of dire wolves. Bears are expert tree climbers and can escape quickly by scaling up trees."

"What animals eat them today, Sasquot?"

"Man is the only real enemy that black bears fear today, Jason—that is, except for grizzly bears. Black bears back down to grizzly bears. Black bears know that grizzlies are too powerful to confront. Come, let us pan fry our trout and salmon. I also brought eggs from your father's hen house so that we can enjoy a full breakfast by the fire."

Sasquot cleaned the fish, teaching Jason each step along the way. When finished, he laid the two down in a skillet which he held six inches above the visible but dying flames.

"There we go; our gourmet breakfast is coming up," Sasquot announced.

"Can I have scrambled eggs, too?"

"Yes, help yourself, Little Hawk. Use the small skillet in my pack."

By the time the fish and eggs had finished cooking, Jason's appetite was enormous. The fresh brook trout and salmon he split with Sasquot were the sweetest and most succulent he had ever tasted. The freshly scrambled eggs were not bad, either.

Sasquot opened his hiking pack and removed some clusters of berries he had picked on his way to Bear Point earlier that morning. Coda munched on wild blackberries, raspberries, and bright red mountain-ash berries while Jason and Sasquot finished their breakfast. Jason felt as though he were the most privileged youth in town, getting to fish and eat with a real, live bear.

"Can I take him to school in a few weeks, Sasquot, to show my friends? Those Stiller twins would never bother me again."

Sasquot shook his head and looked away disapprovingly. "If you want Coda to be your pet, I will raise him myself, Little Hawk. This bear is a wild animal. He needs to learn many things and to hone his skills in order to survive in the wild. To be with many people reduces the cub's odds of surviving on his own. He must not become too familiar with our world. As Coda would have done with his mother in the wild, next year, we must release him to fend for himself."

"Yes, Sasquot," Jason said and turned, expecting to find the ravenous, little cub still gorging himself upon wild berries. However, Coda was nowhere to be seen. "Sasquot, Coda's gone!"

Sasquot sprang up and scanned the area for Coda, but he was nowhere in sight. However, Coda's footprints were clearly visible along the sandy riverbank leading into the woods. Sasquot silently motioned for Jason to follow as he stealthily entered the woods, tracking Coda's broad prints. Except for the claw indentations and lack of a big outer toe, the prints resembled those of a human.

The forest canopy provided instant shade and coolness from the heat of the rising morning sun. As Jason's eyes adjusted to the darker environment, he began to discern Coda's faint trail in the pine-needle floor. Jason wisely followed the nimbly moving Penobscot from the onset rather than waiting for his eyes to adjust. They soon came to a large fir tree, where Sasquot stopped and pointed to a cub comfortably perched upon a branch twenty feet above their heads.

Coda had caught their scent well in advance of their approach. He peered down at them with more curiosity than surprise, as if questioning their intentions in entering his little world.

"Black bears love to explore, my friend," Sasquot said. "This is especially healthy for a young cub."

Coda soon decided that joining his new friends would be more interesting than watching agitated squirrels and chipmunks scamper through neighboring trees. With surprising agility, he descended the tree and approached Sasquot. Sasquot poked at the pine needles with a stick, exposing a couple of beetles and some red ants. Coda obligingly lapped up the insects with his tongue and clawed through the forest floor, searching for more.

Sasquot and Jason patiently wandered through the forest in this manner, entertaining the cub's whims and eating fancies so that he would learn more about his natural environment. Coda sampled just about every berry in sight, exhibiting a particular fondness for blackberries. By the time Coda had satisfied his craving, his little snout was covered with blackberry seeds. Coda didn't seem to mind this one bit, and he lapped up a good many of the juicy seeds as he contentedly sauntered through the forest with his amused companions.

"The forest is a great buffet for bears. Coda is choosing almost everything," Sasquot remarked with wry humor.

Just as they were about to call it a morning, Coda bounded away into the underbrush in the direction of a hollowed-out beech tree. Jason playfully sprinted around the underbrush in an attempt to beat Coda to the tree. Much to Jason's surprise, he got to the tree first. Jason turned around to see the sidetracked cub curiously poking and prodding a pinecone along the ground with his nose. Jason shook his head, laughing to himself.

Only too late did Jason realize that there was a bee's nest in the hollow which his back completely blocked. While Jason considered making a mad dash to safety, a frustrated worker bee, tired of circling the obstructed hive, suddenly alighted upon Jason's arm. Before Jason could react, it stung Jason on his exposed forearm in its final dying act. Jason cried out in pain and anger, immediately slapping the bee off of his arm while lumbering clumsily away from the hive. The bee's stinger lay imbedded in his skin.

Sasquot quickly arrived at Jason's side. The cool-headed Penobscot spotted the tiny black stinger in the red, swelling area and gingerly removed it from Jason's right forearm as if it were but a splinter. The pain lessened instantly.

"You will be fine, Little Hawk," Sasquot remarked. "Our furry friend is the one I am worried about."

Jason turned around and watched an undeterred Coda approach the beehive. Coda extended his paw into the hive without any sign of fear, stirring up a swarm of perturbed honeybees. His paw was rewarded with a rich load of dripping honey. Coda licked his paw contentedly, oblivious to the growing hoard of angry bees. Coda next climbed up a few feet to the hollow and placed his entire head within the hole. The excited cub was poised and ready to feast upon the sweet honey stored within the honeycombs. Before Jason could even process what had happened, a furry, black form streaked in a mad dash away from the hive pursued by an angry swarm of worker bees. Cries of distress rose above the agitated buzzing of bees furiously defending their home.

Burying his head in the underbrush, Coda's nose emerged from a honeysuckle bush wriggling with bees and detached honeysuckle flowers. He was desperately trying to dislodge the handful of remaining bees and stingers from this most sensitive organ. The bees were soon knocked clear of Coda's nose, but the painful stingers remained. Sasquot ran over to Coda, gesturing for Jason to help hold Coda still.

"Hold the cub's paws, so that he doesn't slash me," Sasquot ordered.

Jason lifted Coda up off the ground and held his front paws down. Sasquot gripped Coda with one arm to help keep him still, while his free arm worked adroitly to remove the stingers from the cub's inflamed nose.

Coda yelped and whined pitiably as Sasquot removed each of the six stingers. Jason felt sorry for the overly curious cub.

But, Jason reasoned to himself, *this is part of Coda's learning process, just like what kids have to go through. This is simply part of growing up for him.*

"Let's carry the cub back home," Sasquot instructed, having removed the last stinger. Coda was too agitated and disoriented for Sasquot to even consider letting him return to the shed under his own auspices.

And so, the two teachers carried their injured student through the forest along a lightly traversed path toward Moosehead Lake. Class was over. Coda had learned more than enough for one morning of real-life instruction. Besides, his teachers were exhausted.

CHAPTER 7

As dusk began to fall that Friday, Kyle arrived home from his work downtown soliciting furniture orders. Earlier that day, Sasquot and Jason had returned from the woods and gladly deposited the rambunctious cub at the shed under Autumn's care. In exchange for Autumn taking the cub off their hands, they assumed her duties of watching over Kyle's sheep and repairing the barbed wire fence that enclosed the sheep's wooden pen. Passing by the two, Kyle presently waved and let them know that he would be at the farmhouse, where he planned to do some carpentry work. He would work in peace and solitude on a bedframe he needed to complete for delivery that coming Tuesday.

Minutes later, a phone call interrupted Kyle's work. Kyle assumed it was a business call. He had installed a line in the farmhouse mainly for business purposes, and few people besides customers and suppliers knew the number.

"Hello, Kyle speaking," he said picking up the phone.

"Kyle, it's Cynthia."

"Cynthia, I haven't heard from you for months," Kyle said with mixed emotions.

"Yes, well, you know how it is in my business," she answered coldly. "I'm calling because I'm flying into Bangor for the weekend.

I've been asked to do an article for *Architectural Digest* on New England architecture, and I have to look at a few sites around the area. Bangor has some elegant Victorian, Italianate, Queen Anne, and Greek Revival works worthy of mention."

"I see," Kyle responded, not knowing how to react to her unemotional, business-like tone.

"Yes, and Rick and I would like to see Jason this weekend."

"Who is Rick?" Kyle demanded with unmasked anger in his voice.

"Rick is a friend of mine . . . a doctor from Boston. He thought it would be nice to meet Jason and introduce himself."

"This is unbelievable, just unbelievable," Kyle mouthed half to himself. "Just a minute, I have to see how Jason feels about all of this." Kyle left the phone hanging from the farmhouse wall and called over to Jason, who was busy tying some barbed wire around a stake.

"Jason!" he bellowed out, instantly commanding Jason's attention. "Your mother is on the phone. She wants you to go to Bangor to see her and some doctor friend of hers."

»«»«»«

Jason was perplexed. He hadn't talked to his mother since his twelfth birthday that April, and he certainly had not heard about any *doctor friend* of hers. In fact, for months, he had been expecting her to come back and for everything to return to normal with his family.

"Okay, I'll get it."

"Take it in the farmhouse. I'm taking a walk," his father announced, leaving him to deal with the increasingly awkward situation.

Jason picked up the phone. “Hi, Mom?”

“Hi, honey, it’s great to hear your voice. How’s everything?”

“Good. Everything’s going good.”

“That’s good, sweetie—‘going well’ is how we say it in Boston,” she responded, correcting his grammar. “Now, Jason, I’m flying into Bangor tomorrow morning, and I’d like for you to have dinner with me and a nice friend of mine I’m seeing. How’s that sound?”

“Ah, well, that sounds okay,” Jason answered without much enthusiasm.

“Don’t worry about a thing, Jason. He’s very nice, and he’s a doctor. He just wants to meet you. I’ve told him so much about you.”

“Well, I guess it’s all right.”

“I’m glad to hear that, Jason. You sound so grown-up. It’ll be so nice to see you. Let’s say 6:30 we’ll come around and pick you up, okay?”

“Okay, Mom.”

“Great, honey, you take care and remember to eat right,” she said.

Jason’s mother always was trying to get him to “flesh out.”

“Yes, Mom.”

“Good-bye, honey.”

“Bye, Mom.”

The conversation bothered Jason. He felt like he wanted to make up so much lost time with his mother but not while she was in the company of some guy she was dating. The thought of his mother dating seemed strange and wrong to him. She was part of their family. He was her son.

Absorbed in thoughts of what this all meant, Jason returned to help Sasquot repair the enclosure, absorbed in troubled thoughts.

Jason recalled the words that Sasquot had spoken the day after his mother had left for Boston right before their planned family Thanksgiving last year: "Family is like a rock foundation on which to build a house. A family supports a person's whole being. It is wrong for a mother to be apart from her child."

When Jason had broken down in tears before him, Sasquot had been moved. "You are my family. You are a member of my family, too, from this day on, Jason."

"Jason, you've worked hard today. Go play ball with your friends. I'll finish the work," Sasquot said.

Jason nodded, appreciative of the space to sort through his feelings. He walked inside, wanting to be alone to process the emotions that were welling up inside. He turned on the television and watched baseball in his family room.

How ironic. Watching TV alone in our family room. If Mom changes her mind and returns, could our family ever go back to being normal and happy? he thought to himself.

Two hours later, Jason heard the front door open as his father returned from his "walk." Giving him some hope, Jason observed that his dad's face looked strong and resolved. His father asked him to come out onto the back porch to help with the grill. His dad removed a choice cut of steak from the freezer and some fresh ears of corn from the refrigerator.

"Your mother doesn't think people in Maine have any culture. Let's us two have one great meal."

And so, Jason dined with his father on filet mignon from a cow they had slaughtered earlier that week. Grilled to tender perfection, Jason's cut was one of the best he had ever tasted. Together, they devoured the nearly two-pound steak and three sweet ears of sugar corn picked from their garden the day before. The soft, buttered corn was delicious and felt as though it were melting in their mouths. Between voracious bites of steak and corn, Jason eagerly recounted Coda's progress, or lack thereof, that day.

His father asked a few questions to feign interest, but it was apparent to Jason that his dad's thoughts were elsewhere.

He's probably absorbed in the same thoughts I've been having all evening, Jason thought.

Less than a minute into the dinner, Jason's father looked straight into his eyes and said, "Son, I just want you to know something. Your mother's leaving had nothing to do with you. She loves you. I just don't think she loves me anymore."

Jason felt overpowered with emotion for his father. He could feel his hurt. "She loves you, Dad. I know she does."

His father just nodded slightly and closed his eyes. "She'll always be your mother, Jason. How she feels about me has nothing to do with you. Remember that."

"Yes, Dad," Jason responded, swallowing hard.

Soon afterward, Jason cleared his plate and asked to be excused. He had too many things to think about all at once. To clear his mind of the day's events, Jason decided to begin reading *To Kill a Mockingbird,* one of the books on his summer reading list. Halfway through the first chapter, sleep overwhelmed him. Jason fell into a fretful sleep full of images of his family quarreling and his mother telling his father that she did not love him anymore.

CHAPTER 8

Cynthia and Rick touched down in a twin prop plane at Bangor International Airport shortly after eight o'clock that Saturday morning. Cynthia went from Avis to National to Hertz before finding a car of "suitable luxury" for their Bangor excursion, a black Crown Marquis Cadillac with maroon leather interior, which she proceeded to drive from the airport to the historic Phenix Inn in downtown Bangor.

"How do you think Jason will react to our announcement, hun?" Rick asked Cynthia as they neared the downtown area.

"Jason should understand and be delighted that this will make his mother a very happy woman," Cynthia said and affectionately pinched Rick on the cheek.

"I should think the boy will be a bit shocked," Rick responded with more honesty than Cynthia cared to notice.

"Honey, look over there; that's Bangor House!" exclaimed Cynthia, excitedly pointing to an apartment building converted from a once-famous hotel at which Ulysses S. Grant, Daniel Webster, and Theodore Roosevelt had lodged.

"Cynthia, I was talking about your son."

"Oh, Jason is a smart boy, Rick. He'll understand. Remind me to show you Stephen King's mansion. It so evokes terror, but in such a tasteful and creative manner. You'll just love it."

"Yes, dear," Rick responded, resigned that Cynthia had no clue as to how momentous her announcement would be to her thirteen-year-old son.

For the next nine hours, a self-absorbed Cynthia and an increasingly disinterested Rick traveled all around Bangor's historic districts. Cynthia shot five rolls of film and recorded three mini-cassettes worth of her impressions of various architectural sites, from the Greek revival Zebulon Smith House to the landmark 1898 Bangor Standpipe and Observatory, built on former Native American hunting grounds. Finally, as the sun began to set over the mountains to the west, they headed inland toward Greenville.

"You'll just love the artwork adorning the restaurant, Rick. And the pecan-breaded chicken is to die for. It's The Lemon Tree's signature dish."

"Honey, I think I'll just follow your lead tonight."

"And you must order the cod pâté appetizer. If Maine has any cuisine to speak of, it is seafood."

"Yes, dear."

The conversation continued on in this manner for the next half hour, with Cynthia lecturing Rick on everything he just *had to know* about the restaurant, Bangor's hints of culture, and the lavish 1833 Isaac Farrar Mansion and Greek Revival Hill House that would comprise tomorrow's morning itinerary. Seemingly, the only Maine topic Cynthia did not discuss for Rick's edification was her family.

»«»«»«

Jason was waiting on the front porch for his mother and her doctor friend. As the Cadillac approached the main house, Jason rose from the front steps and quickly walked down the dirt driveway toward the car. Before either Jason's mother or her apparent date had an opportunity to step out to greet him, Jason opened the back door and climbed in. The previous evening had sensitized Jason to how emotional an issue this visit was for his father, and he was determined to conduct himself in a manner that would make his father proud.

"Jason, give your mother a kiss," his mother said, as soon as he had gotten into the car. Jason, a bit shy at Rick's presence, gave his mother a quick peck on the cheek.

"Jason, this is Rick, my doctor friend," she said, presenting Rick.

Rick turned around and shook Jason's hand. "Pleasure to meet you, Jason. I've heard so many good things about you."

"Thanks." The first thing that struck Jason about Rick was how old and refined he looked. Rick had a graying mustache and gold-rimmed glasses, and he appeared to be almost a decade older than his father.

For his part, Jason was a lanky, blue-eyed boy of light complexion with a three-inch height advantage over most thirteen-year-olds. He was clean-cut and casually dressed for the occasion.

"Honey, we're taking you out to The Lemon Tree. You'll just die for the designer breads and desserts. They're so fresh and delicate, they'll just melt in your mouth," his mother exclaimed.

"Okay, Mom," Jason answered without much enthusiasm. He wasn't sure what the evening would bring about, but he already felt bad that his dad wasn't there to spend time with his family.

"Your mother tells me that you're a good student," Rick said, attempting to break the ice.

"I do pretty well, I guess. I'm decent at science and American history."

"He's being modest, dear. Jason earned twice as many A's as B's this past semester and is working hard to be a straight-A student for the year," Jason's mother boasted, much to his chagrin.

"A lot of students get A's," Jason said, uncomfortable with the stellar student portrait his mother was painting of him.

"Yes, well, a boy like you can do very well in this world," Rick observed matter-of-factly.

"What Rick means, Jason, is that with the proper education, you can become someone respected in society. Rick and I are proud of your schoolwork, but we want you to be challenged more. I've had Rick set up an entrance interview with an admissions officer he knows at Exeter."

"Exeter? Where's that?" Jason asked, not liking what he was hearing in the least.

"Phillips Exeter Academy is in Exeter, New Hampshire, honey. It is an excellent school and has such a pretty campus. You'll just love its wonderfully reconstructed English Gothic church," his mom stated.

"I like my school, and I want to go to high school at Greenville," Jason responded with an edge of defiance.

"Jason, please, we are only discussing things. Now, I think it would be better for your education for you to go to school with well-taught children from good families. Greenville

Consolidated School has too many lower-class children, not to mention Native Americans."

Jason glared at his mother, half in anger and half in disbelief. "You mean like Autumn and Sasquot?"

"Jason, Autumn and Sasquot are nice, but they are crude and uneducated. They will never amount to much in society. We need to send you to a good school where you can learn what society really values."

"Sasquot and Autumn are like family to us. I can't believe you are saying things like that about them," Jason countered. "Besides, I want to be like Dad when I grow up." For a rare moment, Jason's mother seemed to be at a loss for words. She sighed disappointedly and did not address Jason the rest of the way to the restaurant. Instead, Rick attempted to make small talk with Jason with mixed success.

When they finally arrived at The Lemon Tree, the first thing Jason noticed was how many paintings decorated the walls of the intimate, thirteen-table restaurant. Jason's mother bubbled with excitement, explaining the styles and schools of art represented by each painting as she led Jason and Rick on an impromptu art tour. His mother explained that most of the paintings were signed by local artists, a few recognized even in Boston's art circles. She singled out one oil on canvas seascape painting to Jason and noted that it was on sale for "just" a few hundred dollars.

"How would you like to take that one home with you, young man?" Rick asked Jason with an air of wanting to impress.

"That's okay. I like my U of Maine hockey posters. Paintings are for women," Jason pronounced.

Rick gulped some air in surprise, looking as though someone had knocked the wind out of him.

Jason's mother immediately sought to gain the upper hand. "Jason, that was uncalled for. Rick is an extremely cultured and well-mannered gentleman, and I hope that one day you will be, too."

"Sorry, Mom," Jason said, feeling a bit guilty.

"It's not me you should be apologizing to," Jason's mom stated sharply.

"I'm sorry, Rick," Jason said. "Thanks for the offer. But I'm good for now."

"Well, now, that's all right, young man," Rick offered, regaining his composure.

"Let's take a seat and look over the menu," his mother suggested.

Jason deliberately sat closer to his mom, leaving ample space where an extra chair had been removed between him and Rick. He quickly picked up and scanned the menu, hoping not to have to talk to his mom's friend any further. Jason's mother suggested the pecan-breaded chicken, but he decided to show his independence and instead chose prime rib with a baked potato and New England clam chowder. Rick, by contrast, dutifully followed his mother's lead in ordering the signature dish with a smoked cod pâté appetizer to start.

"How about a good wine," Rick suggested, then quickly caught himself. "But I suppose that could set a bad example for the young chap."

"My friend Paul's family serves wine with their dinner whenever I eat with them," Jason stated. "I don't drink any, of course . . . "

"I didn't know that," Jason's mother snappily interrupted, without masking her disapproval. "Jason, you know very well that Paul—and any boy for that matter—should not drink wine."

"Yes, ma'am, I mean, Mom," Jason stammered, a bit embarrassed.

"That settles it. Please bring us your best bottle of Chardonnay for the two of us and some sparkling cider for the boy," Rick requested, as Jason bristled at being called a boy.

"Very well, sir."

The overwrought pleasantries and strict etiquette of an upscale restaurant were quite foreign and uncomfortable to Jason, who much preferred an outdoor grill to formal indoor dining. In fact, Jason had not been to any restaurant, let alone a formal, highly-rated one, since his mother's birthday last November. She had departed for Boston a week following her birthday and just prior to their highly anticipated family Thanksgiving. Thanksgiving without her had sorely tested his father's cooking skills, ultimately leading to their sharing take-out chicken wings after the turkey erupted in a grease fire. This year, the two of them planned to share Thanksgiving with Sasquot and Zephyr, who had heard about last year's debacle and kindly offered to host them.

"Now, Jason, let me tell you a little bit about Rick. He's a radiologist at New England Medical Center in Boston. His family has lived in Beacon Hill for generations."

"What's Beacon Hill?" Jason asked.

"It's a very nice place to live," his mother answered. "Much more art and theater than in Maine and so much history, honey. We think you'd love it there."

Jason's jaw dropped noticeably, and his facial muscles tightened.

"Jason, what we are saying is that you're welcome to come live with us . . . in Boston," she continued.

The agitation on Jason's face deepened, evidencing disgust and horror.

"If you like, you can finish your eighth-grade studies in Greenville and then move down in June," his mother offered in a tone of voice which conveyed how perfectly reasonable she felt she was being in extending the offer. "It'll be a great opportunity for you and Rick to bond." Then, patting him on the knee, she said, "Jason, I have something very special to tell you. Honey, Rick and I are engaged to be married!"

Jason stammered as he rose from his seat. "You're—you're married to Dad," he managed to say.

"Please, Jason, sit down," she said, taken aback by Jason's reaction. "That's in the past. There is no longer any future between your father and me. I am moving on with my life, and he needs to move on with his. You must understand, Jason, that my relationship is with only you now."

The one thing Jason knew for certain was that he did *not* understand this.

"I've filed for divorce. Your father will be served with the papers on Tuesday." The words sounded remote, as if Jason were far removed from the scene.

Returning to the dinner table in mind and spirit, Jason shook his head in disbelief. "How can you do this to our family?" he demanded. Jason was furious, and his voice trembled with anger.

Her eyes bulged with surprise. "Jason, please, you're making a scene," she pleaded. "This is what's best—for all of us."

Jason's mind reeled with the brunt of his mother's leaving them—her own son and her loyal husband—for someone else.

How could she even dare to think I would be happy about this? he thought. *Doesn't she understand how much I love Dad and want us to be a family again?* Jason's mind flashed in anger, hurt, and disappointment.

His whole body suddenly felt sick, nausea flooding his stomach. Propelled by the power of emotions that Jason could neither fully control nor understand, he stammered to his feet, breathing hard.

"Ja—"

Before his stunned mother could even complete his name, Jason had bolted out of the restaurant and down the street, disappearing into the night. He rounded a corner and did not stop until he reached a pay phone four blocks away.

His heart pounding, Jason inserted all the change he had in his pocket into the pay phone and dialed Sasquot's number.

Sasquot answered the phone in a deep, calm voice. "Hello."

"Sasquot, it's Jason! I . . . I need you to pick me up . . . I'm . . . I just need to go home."

"Jason, what is wrong? Are you okay?" Sasquot asked with great concern.

"I'm okay. Really. I just have to go home."

"Where are you, Little Hawk?"

"On Center Street in Bangor . . . at a pay phone somewhere near The Lemon Tree Restaurant. I'll walk to the convenience store on the corner of Garland and Center Street. Can you pick me up there?"

"Yes, Little Hawk. It's a long drive, but I will be there as quickly as possible. Don't worry. I will call your father to tell him I'm picking you up."

"No, Sasquot. Please. Don't worry my dad. I'm fine. I just need to get away from my mom and her . . . friend, that's all."

"Okay. I'll leave now, Jason."

"Thanks, Sasquot. I really appreciate it."

"Say no more. I'll see you soon, Little Hawk."

The evening ended in anger and frustration. Jason felt discarded and abandoned, a child whom his mother had voluntarily chosen to leave behind for convenience in order to start a new life without him. What pained Jason most deeply was the terrible realization that his mother had betrayed those closest to her: her husband and him, her only child.

She always knew she wasn't coming back, Jason reasoned, sickened by the thought. *She started a new life in Boston without us.*

CHAPTER 9

The next morning before dawn, Jason began an ascent of Mount Katahdin with his father, hoping to find healing and revitalization along the way. He breathed in the cool air of the morning as the rays of the sun dissipated the mountain mist enveloping the waking forest and lake. The welcome warmth of the sun radiated heat and light upon his skin, invigorating his whole being.

With a host of grateful forest creatures awakening to a new day full of possibilities and fresh beginnings, there seemed to be a oneness with nature. The mountain's peak alternately glowed and flashed in long rays of early morning light that seemed to beckon him and the world surrounding him to emerge and partake of awaiting wonders.

If only my mother could appreciate this, he thought. Jason was transfixed by the raw beauty that enveloped him.

Before Jason and his father stood Katahdin, which means "greatest mountain." As Sasquot had taught Jason ever since he first gazed upon it in amazement, Katahdin was the mightiest peak in all of Maine, towering a mile into the sky. As such, Sasquot had pointed out, the heavens reward its lofty heights by casting upon its summit some of the first rays of sunlight in the United States each morning as dawn breaks. Jason was eager to show his mountaineering father that he, too, could successfully navigate Katahdin's strenuous trails, ascending its crown with him to share its regal majesty.

The night before, Sasquot had dropped Jason off at home around 9:30. His dad had been waiting up for him in the den, re-reading an old hiking guide. Jason had not said much. He simply had told his father that his mom seemed changed and that he did not want to see her for a while. His dad had nodded and not pressed Jason. Instead, he had said that while Jason had been gone, he had decided they should rise very early the next morning and head out to summit Katahdin. Jason had seen this imposing mountain from a distance and had always wanted to climb it. He had excitedly agreed to make the full-day hike.

Sasquot and his family regarded Katahdin as a sacred mountain, as did many of the surviving members of the Abenaki Confederacy. Sitting next to Jason on the shore of Moosehead Lake one morning, Sasquot had shared with Jason the mountain's legend—that it was the home of the Mountain King; his sons, the Thunders; and his daughter, Lightning. Sasquot had even confided in Jason that years ago, he had honored his father's dying wishes and buried him just off of its summit.

"My father," Sasquot had shared with a mesmerized Jason, "was a great shaman of our tribe and told me that he wanted for eternity to be able to 'see our People from above.'" Katahdin was the perfect place of rest for him, providing a spectacular view of more land and lakes than any other point in North America.

Recalling Sasquot's words, Jason was nearly overwhelmed with reverence for the mountain he now climbed. If he were to reach its pinnacle, he would achieve a goal that even Thoreau, the great naturalist Jason much admired, had never attained.

Jason and his father began their ascent at Katahdin Stream Campground, carrying flashlights to light their way through the moonlit forest. They wore jackets that were insulated against the pre-dawn chill and any passing rain or winds they might encounter. Following Hunt Trail along the west side of the mountain, they crossed through forest growths of spruce, pine, and maple that peacefully cast their silhouettes against the softening blue of the morning twilight. Jason heard soft low hoots coming from the pine trees ahead.

"Dad, I think there's an owl up ahead," Jason whispered.

Jason's father paused and examined the ground beneath the pines with his flashlight, revealing bundles of undigested fur and bones. He pointed to a branch in a pine directly above. Jason could see a crow-sized owl with mottled brown-gray feathers and a strikingly round face peering down at them with large, yellow eyes. It evidently had been feasting on mice and rabbits from its perch.

"A short-eared owl," his dad said with a smile before signaling to move on. "Let's keep going. We have much more to see, son."

The two continued on the rocky Appalachian Trail as the orange glow of dawn began to illuminate the sky. From time to time, they could see Katahdin Stream gurgling down the mountain not far from the trail. The rains had been mild that August, rendering the stream safe and tame compared to the treacherous torrent it became during Maine's infamously wet springs.

Hunt Trail led over a rustic bridge and bore left, tracking along the banks of Katahdin Stream.

"Dad, can I try to catch some crayfish?" Jason asked, eyeing the clear, shallow water lined with rocks. He knew that crayfish lurked under such rocks, hiding from brook trout and other predators.

"Why not? We already passed the one-mile point at the bridge. Let's have some trail mix and then you can test your luck with the crayfish."

His dad opened a bag filled with raisins, coconut, peanuts, almonds, dried apricots, and bananas. It never ceased to amaze Jason how refreshing trail mix tasted in the middle of a good hike.

After taking a couple handfuls of trail mix and a swig of water from his canteen, Jason removed his pack and lumbered down to the stream bank. He hunched over a large granite rock bordering a shallow pool, rolled up his sleeves, and peered into the water. Spotting a potential crayfish hideout, Jason overturned a rock in the middle of the pool, revealing two crayfish. The crayfish instinctively darted backward toward other rocks, difficult to discern along a pebbly bottom which camouflaged them extremely well.

Choosing one to intercept, Jason quickly placed one hand before the rock that the crayfish was positioned to back under and his other hand directly in front of the crayfish. Then he deftly trapped the elusive creature in his hands. He brought the three-and-a-half-inch crayfish out of the water and placed it in a plastic bag, which he tied and put inside his hiking pack.

"What do you intend to do with that?" his father asked.

"I'll see if Coda likes to eat crayfish."

"That cub never seems to satisfy its appetite."

"Coda's a he, Dad. Sasquot told me bears eat many times what an average human eats every day. Especially during the fall, when they're storing up food for the winter."

"At least, Coda's not eating me out of house and home," his father remarked. "Okay, son, let's move on. We still have more than four miles to go to get to the summit."

Katahdin Stream continued to run parallel to Hunt Trail for several hundred meters further.

"This hike is not that hard, Dad," Jason observed.

"Just wait until we start our real ascent," his father cautioned. "Remember to lean slightly into the upgrades so that you reduce strain on your back and don't end up tumbling backward from the weight of the pack."

The trail soon cut off from the stream and led upward to an altitude of roughly eighteen hundred feet. Jason's quadriceps began to register the exertion of carrying his body and equipment up the mountainside. The burning sensation in his legs was similar to what he had experienced while running the mile in seventh grade. During that time, he had run a little over five miles, just twelve seconds off of the junior high record, and his weary legs had grown increasingly heavy during the bell lap.

He had dug deep within himself in a last-ditch effort to outkick his nemesis, Matthew Stiller, in the home stretch. Coming off the final turn, Jason had commanded his body into a labored sprint. His throat had felt parched, his lungs as though they would collapse. He had reached the dreaded *wall*—that point at which the body overrode the mind and forced the runner to respect its limits. The pain and nausea after the race had almost been as bad as the humiliation he'd had to endure. Stiller had gloated over his three-second victory, ridiculing Jason as Jason collapsed to his knees in exhaustion just past the finish line.

"Whatsa' matter, sissy? Can't hack a little race? Go train with your . . . " Stiller had taunted, proceeding to deride Jason's association with Autumn and her family.

As Jason negotiated the upgrades, he envisioned how it would feel to beat Stiller and be the team's top runner. *This hike will get me in shape for the fall cross-country and spring track teams. There's no way Stiller is going to out-kick me this year,* he thought as he climbed.

After almost twenty minutes of steady climbing, Jason finally spotted a charred wooden structure just off the trail ahead.

"Let's stop for another snack and water break," Jason's father said as they arrived at the Seven Pennies Shelter. Though the shelter had burned to the ground, its remnants marked the point that was two miles from the mountain's base.

Jason drank deeply from his canteen, quenching his thirst. "Dad, do you think I can beat Stiller this year?"

"Well, I think you can do almost anything you put your mind to, Jason. You're a Wilson, aren't you? And we Wilsons are a hardy stock," his dad stated confidently, slapping Jason on the back.

"I know. It's just that being a Wilson can be a lot to live up to sometimes."

His dad looked at him, seeming to collect his thoughts, then slowly nodded. "Yes, I know what you mean. Your grandpa was quite a man. He had great character, and the whole community respected him."

"What made him so respected, Dad?"

"When Grandpa set his mind to do something, he would do it; and when he gave a man his word, I never once saw him break it. He could warm a room with his smile and make strangers feel at home. He was handsome and athletic and cared about his family. I'd be happy to be half the man Grandpa was," his father mused.

"I think you're a lot like Grandpa," Jason said with sincerity. "What sports did you do at school, Dad?"

"I didn't run, but I did cross-country skiing. Placed best in Piscataquis County my junior year of high school and second in Maine my senior year," his father reminisced. "Even won a biathlon or two back in my day."

"Cross-country skiing is a tough sport." Jason nodded, knowing it required tremendous endurance to cross-country ski.

"Yes, you're sure right about that; the races can be grueling. Well, your Wilson lineage surely passed down to you some good endurance genes, son. Keep training like this, and eventually, you'll be greeting Stiller at the finish line."

Jason smiled, proud to be a hardy Wilson man or one in formation. Climbing Katahdin and vanquishing his athletic rival would each be major steps in claiming manhood status. Unfortunately, both of the Stiller boys were itching for a fight with Jason.

I might have to face and confront them before I ever get the chance to beat either one of them at a sport, he thought.

"Would you ever fight someone, Dad?" Jason asked.

"Everyone has got to pick his fights, son. Some fights can be avoided. Others have to be fought."

I'll probably have to fight the Stillers then. They are not the type to back down from a fight, especially one they've already told me they want.

"Yeah, I think I know what you mean," Jason stated.

"What I mean, son, is that you have to stick up for your principles. If someone challenges what you stand for, you can't back down. What you believe in is what makes you a man."

Jason had never before heard his father speak like this. For as long as Jason could remember, his dad had been a private man who kept most of his life philosophy to himself.

"If a person does not like or respect you because of something that doesn't go to the heart of who you are, let that pass; but if a person insults your family, your God, your country, your core life beliefs, that's something to stick up for, even if that means a fight."

"I guess I kind of did that yesterday," Jason responded.

Jason's answer took his father by surprise. "What do you mean, son?"

Jason then told his dad what had transpired Saturday evening, from the uncomfortable car ride into Bangor to his furious confrontation with Cynthia over the shocking announcement of her engagement and filing for divorce. Jason's dad appeared to be riveted by every word Jason had to tell him. So riveted, in fact, that he permitted Jason to tell the entire story uninterrupted from Jason's conversations with his mother and her doctor friend en route to The Lemon Tree through the moment Jason abruptly departed the restaurant following his mother's shocking announcement.

Once Jason had finished, his father paused for moment while he gathered his feelings and said, "Son, you make me proud to be your father. You stood up for what you believed in, for what was important to you."

"Thanks, Dad," Jason replied, as the two briefly embraced for the first time since his mother had left.

"Now, I want to make sure you know, son, that I'm not pressuring you to live here with me. I want you to be happy, to grow up where you want to. You can choose to live here with me or with your mother . . . But I do think I can give you a good upbringing right here in Maine."

"I love it here, Dad. I want to stay here 'til I die."

"Hey, now, let's not pass any life sentences out today," his dad said, seeming to want to lighten the mood while, at the same time, there was a touch of emotion in his voice. "But I think this year and high school would be a good start. Come on, let's continue your mountain training."

Just beyond the Seven Pennies Shelter, they encountered steep terrain, which forced them to navigate on all fours for several stretches. These inclines, known as the Pitches, were notoriously slippery during inclement weather.

The two continued for another twenty minutes until they came to a gargantuan slab of rock projecting from the mountainside, commonly referred to as the Cave, where his dad signaled for another rest. The Cave marked the half-way point of their ascent.

Peering inside, Jason imagined brave explorers holed up in the Cave during a Maine blizzard. Many hikers had perished in white-outs on Mount Katahdin. In such conditions, the Cave could serve as an invaluable sanctuary, sheltering those hunted by the fierce mountain weather.

Stepping inside, Jason turned on his flashlight in order to examine the Cave's innermost crevices. His eyes began to adjust to the eerie darkness, one pierced only by the tiny cone of light from his flashlight and the dull light of morning at the entrance to the lair. Suddenly, Jason tracked movement in the inner recesses of the Cave. Three furry creatures emerged from interior crevices, hanging upside down with their wings folded.

His father entered the Cave. In the dim natural light, Jason first heard, then saw, a tiny creature fluttering around the back of the Cave. Abruptly, the creature changed course and headed straight for them. Its mouth agape, Jason could see the creature's tiny teeth as it swooped down within inches of their heads. Jason instinctively ducked, repulsed and frightened by the creature. Jason noted that his father, by contrast, barely moved a muscle even as the same dank air that had repulsed Jason undoubtedly pressed upon his father's hair and neck.

"Hey, that bat almost flew into my head!" Jason exclaimed.

"Calm down, son," his dad commanded with the same calm he presently demanded. "First of all, that bat is not more than four inches long. Secondly, bats don't just crash into things, unless they happen to be insects."

"But aren't bats blind or almost blind?" Jason asked, ducking down as another bat began to fly overhead.

"That's a myth, son. Bats actually have great eyesight. Plus, they make sounds through their mouths or noses which echo off objects and let them know where things are located. These bats eat insects like flies, mosquitoes, and moths. In fact, I think they're dining on the mosquitoes swarming above our heads."

With his arms covered by his jacket, Jason had not realized that hundreds of mosquitoes had been hovering above the duo since they had entered the Cave.

"Watch carefully as the bats feed, son."

Jason mustered enough courage not to flinch as the two bats flew back and forth through the mosquito swarms. The bats rotated their wings rather than flapping them up and down, and he saw one do a somersault in the air.

"What was that somersault all about?" Jason asked in mild amazement.

"Bats sometimes scoop mosquitoes into their wings. They somersault around to free these insects from their wings so that they can feed upon them," his dad answered.

Jason watched the bats, fascinated by their skill in catching the minuscule mosquitoes in midair. The bats were a light brown color with pale yellow bellies and ears protruding beyond their noses. Their noses, ears, and wings were a brownish-pink and seemed to consist of some sort of membrane, while the rest of their bodies were covered with fur.

"Well, son, I think it's time to do some feeding of our own. Let's get out of here to regain some appetite."

"Yeah, I don't think I can eat in here," Jason agreed.

Jason followed his father out of the Cave and back into the morning sunlight. The air was rapidly warming.

"I don't think we'll need our jackets," his dad said. "Here, let's trade these in for some light windbreakers."

The two took off their all-weather jackets and put on nylon windbreakers.

"With a wind and water-proof jacket, I can train for track this winter," Jason said, considering all-year training for the first time.

"Of course, you can. That's where you get an edge on the competition in any sport—training year-round and being in good shape to start each season. All right now . . . time for some granola bars."

They munched on granola bars and drank from their canteens.

"Drink some more here, son. The going gets very rocky, and we're not going to stop again before we hit the summit," his father warned.

Jason drank deeply, beyond what he needed to quench his thirst at the moment. Jason's coach had always told him to do this before practices and meets, explaining that a runner did not become thirsty until well after his body needed refreshment. Ingrained in him was Coach Sullivan's admonition that hydrating well was the key to avoid overheating and to mitigate the chances of even passing out from heat exhaustion.

Temporarily refreshed, the two pressed on for the summit, treading over rocky trail as the trees thinned all around them. Soon, they came to a bleak stretch of granite rocks called the Boulders, where they halved their pace in order to navigate over and around the rough terrain. Jason's calf muscles burned with exertion from the relentless demands of the steep climb.

At long last, they came to what his dad called the Gateway, a moss-carpeted plateau leading to very graduated upturns.

Heartened by the decreasing difficulty of the trail, the two quickened their pace.

"We'll make the summit by noon at this rate," his dad announced with a tone of satisfaction.

Less than half an hour at this speed brought them to Thoreau Spring at the end of the plateau. The spring was almost dry due to the scant August rainfall, although the area was covered with tall grass and moss. A bronze marker commemorated the naming of the spring in honor of Henry David Thoreau during the Great Depression.

Jason peered upward to behold Katahdin's lofty summit rising before them. The summit appeared deceptively close, but in actuality, it stood a full hiking mile away. As Jason gazed out into the morning, he observed a rich view of lakes, streams, and mountain peaks extending in all directions as far as he could see. He could not wait to experience the view from the summit.

"Baxter Peak isn't much higher than this, son," his dad said. "We've almost ascended Mount Katahdin, the highest peak in all of Maine."

This is the last leg. Jason refocused his mind and body on the task at hand. "Let's do it, Dad."

Jason and his father forged ahead at a brisk pace, determined to conquer the mountain by noon. The sky looked clear for miles in all directions. Nothing could stop them now.

As they neared the summit, seemingly out of nowhere, a storm cloud appeared. There were no other clouds in sight. Before they could react, thunder clapped, and a streak of lightning flashed across the sky. Terrified, believing that they were in a most dangerous position so high upon the mountain, Jason crouched to the ground next to his dad, trying to keep as low as possible. They braced for an onslaught of rain. However, only a light, misty rain fell upon them and the adjoining ground. Soon, the mist dissipated, revealing a clear blue sky in all directions. The two looked about them in amazement.

Jason saw it first. They were standing before the graves of Sasquot's father, grandfather, and great-grandfather, each formerly revered as a shaman of the Penobscot people. Distinguished even among their tribe for their deep ties to Mount Katahdin, Sasquot's ancestors had summited the lofty peak for generations before the likes of Henry David Thoreau and Theodore Roosevelt. In fact, so ardent were his great-grandfather's efforts to preserve and protect Katahdin from the ravages of over-logging that plagued early twentieth century Maine that its famed conservationist governor recognized and rewarded his devotion. In a remarkable gesture, when the trailblazing governor and philanthropist, Percival Baxter, donated Baxter State Park, he granted special dispensation for Sasquot's great-grandfather and lineage to be buried just off of the summit of Katahdin's regal crown. Fittingly, it later was named Baxter Peak in Percival's honor. This burial right only served to deepen the aura that enveloped Sasquot's forefathers in their Bear Family clan.

Although Sasquot denied that any of his ancestors had possessed supernatural powers, he told Jason that they had been gifted with great wisdom and an uncanny ability to interpret and discern nature. In Jason's eyes, Sasquot likewise appeared to be endowed with a remarkable ability to comprehend the mysteries of nature.

Jason's father turned toward him with a dumbfounded look on his face. "We must have gotten sidetracked from the trail because this is the first time I've ever seen these graves."

There were stone markers at the head of each grave with symbols and decorations engraved upon them. Each also bore an inscription in the Abenaki language, which neither of them could read. There were also stunning, white feathers sewn together and tied to a wooden stake in front of the graves opposite the markers.

Jason's dad knelt and touched the feathers. "These are feathers from the crown of a bald eagle."

Jason and his father looked out from the mountain downward at the peaks of the thirty other mountains of Baxter State Park—a string of serene, rounded gems crowned by the king of them all: Katahdin. Ponds, rivers, and lakes stretched out in all directions: Katahdin Lake to the east; Millinocket, Nahmakanta, and Pamadumcook Lakes to the south; the western branch of the mighty Penobscot River to the west; and Grand Lake Matagamon and the eastern branch of the Penobscot to the north and east. Never before had Jason seen such a panoramic view of Maine's rich and pristine, glacier-created topography. With the wind and sunlight striking his face as he gazed out upon the expanses below, Jason felt what he would later call "the majesty of Maine from above." Jason could now appreciate why Sasquot's father had asked to be buried here atop Maine's sapphire sky.

Deep in thought, Jason and his father turned and slowly walked back to the trail. Humbled and sobered by the terrifying yet hauntingly beautiful experience, neither could explain the strange storm cloud and mist which had appeared and disappeared so mysteriously. And neither could recall having left the trail at any point in their final approach to the summit.

Minutes later, they came to a sign bearing the legend, "Terminus of the Appalachian Trail, A Mountain Footpath 2054 Miles Long to Springer Mountain, Georgia." They had reached the summit. Jason had conquered Katahdin.

CHAPTER 10

Early the next morning, Jason strolled through the woods toward Sasquot's cabin, immensely proud of his climbing feat. Sasquot would surely appreciate how exhilarating it had been for Jason to mount Katahdin's lofty summit and gaze down upon the land his forefathers had cleared and settled nearly a century ago. Jason was likewise certain that Sasquot would understand how powerful the scene had been that unfolded so mysteriously before him and his father as they neared the final peak—an almost mystical transportation into the world of Sasquot's ancestors, the revered shamans of the Penobscot people. He would question Sasquot how it was possible that one moment they had been on the trail toward Baxter Peak and the next moment found themselves standing before the graves of Sasquot's forebears. After relating these experiences and hearing Sasquot's insights into them, Jason hoped that he and Sasquot would take full advantage of the perfect Labor Day weather to sojourn together into the woods with Coda. He was so consumed with sharing his adventures with his wise old friend and earning his praise and recognition that he could barely concentrate enough to find his way through the forest to Sasquot's home.

Jason turned from the forest path onto the dirt road that led directly to Sasquot's abode. He gazed toward Coda's shed as he approached the dwelling. Suddenly, out of the corner of Jason's eye, he saw a small, black form dart into the woods to the east.

Jason stopped for a split second, questioning whether it could have been Coda. Then he bolted for the woods in pursuit of the animal, convinced Coda had somehow managed to escape from the shed.

"Coda! Coda!" Jason shouted as he shunted aside brambles and brush, frantically trying to get within sight of the cub. He could not see Coda anywhere in the thick forest cover.

Then the sound of laughter stopped Jason dead in his tracks.

"Awasosis, Awasosis," a female voice called out in amusement.

Not more than thirty feet ahead and to his right, Autumn lay on a bed of forest moss, looking up at a small pine tree above. Jason followed her line of sight and saw Coda racing up the tree.

What in the world has frightened or inspired Coda to climb at that speed?

Jason soon spied his answer scurrying up the tree five to ten feet in front of Coda. It was a gray squirrel fleeing from a potentially fatal encounter with the curious cub.

Coda's ascent was remarkably quick and agile. His front paws gripped the tree on either side as Coda thrust his hind legs forward under his belly. Then Coda extended his hind legs and reached up for another hold with his short, sharply curved front claws. With Coda in hot pursuit, the squirrel climbed to the topmost branches of the thirty-foot pine. Unfortunately for the squirrel, it was running out of tree, and there were no trees within leaping distance, either.

Coda closed in on his prey, enticed by the reward of his first solo hunt that helplessly awaited him only three—now two—feet out of reach. Another lunge and one quick swipe and the squirrel would meet his Maker.

Desperate, the squirrel abruptly turned its body and faced its foe. Coda let out a bark-like cry of excitement. Then, without warning, the squirrel stunned all concerned. It bolted down over Coda's head and belly and scrambled down the tree in seconds flat. Coda continued to grip the top mast of the tree in disbelief.

Autumn burst into a fit of laughter. "Poor Awasosis!" she cried out.

Jason could not contain his anger any longer. "What are you doing with Coda?" he demanded. "And what in the world are you calling him?"

Autumn turned toward Jason in frightened surprise. "Jason, I was just taking Coda out for a walk. Coda saw a squirrel running along the ground and chased it up this tree."

"What were you calling him?" Jason asked again in anger.

"I called him Little Bear in Abenaki," Autumn answered.

"Well, I am the bear's owner," Jason proclaimed. "And his name is Coda. Coda won't be going into the woods to hunt with a girl. He needs someone to take care of him, not someone he has to take care of."

Autumn looked at Jason with an expression of anger and hurt. "I thought you were different from the rest," she said. "You're . . . you're no better than any of them!" Autumn sprang to her feet and ran back toward the cabin, leaving Jason alone with Coda to consider his harsh words and actions.

Jason couldn't be sure, but he thought he heard the sound of muffled sobbing before the cabin door slammed shut. He felt bad but also felt certain that taking a bear out into the woods to hunt and forage was a man's job.

My father would never approve of a young girl taking a bear out like that. In doing so, she would only injure Coda or, even worse, herself, in some manner. The woods are a dangerous place.

Jason peered back up into the pine tree only to observe Coda sliding down the tree in what appeared to be a controlled fall. Coda's sharp claws scratched the pine's bark just enough to keep the descent at a manageable speed. Once Coda got to within three feet of the ground, he released his grip and landed safely, but awkwardly, on his haunches.

Now on the ground, Coda scanned the area in a perplexed manner, searching for Autumn. When he spotted Jason, Coda eagerly made his way over to Jason in the black bear's patented shuffle, hoping for some food and refreshment. The cub appeared healthy and content. At close to forty pounds of weight, Coda hardly lacked for nourishment. Within the short span of time since his capture, the young cub had gained almost four pounds—a very encouraging sign that he would survive his first winter.

Coda's rapid growth continually amazed him. And this was despite Sasquot's having prepared him for it with numerous nuggets of information. For Sasquot had taught him from the first week Jason had set eyes upon the adorably small cub that his very survival depended upon a healthy diet and steady weight gain. In response to Jason's eager follow-up questions, his Penobscot mentor had explained that Coda instinctively would eat more during the fall as his body attempted to store up a sufficient layer of fat beneath his fur to survive a winter of deep sleep and the scarcity of early spring food which would follow his winter dormancy. As with all black bears, Sasquot elaborated, Coda would not hibernate in the traditional sense. Rather, the cub would gradually fall off into a deeper and deeper sleep as the days shortened and the temperatures dropped. If there were a warm spell during the winter, Coda might awaken and wander around for a while before returning to his sleep. Likewise, if Coda were disturbed during his winter sleep by the noise or scent of an intruder, he would awaken and take action to protect himself, whether it be to stand and fight or, more likely, to flee to another den.

It astounded Jason to hear that Coda had been born blind, deaf, and toothless, measuring only roughly eight inches in length and weighing a mere eight ounces. Earlier that week, Sasquot had pointed out that the once-miniscule cub was now approaching a healthy forty pounds. If Jason had performed the math, he would have calculated that at birth, Coda had weighed only one four-hundredth of his mother's two-hundred-pound weight, whereas now, he weighed nearly one-fifth of it, an eighty-fold increase. To Jason's delight, Sasquot had further informed him that Coda could very well dwarf his late mother's two-hundred-pound weight and attain a weight of up to six hundred pounds when fully grown.

So, it was with hungry and eager eyes that Coda approached Jason. Perhaps Jason would have something even tastier than the elusive squirrel for him.

Jason rummaged through the pockets of his pants but could find nothing. Then he remembered that he had a half-eaten granola bar in his jacket pocket. He took out the granola bar, removed the remainder from its wrapper, and was about to hold it out to Coda when a deep voice rumbled, “Bear cubs do not eat granola bars.”

Jason looked up into the stern eyes of Sasquot, who stood above him with arms crossed in disapproval.

“Sorry, Sasquot, I just thought he might be hungry.”

“A bear is always hungry, Jason, but Coda needs to eat wild food, not human food. Now, come with me; there is an important matter we must discuss.” Sasquot gestured for Jason to follow as he led Coda back to the shed.

Sasquot opened the old, wooden shed, revealing plenty of natural foods for Coda to feast upon, ranging from a rotten log full of grubs and other protein-rich insects to acorns and beechnuts, blackberries and raspberries, and wild grasses and plant roots.

“Coda will be fine here for now. Let us go to the edge of the lake together,” Sasquot instructed, closing the latch on the shed.

Jason obediently followed Sasquot to a large slate formation by the edge of the lake and took a seat beside his pensive father-figure. The expansive lake shimmered in a vibrant radiance of sunlight reflecting blue and green hues cast by Big Squaw Mountain.

“Little Hawk, have I told you the legend of the bear? How a black bear family raised a Penobscot boy until the whole bear family was needlessly slain by a Penobscot man? The wrongful rescuer returned the child to his human family, and the child grew bear bristles and began to act like a bear. Eventually, though, the child did grow up to be a Penobscot man, rather than a bear. The grown man, however, wisely remembered his upbringing by the kind bear family and vowed to treat bears like members of his human family from that day forward. That man was the founder of the Bear Family, the most important family of the entire Penobscot tribe. Zephyr, Autumn, and I are descendants of this man. We are the last survivors of the Bear Family." Sasquot paused and then turned from the waters to look directly into Jason's eyes.

"The black bear is a sacred animal to my family and me. A bear is my brother." Jason could no longer look into Sasquot's intense gaze. He could only look down, shameful of his actions earlier that day.

"My family took a solemn vow never to harm a bear. If a bear attacks me, that will be my fate." The creases around Sasquot's eyes deepened. "Autumn is my blood. Black bears are her kin. Our Bear Family has a solemn duty to save the cub from starvation this winter. No one man or boy owns any bear in Maine or anywhere else in this world. It is a wonderful, wild creature belonging ultimately only to God. Do you understand, Little Hawk?"

Jason nodded, panged at the hurt he had caused Sasquot and Autumn. "I am very sorry, Sasquot, very sorry," Jason said.

Sasquot nodded slightly and continued, "Little Hawk, in my tribe, it is taboo for a man to use foul words or to tease or insult a woman. It is, as you know, hard for Autumn at school. Some ignorant people there who do not respect my people mistreat her."

Then, once again, he looked directly into Jason's eyes. "Little Hawk, God adopted me to be part of His family. Likewise, I adopt you to be an honorary member of my family. You are like a son to me—part of my blood. My heart grows very sad to hear of how you treated my daughter earlier today—my very blood."

Jason felt as though Sasquot's eyes had pierced his soul. He felt numb all over his body and could not utter a word.

In that silence, Sasquot arose and left him, his "son," to contemplate his words.

CHAPTER 11

The next morning, Jason stood alongside Autumn waiting for the school bus to take them to Greenville Consolidated School. School officials had told Sasquot that the dirt road to his shorefront cabin was too rough and the location too remote to place Autumn on the bus schedule. So, every morning during the school year, Sasquot would drop Autumn off at Jason's house and then begin his ten-hour workday on his father's farm.

Both Jason and Autumn were entering the eighth grade, the last year in which they would be considered part of the school's junior high. Jason anticipated that this first day of school would be especially awkward. First, he would have to wait with Autumn for the bus to arrive, with the events of yesterday still prominent in both of their minds. Then, once he arrived at school, the Stiller twins would be sure to reiterate their challenge to meet after school in order to teach him a lesson about associating with the Autumn and her family. Lastly, Jason remembered that his mother planned to have his father served with divorce papers sometime that day.

This is going to be one of the worst days of my life.

Jason anxiously awaited alongside Autumn for the bus to arrive. He had apologized to Autumn as soon as Sasquot had dropped her off five minutes ago. However, Autumn had only mouthed, "Okay," and then proceeded to ignore Jason.

She really must have taken it hard. I wonder why?

Jason endured the ten long minutes waiting for the bus beside Autumn without further conversation. Once on the bus, he sat alone, relishing the silence of the twenty-minute bus ride to school. He sensed that the relative tranquility could soon shatter all around him.

There are some things worth fighting for, he thought. Jason recalled his father's words as he tried to fortify himself for what he viewed as an inevitable confrontation with Matt Stiller. *I can only emerge from so many battles unscathed.*

The bus pulled into the school parking lot off Pritham Avenue, just a couple hundred feet from Moosehead Lake's southern shore. The lake glistened in the morning light, rippling with gentle waves.

Yet home seems so far away, Jason thought as he gazed out upon the lake. *At least, I'll see Scott and Paul at school.* The only thing Jason did look forward to that day was seeing them.

To Jason's surprise, his school day began very pleasantly. The first thing he did was catch up on Scott and Paul's summer adventures at Camp Deerpoint. He listened in mild amusement to their predictable tales of camp pranks and their unit's spying on its "sister" camp. Fortunately, the stories did not amount to anything even remotely as exciting as the stories Jason had to tell.

Once both Scott and Paul were done, Jason told the story of the bear attack in as nonchalant a manner as possible, embellishing several aspects of the story. The bear went from weighing two hundred pounds to weighing four hundred pounds, and Jason's role morphed from that of firing the initial shot to that of firing the fatal shot moments before the ferocious beast was about to devour the entire party. Moving on to current circumstances, Jason proceeded to inform his friends of his crucial role in raising the cub and teaching it how to hunt big game.

"Yeah, I've taught Coda to fish and track small animals, and now I think he's ready for some serious game," Jason told his mesmerized audience. "He's already hunted small rodents like squirrels and woodchucks, and now he's all set to move up to the big league, you know, bringing down deer fawn and moose calves."

"Wow, that'd be really cool. But think about it. Man, there's a big size difference between a squirrel and a moose," Paul cautioned. "A newborn moose weighs almost as much as your cub."

"Yeah, but this bear is really smart and much stronger than you'd think for his size. I betcha he could bring down a moose calf without a problem," Jason boasted.

"Let's take him down to Lazy Tom's Bog and see whether he can down a moose," Scott suggested.

"Hey, guys, this bear is not a toy. He has to be expertly trained. Sasquot and I are handling his development. Once we've trained him, you'll get to see him in action," Jason stated with the air of a professional trainer.

"Expert training," Paul said and laughed. "Since when were you a bear trainer? Been working at the circus or something?"

Paul and Scott good-naturedly gave Jason a poke in the ribs and chuckled.

Then a big storm cloud began to rain on Jason's day.

"Hey, punk, you should be training *yourself* to survive, if you know what I mean. Not messing with some *Injun* and his collection of wild animals."

It was Matthew Stiller, who, amazingly, was the more intelligent of the Stiller twins, although the measurement was a relative one.

"Matt, no one was talking to you," Scott, the largest of the three, answered back.

"I don't need your permission to do squat, Jack," Matt said as he rolled up his sleeves to show two bulging biceps. For a cross-country and track runner, his upper body was ripped beyond belief. "I was talking to my friend here. So, what do you say, punk, are you ready to show me something after school, or are you still the yellow-bellied, *Injun*-loving wuss you've always been?"

"My boy could kick your butt out there on the track any day," Scott asserted.

Matt directed a scornful laugh at the three of them. Then his face suddenly reddened with anger. "You better not be talking smack behind my back, punk, because I'll eat you for lunch out there on our track or home course any day."

Jason decided to play the game. "Yeah, well we've got time trials coming up next Monday. We'll see who's the better man." The cross-country time trials, which they used to seed the varsity team for meets, held significant bragging rights for the winner. The winner would be looked upon to lead the team in every race that season.

"Lot of talk, no action . . . just like your *Injun* girlfriend told me you were all about," Matt said with an evil smile.

"You leave her out of this, you hear!" Jason said, his voice rising. "She's a proper woman. Don't you dare speak about her like that!" He had never spoken to Matt with such boldness and emotion.

Matt brought back his right arm, ready to pulverize Autumn's defender. Scott and Paul instinctively each grabbed one of Matt's arms and, working together with all their might, managed to slowly pull them behind his back. Jason's eyes widened as he witnessed their grips trembling with tension and realized that they were all that held Stiller back from unleashing a fury of brute force upon him.

Just then, a hall monitor spotted them and demanded, "What's going on over there?"

Before anyone could be caught, the four of them immediately dispersed. Scott, Paul, and Jason headed for the cafeteria, while Matt beelined in the opposite direction for the gym.

No doubt Matt needs an immediate outlet for his soaring testosterone level, Jason reasoned. Out of the corner of his eye, he glimpsed a tightly muscled form sprinting away at breakneck speed. *If he is not on steroids, he doesn't need to be.*

The three arrived at the cafeteria out of breath.

"Jason, are you trying to get us killed?" Paul demanded.

"Some things are worth fighting for," Jason answered, surprising even himself with his statement of principle.

CHAPTER 12

Scott's mother dropped Jason off at home after practice that afternoon. As Jason turned to wave goodbye to Scott and his mother, he felt a sharp pain in his lower ribs. Much to Jason' dismay, the newly discovered pain recurred when he rotated his torso.

I know the culprit. That low blow from Stiller must have done it.

While training on a forest trail on their home course that day, Stiller had come up from behind and elbowed Jason sharply in the ribs before passing him to take the lead. The blow had momentarily knocked the wind out of Jason, forcing him to the side of the course to stop and recover. Jason's teammates, characteristically trailing the faster duo, had rounded the bend to find Jason arched over in pain beside a tree, struggling to regain his breath. Seeing Jason in that condition, they had assumed he had cramped up from being out of shape or pushing himself beyond his limits. Red-faced with shame, Jason had joined the main pack without mentioning the incident.

At least, Stiller had not attempted to resume their confrontation anymore from earlier that day. With a coach who had served as an army drill sergeant watching over the team, Stiller had uncharacteristically exercised reasoned restraint.

Stiller's brain cells must have been operating at close to maximum capacity when he decided that the risks outweighed the reward of trying to beat me up while at practice. Besides, he probably realizes he will have plenty of other opportunities to confront me when Coach Sullivan is not around.

As Jason entered his house, Max barked a worried bark, indicating that Jason should follow. Jason trekked down the basement stairs behind Max to find his dad seated on a stool facing the liquor cabinet. On the bar counter was a bottle of Jack Daniels a little more than two-thirds full with an empty shot glass beside it. His father's face appeared expressionless, as if he were gazing into a void. A shattered picture frame of his parents dressed in their wedding finery lay on the floor just a few feet away. The culprits—divorce papers notifying his father of an impending hearing to decide whether to grant his mother's petition for divorce—were strewn across the room. Most had landed on the floor. A few had found their way onto the well-worn couch. Two lay on the black-and-white TV, and one had even found its way onto their ping-pong table.

The basement was seldom used these days. It had once been a kind of family recreation area, where they had vied for supremacy on the ping-pong table, played king-queen-jack, or brokered Monopoly deals while watching re-runs of *MASH*. The place now looked forgotten and neglected, a sad reminder of what it had once been to them.

"Dad," Jason called out softly. "Dad, are you okay?"

Jason's father turned slowly toward him, a forced smile on his face. "I'm okay, son. I'm okay."

"Dad, don't blame yourself for the divorce," Jason begged. "Mom doesn't deserve you anymore, anyway. She . . . isn't family," he gushed out.

"Oh, Jason. Things used to be so different. You should have been there when . . . "

»«»«»«

A chestnut steed galloped through the woods toward Moosehead Lake, head held high as if it were well aware of its magnificent beauty. Kyle rode upon its back, confident and in control. The horse broke out of the forest onto open ground alongside the lake, a picturesque vista of lake against mountains.

In the distance, Kyle saw two people laying upon a blanket near the shore. As the horse neared the two individuals, he realized that they were two young ladies enjoying a midday picnic. He was about to continue past them when he was struck by the breathtaking face which turned toward him and smiled blushingly. In a matter of moments, he had reined in the horse and turned it around to face this woman, this goddess of the lake. She had long, flowing, blonde hair; sky-blue eyes; and a radiant smile that gave color to her delicate face.

"Hello, stranger," she said in a flirtatious voice.

Kyle held his breath in blissful amazement. Then, once he had gathered himself enough to speak, he said, "Good afternoon, ladies. Allow me to introduce Untamed Heart."

"Hello, Untamed Heart. What a beautiful name," the goddess observed, stroking the horse's face. "And what name shall we call you, bright-eyed stranger?"

"I'm Kyle. And who do I have the pleasure of meeting this fine day?"

"I'm Cynthia. And this is my college roommate, Judy."

"My pleasure to meet both of you. Now, college did you say? With both brains and beauty, you're surely aiming to be women of high

society," Kyle coyly observed. "I, on the other hand, am a man of the woods, born and raised in these wild lands."

"A mysterious man of the woods of uneven shave and dark complexion," Cynthia noted. "A true-to-life Paul Bunyan, are you? Why, you're certainly built like a man of the woods, Kyle."

"Yes, ma'am, that's the reward of living off the land. I work my father's farm and do some carpentry on the side. I hunt, fish, ride, and roam these parts unafraid of man or beast."

"That sounds a lot more exciting than studying architecture down at school. Say, Kyle, I've always wanted to ride a horse."

"Nothing to it, Cynthia. I'll give you and Judy a free lesson. How's that sound?"

"Wonderful. You up for it, Judy? A free lesson from this handsome stranger?"

Judy nodded, excited yet seemingly unsure of what they were getting themselves into.

"We're in."

»«»«»«

"That afternoon was one of the happiest in my life, Jason. We rode the trails along the lake until sunset and then grilled steaks out on the back porch. Your mother fell in love with Untamed Heart and the farm. She said the whole thing was so romantic, just like a scene out of a book. She just didn't see all of the work and toil that went into everything. And the wilderness, the roughness of the wilderness . . . "

»«»«»«

There was a blizzard that year, one of those terrible February blizzards that erases all vestiges of roadways and trails. The electricity had been out for days, and Kyle had chopped his reserves of wood to fuel their wood-burning stove. The cold was so extreme that three sheep had frozen to death in the barn. Kyle had trudged into town on snowshoes, leading an old packhorse tied to a sled. The sled was laden with an oak bedframe and end-table that Kyle had just completed and needed to market in order to buy essentials to make it through the coming weeks. Cynthia, a woolen shawl wrapped around her, sat upon the packhorse. She had placed a basket upon the sled with which to bring back meat, milk, canned goods, and other foods from Greenville's general store.

The journey into town was long but uneventful, and they did not pass a soul on the way. Once in town, Kyle unloaded the bedframe and carried it into the Greenville Furniture Store. After minutes of haggling, Kyle walked out of the store with less than two-thirds of what he would normally get for the frame. The facts were that people were desperate to just make it through the winter and that prices for anything but essentials were dirt cheap. Kyle was grateful that at least the owner had promised to buy either the end table or another piece of furniture from him the following week.

Meanwhile, Cynthia had found enough food at the general store to last them through the week. If another blizzard made their return to town impossible next week, Kyle would have to hunt deer or slaughter his own livestock for food.

As they made their way back toward home, a light snow began to descend. The clouds darkened the afternoon sky, casting a gray pallor upon the freshly fallen blanket of snow. Ever alert, Kyle presently spotted a fallen moose calf ahead and just off the elevated snow-covered road upon which they were traveling. He reached into his pack and removed his rifle, fearing predators lurking nearby.

Soon, he observed a gray form stealthily slinking through the forest toward the snow-trapped moose calf. It was a lynx traveling with remarkable agility over the thick snow. The moose-calf bleated, attracting unknown predators whose shadowy forms could be seen darting through the forest.

Suddenly the horse reared, throwing off the sled. Cynthia clung onto the packhorse, screaming in fright. Attracted by the scent of store-bought meat, a pack of gray wolves rarely observed in these parts emerged from the woods and rushed for the sled. Ravenous from months of blizzards and unusually bleak conditions, they were eager to feast upon a ready meal of chicken and lamb.

Kyle immediately sprang to his feet and raised his rifle, aiming at the closest wolf. The shot dropped the howling canine instantly, prompting its companions to slow their approach and growl menacingly. The packhorse whinnied and reared, trying desperately to throw Cynthia off and flee for safety. Cynthia gripped the reins in one hand but was slipping off to the side. She couldn't hold on much longer.

Without warning, a wolf lunged again for the sled. Kyle's rifle misfired, and he desperately beat the wolf off with the butt of his rifle. Terrified, the packhorse violently lurched, hurling Cynthia to the frozen ground. Her side ached with pain, having borne the brunt of the impact. Panicked, Kyle reloaded and shot at the attacking alpha wolf, injuring its leg. Limping, it bled a trail of blood away from the sled, unlikely to survive the night. However, in return, it had mortally wounded the packhorse and thrown it into a panic.

Kyle rushed to where his wife lay. The packhorse is dangerously close; one kick could be fatal *flashed through his mind. He had no choice but to bring it down. He took steady aim and brought down the panicked creature with two shots in rapid succession to the head.*

The wolves cowered back in fear, unwilling to continue the attack. The male and female alpha pair of the pack had been grievously wounded. They paused for a moment before fleeing back into the cover of the forest.

Having secured the area of immediate danger, Kyle carefully carried Cynthia to the sled and gently laid her on top of a blanket he had brought to cushion the furniture.

"You're all right, Cynthia. Nothing looks broken," Kyle said.

Cynthia sobbed back, "I'm not all right. I think I've lost the baby!"

"The baby! Oh, no, it can't be! I . . . didn't know. I didn't know," Kyle wailed. Gnashing his teeth in grief, Kyle pulled Cynthia and the sled three excruciatingly painful miles through the snow back to the farm. When they arrived back home, he immediately called a doctor who lived but a mile away. The worst was soon confirmed. Cynthia had miscarried.

»«»«»«

"When we got home, your mother explained that she had deliberately shielded me from knowing about her pregnancy, hoping our fortunes would turn and there would be a happier time to let me know the joyous news. As it was, your mother feared I would work myself to the bone if she made known her pregnancy to me during those lean, stressful times. Despite my best intentions in trying to protect her, our horse, and our cargo of food from the vicious pack of wolves, your mother has always held me responsible for her miscarriage," his father explained in a low voice. "I really can't blame her much for that."

"You mean, I would have had an older sibling?" Jason asked incredulously.

Jason's dad nodded, looking Jason squarely in the eye. "Yes, son. I'm so sorry." In a rare expression of emotion, Jason's father hugged him, bringing Jason's head close to his, softly sobbing. "I should never have let your mother go out in that weather."

"You didn't know, Dad . . . You just didn't know."

Nodding with a forced smile, his father managed to compose himself before continuing. "Your mother mostly kept her feelings about living out here to herself. Sometimes, though, I saw her explode at the tiniest thing, and it was then that I realized just how much she resented living on our farm . . . "

»«»«»«

It was a brisk November morning, one week before Thanksgiving. Cynthia was walking back from the barn bearing a metal pail full of fresh milk in each hand. Meanwhile, Kyle had just returned from a successful pre-dawn deer hunt, and he, Sasquot, and his husky friend, Lester, were carrying a 225-pound buck to the barn to be gutted.

Mitch and Max proudly trailed the train of hunters as they made their way past the main house. Then, spotting Cynthia, they enthusiastically bounded her way. Mitch, an overgrown puppy, darted right into Cynthia's path and eagerly jumped up onto her. Momentarily startled, Cynthia stepped backward, upsetting her balance and spilling the milk all over herself and the frightened pup. Kyle signaled the men to place the buck down and then ran over to Cynthia to make sure she wasn't hurt.

Cynthia was angrily swearing at Mitch. When Kyle arrived at the scene and saw that Cynthia was fine, he burst out laughing at the spectacle: here she was, drenched in milk and cursing at a bewildered puppy who was flinging milk in all directions as he shook himself off.

"How dare you!" Cynthia burst out. "I am sick and tired of this farm-girl life dealing with stupid animals and stupid people day in and day out."

"Easy, Cynthia, Mitch is only a puppy. He doesn't know any better."

"That isn't the point, 'Mister Man of the Woods.' To you, my life out here is one big joke. You don't take my life and my career seriously, and I've had it. You've pushed me over the edge!"

"Cynthia, please, you know that's not true. Can we please talk about this later on in private?" Kyle was not only completely taken aback by what Cynthia was saying, but he was mortified that Sasquot and Lester could overhear her tongue-lashing.

"There's no later time to discuss this, Kyle. I've made up my mind. I've sent my portfolio to an architectural firm in Boston, and they've offered me a position. I've decided to take it. I'll be leaving this week."

"What? I can't believe this! What are you talking about?" Kyle demanded.

"I just need a break, Kyle, a hiatus from my mundane existence here on this farm. I want to be part of something important, to be part of real society. I just need to do this for me."

"Do this for you? You're a mother and a wife. You can't walk away from your life and your responsibilities like that."

"I have to think about myself first and foremost. I've been thinking about everyone else for too long and neglecting myself. It's time for me to focus on my needs. And besides, I'm coming back. I just need some time alone."

»«»«»«

"Your mother left that night, Jason. Nothing I could do or say would dissuade her from leaving."

"Mom told me she was taking a vacation, a long vacation. For the first two months, I thought she was coming back any day," Jason recalled aloud.

"I'm sorry, son. I couldn't bring myself to tell you that it was more than that. I couldn't even tell myself that things were over between your mother and me. I believed the lie she fed me that she was coming back and that everything would be okay with our family once she got this architecture bug out of her system. Now, I see what she had in mind: a new career, a new husband, a whole new life . . . "

"It's just wrong, so wrong," Jason said, shaking his head in agitation. "It's not right to leave people who love you like that."

"I know, son. It eats me up inside, too. We've got to be strong. We've got to be there for each other, so that we make it through this. We're tough enough, aren't we, son?"

"We don't need her. She was just making you miserable, Dad. I'll always stick by you," Jason vowed.

"Son, you're a keeper. I've always loved you, but until today, I didn't appreciate just how *much* you mean to me. I had no clue how deeply you cared about all of this; you were just storing it inside. Son, I know I can pull through this okay. I owe you one," Jason's father said, giving voice to an unsteady stream of feelings he rarely let flow.

"Of course, you'll make it through, Dad. We Wilsons are a hardy stock," Jason pronounced, confidently repeating his father's words of inspiration from their mountain hike.

Father and son embraced. It was a sad and heart-warming scene all at once. They were there for each other. Neither had felt such a sense of being loved unconditionally in a long, long time.

CHAPTER 13

For the rest of the week, the school was abuzz over Jason's confrontation with Matt Stiller. Although there were several variations to it, the core of the gossip was that Jason had stood up to Stiller and challenged him to a race to determine who was the better man. Some said that the incident amounted to a dispute over a girl, others that it centered around Jason's association with Native Americans. No matter which variation was told, the effect was the same: Jason's estimation in the eyes of his classmates shot way up. No longer an average kid who minded his own business, Jason was now seen as a real leader—someone with a lot of backbone.

For Jason, this was a mixed blessing. He basked in the respect and admiration of his peers but secretly feared a physical fight with his dreaded nemesis. Perhaps even more, he feared the humiliation of losing the race and consequently being thought of as a loser rather than as the winner who had taught Stiller a lesson in humility.

Overnight, Autumn's attitude toward Jason transformed from one of pained and angry disappointment to one of fawning respect. He sensed that she might even be developing a crush on him based on his bold challenge to Stiller's verbal onslaught.

More important to Jason than any of this attention was that by confronting Stiller, he had taken one additional step to becoming a real man. Once accomplished, he hoped it would bring both pride and honor to his father and to his beloved mentor, Sasquot.

During practice that Wednesday, Thursday, and Friday, Jason trained with unprecedented focus and commitment. He arose early each morning to get in an extra three-mile jog and, after practice each day, lifted weights, alternating upper and lower body workouts. During practice, he exceeded whatever workout the coach instructed the team to do.

On Wednesday, the coach told the team to run four to six miles at a seven-minute mile pace. Instead, Jason ran seven miles at a six-minute, thirty-second mile pace. The coach and the team in general were mildly impressed. Then on Thursday, the coach instructed them to do a "speed workout": eight quarter-mile laps at an eighty to eighty-five-second pace with a full recovery lap in between each quarter. Jason ran ten quarter-mile laps averaging seventy-eight second clips with a brisk jog in between each one. His teammates, and especially Stiller, now took serious notice of Jason's performance.

Unwilling to be outdone, Stiller did an extra workout session in the pool after practice and lifted weights early Friday morning. At practice, Stiller hung with Jason during Friday's six miles of rolling hills at a grueling six-minute, twenty-second mile clip.

Jason's gauntlet had been thrown, and Stiller had accepted the challenge. Monday would be the day of reckoning.

That weekend, Jason asked Sasquot how he could build his strength, speed, and stamina. Sasquot taught him to take short breaths from his diaphragm rather than deep breaths from his chest, which were slower and less efficient in a race. He also taught Jason to run with his weight borne by the forward part of his foot and toes rather than by his heels, which would help to propel Jason onward and sustain forward momentum. With regard to pre-race diet, Sasquot told Jason to eat foods that were low in fats but high in carbohydrates, which, as Sasquot explained, were "fuel for his body." And most importantly, Sasquot told Jason how to prepare his mind for a race.

"For my people, Little Hawk, speed in the forest sometimes spelled the difference between life and death. Many years ago, young warriors fleet of foot would spy enemy Mohawks canoeing down the Penobscot River or making camp upriver. If the warriors did not reach my people before the Mohawks, it could have terrible consequences. If most of the men were out hunting or on patrol, this would leave our squaws and children without enough protection. Our tribesmen would return to see our village burned, women and children killed."

"Wow! Sounds like training was necessary just to survive back then, Sasquot."

"Yes, little warrior. Tough physical games prepared youth for battle. Young boys played a game similar to lacrosse and hurled sticks much like javelins in another game. The winners received much admiration and respect. But physical strength alone is not sufficient to be a good warrior. Most important is a person's strength of mind. Great warriors knew no fear in battle. They had confidence in their skills. Their minds controlled their actions in battle, enabling them to fight without fear of death."

"How can I build up strength of mind, Sasquot?"

"This is a process, Jason. First, you need to grasp the power of your mind. Then you need to focus on the task before you. Watch the race play out in your mind. Imagine yourself winning the race. Conquer all of your fears by visualizing in your mind what you must do to prevail."

"How do I do this?"

"You must clear your mind of all other things and focus it solely on the race ahead," Sasquot pronounced, gazing intently into the distance. "When my father, a great medicine man, visited sick members of our tribe, he saw the injury heal in his mind before he treated the person. He concentrated his strength of mind in order to heal the person. A sick person needs to have the will to get well. The spirit and mind must be as one."

Jason closed his eyes and visualized Greenville's home cross-country course. He could see the fastest runners being aligned by the coach on the starting line, with Stiller getting the best position as the pre-race favorite and him getting the adjacent starting block.

"Sense the power and strength you have," Sasquot intoned. "See the woods before you as you run like a deer through them. Feel how fleet of foot you are, your feet like feathers being carried by the wind. Feel your breaths as you run. Control them. Feel your heartbeat. Control each beat."

Jason saw and felt the race before him. He traversed the course through the woods onto a stone bridge overlooking a stream, then up a gradual hill, along a stone wall, and back onto a wooded trail laden with moss, roots, and stone which he deftly navigated, his mind one step ahead of his feet. He saw Amazon Hill, a steep incline that he leaned into in his ascent, making an extra effort to lift his knees higher and push off the ground with power from his toes. He felt the rush of the wind, heard the cheers of spectators lining the course, and felt the pounding of his heart as he raced well ahead of the pack.

A figure ahead grew larger and more distinct. It was Stiller. He was closing in on the front-runner with only a mile to go. Stiller followed a thin dirt path which wove its way in alternating right-left curves around small fir trees, creating a running slalom. Jason methodically shifted his body weight to lean into the turns and accelerate out of each one. After clearing the last of the line of fir trees, he shifted his weight sharply to the left and began to ascend the final hill. The quarter mile monster started gradually but became steeper as Jason neared the top. He was now close enough to Stiller to hear him panting ahead. As he crested the hill, Jason lengthened his stride, causing his hamstrings to burn from the exertion. Stiller was now but thirty feet ahead with one half-mile to go.

Jason could see his coach, alternating glances at his stopwatch and Stiller, the lead runner. "Fourteen minutes, forty-eight seconds—half a mile to go. You can break the course record!" Coach Sullivan shouted.

If Jason could summon the courage and strength to pass Stiller, he would win the race while setting a new course record. His spine tingled with excitement. A shot of adrenaline surged through his body. He willed his body to close the gap with Stiller. The ground between them shortened. With a quarter mile remaining, fifteen feet separated the two runners. One surge—one excruciatingly painful, sustained surge—would propel Jason to victory.

Stiller rounded the soccer goal and began his final kick to the finish line. Spectators lined the back straightaway of the deco-turf track in anticipation of a close finish. Jason had to move now or never. He heard Sasquot's words, "Concentrate your strength of mind . . . Your spirit and mind must be as one." His spirit would brook no defeat.

He envisioned himself a Penobscot scout racing an enemy party back to his home camp with everyone and everything he knew and loved depending upon his speed and willpower to save them from otherwise certain death. His lungs felt as though they were on fire, his legs as heavy as logs. He was burning fumes, but he would not give up. He could not, and would not, surrender.

Jason and Stiller were side by side as they hit the deco-turf of the final straightaway. There were only 150 feet to the bright white finish line where the coach awaited the winner, eyes fixated upon his stopwatch.

"Seventeen minutes even. The winner will shatter the course record!" Coach Sullivan bellowed.

They were traversing the final half mile at a blistering speed. Jason kicked with every stride, his tiny spikes digging into the track for extra traction. Sweat dripped from his face onto the track. The finish line became larger than life. Jason closed his eyes to block out the pain. He thrust his chest forward to break the plane of the finish line first.

"Wilson, first! Seventeen minutes, eight seconds. A new course record!" the coach announced.

Jason's face beamed. He was the new school champion. He had vanquished Stiller and humbled him. He would be a school hero.

"Little Hawk, Little Hawk," Sasquot called out. "Your eyes are closed, but your face beams like the noon sun. What did you see?"

"I won, Sasquot! I beat Stiller and set a course record. That would be incredible! I hope this stuff works."

"It will not work unless your mind wills it to work. Your mind and spirit command your body. You need the will to win before you can win the race, young warrior," Sasquot coached. "God gave you the gift of being fleet of foot. By using that gift, you honor Him."

"Yes, Sasquot," Jason said, his mind focused upon willing himself to victory. By uniting his mind and spirit behind an unshakable will to win, he was confident that he could forge his God-given talent into a school championship. He would fear Stiller no longer. Stiller would be vanquished in mind, body, and spirit.

CHAPTER 14

Autumn led Coda out of the shed for a Sunday frolic in the woods. Coda had quickly grown accustomed to Autumn and loved to follow her into the forest to find new creatures with which to play. Unfortunately for these creatures, play often meant chasing them through the forest undergrowth or treeing them in a towering pine or maple. Fortunately for these harried creatures, the cub still had much to learn regarding how to hunt and quarry his prey.

Autumn was in a particularly cheerful mood this Sunday afternoon. No one at school had ever stood up in her name to Matt Stiller or, for that matter, to any of the teachers or students who mistook her quietness for lack of ability or ignorantly patronized her. She was proud of the Penobscots and their role in fighting for American independence from the British and did not understand why so many at the school resented her tribe for finally receiving compensation for the millions of acres of land it had inhabited for generations prior to European settlement. It had especially pained Autumn when a couple of her classmates asserted that she was not a real American.

How can they say such a thing when Native Americans had lived and died throughout North America for thousands of years before the

Europeans even realized that there was a North America? This was something she asked herself over and over.

But this school year had begun differently. On the very first day of eighth grade, Jason had shown that he appreciated Autumn and Native Americans and that she and Sasquot were important enough for Jason to risk his reputation and well-being in their defense. Jason finally had demonstrated that he thought of Autumn as someone special and that he cared what people said about her. Autumn's crush on Jason deepened, since it now stemmed not only from Jason's good heart and looks but from his heroic championing of her people's dignity. Autumn made up her mind to go to the home course after school Monday to cheer on her newfound hero in his athletic showdown with Stiller.

Autumn watched as Coda nosed his way into a damp, rotted tree within sight of the lakeshore. Coda seemed fully immersed in finding some creature or thing hiding within it. Suddenly, a green frog leaped from his daytime sanctuary into the surrounding grass.

Coda instantly abandoned the rotted tree and took notice of the fleeing frog. The frog leaped into an area of tall grass. Coda pawed at a tuft of high-growing grass before even establishing where his playmate lay. Close enough to alarm the frog, Coda watched as the creature bounded in two quick leaps toward a naturally occurring pile of rocks in the middle of the forest. The frog now lay perilously exposed.

Not one to waste the opportunity, Coda sprang after the frog and eagerly pawed at its right hind leg. Injured, the frog took a spastic jump. Coda gave the unfortunate frog one final smack and quickly decided to sample this new morsel.

Autumn bounded after Coda, who now had the dead creature hanging from his mouth with only its legs visible. Autumn laughed as if at a naughty child. "Coda, you silly thing, what in the world do you . . ."

Just then, Autumn heard a rattling sound which instantly froze her mid-stride. A brown and black crossbanded snake lay coiled not more than three feet away, the hollow segments of its tail ominously signaling its warning to strike. She had inadvertently stepped by a rare timber rattlesnake as she ran past the rock pile, rousing the predator to action.

Autumn shuddered as she recalled her father's warning years ago that a single injection of its venom would bring pain, swelling, and blistering and could even potentially paralyze her lungs from neurotoxins in its venom. A strike that penetrated only her muscle tissue could leave discoloration and blistering scar tissue comparable to third degree burns, he had somberly warned.

The viper's elliptical eyes struck terror into Autumn as it elevated its head to pinpoint her location. Its forked tongue darted in and out of its mouth, smelling out its adversary.

Autumn cried out in fear. The rattler raised its head higher, curling back onto itself as its rattle shook with increasing ferocity.

Suddenly, Coda pounced on the rattler from behind. The rattlesnake lashed out at Autumn but fell short of her body due to Coda's attack. Coda's pounce had thrust the four-foot body of the snake backward, away from its quarry. Its flesh had been pierced by Coda's razor-sharp claws. Momentarily stunned, the snake's head crashed against the forest floor. In a matter of seconds, the embattled reptile had recovered its bearings and smelled out the location of its new adversary.

Without waiting for the enraged creature to make a second strike, Coda bit into its black tail. The wounded rattler viciously lashed out at Coda, its gaping mouth exposing fangs poised to inject the outmatched cub with paralyzing venom. Coda instinctively swiped at the rattler's lunging head. The paw sliced open the rattler's neck, dropping its body and head to the ground once again. The snake writhed in excruciating pain, its rattles vibrating yet louder and faster.

The snake was grievously wounded but would not die without a final attempt to strike its slayer. The snake raised its trembling head and flicked its tongue, zeroing in on Coda's location only two feet away.

"Oh, no!" she cried out as Coda raised his paws in self-defense, unwittingly exposing his underbelly to the springing rattler. Too slow to avert this attack, Coda's paws were not readied in time to parry its blow. The rattler's head accelerated, thrusting toward the furry underside of the creature she held most dear. Surging with pure adrenaline, Autumn snapped a branch off a rotting tree and thrust it through the body of the snake with tremendous force. Pinned to the damp forest floor, the rattler spasmed uncontrollably. Then, abruptly, its body went limp, putting an end to its death throes.

Coda fell over backwards in anticipation of the attack on his underside. The bear looked comical as he lay on his back, visibly puzzled that he had averted the rattler's strike. Coda soon regained his composure, rolled over, and sprang to his feet. When Coda's eyes alighted upon the snake, now pinned to the ground and dead to the world, he became furious. He mutilated the rattler, decapitating it with his paws and biting viciously into its underbelly.

Autumn stared with pride at the spear she had created by snapping an inch-thick branch off an aging elm. She beamed with satisfaction that she had summoned the strength and courage for this feat.

Coda had helped save Autumn from a dangerous attack, one that could have potentially been deadly. But even more surely, Autumn had saved Coda's life. Whether or not Coda realized this at some conscious or subconscious level, she could not say; but that day, a special bond developed between the two that neither man nor beast could break. Coda was her protector, and she was his.

CHAPTER 15

Today is the day of reckoning was Jason's first waking thought. Energized from race-day anticipation, he quickly dressed and sat down to a breakfast of yogurt, Cheerios, a plain bagel, and a banana. He washed the breakfast down with a twelve-ounce bottle of a high-carbohydrate sports drink, which would provide extra energy for his body to burn that afternoon. Even though he was no longer thirsty, he forced himself to gulp down a glass of water as well. There was no such thing as being over-hydrated, he recalled Coach Sullivan lecturing him.

Autumn excitedly greeted Jason at their bus stop without mentioning the rattlesnake encounter for the time being. *I don't want to distract Jason,* she reasoned with herself. *He needs to focus on the task at hand—defeating the* school *bully, who's just as venomous.*

"I'm really happy you're standing up to Matt," she said instead. "That takes a lot of guts."

"Oh, it's just a race," Jason answered, trying to downplay the situation—partly to keep himself as cool and collected as possible and partly to mask his embarrassment at receiving such a compliment from a girl his age. Despite the effort, he could not help but blush slightly at her praise.

"It's not just another race, Jason. I mean, the whole school is talking about it," Autumn stated.

"Yeah, it's nice that people are taking an interest; but win or lose, it's no big deal. I'll just do my best." Jason's stomach churned at the thought that he had set himself up to either be a hero or a goat in a matter of hours from now.

Autumn looked up at Jason with a smile. "I know you'll do great," she said.

"Thanks, Autumn. So, which explorer did you end up choosing to present for our history project?" Jason asked, looking to change the subject.

The two proceeded to discuss their favorite explorers with Autumn explaining why she had selected Sacagawea of the Lemhi Shoshone tribe. Autumn informed Jason, Sacagawea had traveled across the continent with the Lewis and Clark Expedition, serving as their sole female interpreter and, at times, their guide.

"Her wisdom and kindness helped them to befriend, trade with, and pass through the lands of new tribes they encountered along the way, crossing the Western wilderness. They even named a river in honor of her after she saved the journals of the expedition from a capsized boat," Autumn explained to Jason.

"Wow, I never realized that," Jason said. "The history books focus on Lewis and Clark. They should give her some credit. I wanted to present Paul Bunyan, but Ms. Lavigne told me that he may be more of a legendary figure than a historical person. So, I ended up choosing Samuel de Champlain. Besides being the founder of Quebec and New France in the New World, which included parts of Maine, he treated Native Americans with respect and even formed alliances with many tribes against the warlike Iroquois."

To Jason's liking—as he was happy to focus on anything but the race that loomed before him—he and Autumn discussed their favorite teachers and electives and other safe, school-related subjects. Jason even shared the latest gossip about their school's cheerleading squad, which reportedly would go on strike if their junior high football team did not engineer a major turnaround this season.

Last year, under Coach Tim Owen, the listless team had gone winless in all ten games on their schedule. After it became apparent that the team would lose for a record tenth time in a row, the few students left in the football stands had chanted, "O-ten, O-ten!" in a derisive play on his name. Jason wondered what creative nickname he might soon garner if he lost the race.

Once aboard the bus, Jason was oblivious to his classmates, consciously blocking out everything but the time trials from his mind. *Focus on the task before you. Prepare your mind, and your body will be ready,* Jason told himself, feeding off Sasquot's lesson from that weekend.

Preoccupied with his thoughts, Jason exited the school bus, oblivious to an out-of-place youth who suddenly emerged from around the corner of the main building. The secretive figure followed him at a narrowing distance through the front door, up the stairs of the front hall, and down a corridor toward Jason's locker. Just a few feet from his locker, Jason was shoved into it with unusual force. Reflexively, Jason used his hands to brace his body from the impact, then turned his head to see who the perpetrator was, figuring it was Matt Stiller or his muscle-head brother, Glen.

What he saw made him shiver in fear. The attacker was a hulking mass wearing a black ski mask, which revealed only dark, stone-cold eyes and a thick, reddened neck. Jason swung his body around to the adjoining locker, a mere instant before the thug's steel-toed boot made a huge dent in Jason's locker.

He's trying to hobble me!

Terrified, his heart pounded, and his breathing quickened. Jason bolted down the hallway in the direction from which he had come. Another student rounded the corner, walking in Jason's direction.

"What's the matter, Jason?" the consummate class nerd, Simon, asked Jason, who stood unsteadily before him.

"That cretin is trying to injure me!" Jason exclaimed, turning around and pointing in the direction of an empty hallway.

"Who exactly are you talking about? There is not a single soul here but you and me," a perplexed Simon observed in a whiny tone of voice. "For goodness' sake, Jason. You're becoming paranoid from all the hoopla around here."

"I'm not paranoid. There was a big guy in a ski mask who pushed me into my locker and tried to injure my leg," Jason said angrily. "Look over there!"

Jason pointed to a fire exit door, which was propped open with a newspaper. The alarm had been disabled.

"See, I'm not imagining things!" Jason shouted at Simon, who cowered back from him.

"Okay, Jason, okay, just don't hurt me. I didn't do anything to you," Simon cried out in a pitifully weak voice.

Disgusted at the incident and at Simon, Jason shook his head and proceeded to his homeroom to talk things over with Paul and Scott. Jason had no doubt that Stiller had orchestrated the attack. Stiller had stooped to the lowest level imaginable—and for what? To send a message loud and clear to everyone not to mess with tough-guy Stiller and to ensure that Jason did not humiliate him before the whole school by beating him in a race.

"It's only a race among teammates. That thug tried to take out my knee to win an intra-squad race," Jason fumed, furious that Stiller would try to pull off something so brazen and so dangerous to him.

Jason signaled to Paul and Scott to meet him at the back of homeroom to talk things over.

"What's going on, Jason?" Paul asked.

Jason proceeded to tell them everything that had happened that morning from the moment he had gotten off the bus.

"That must have been some stooge paid by Stiller," Scott stated. "Did he talk at all?"

"He didn't say a word and, like I said, wore a ski mask, so I have no way to pin it on Stiller or his buddies," Jason answered.

"There must be some way to track down who this guy was," Scott said, thinking aloud.

"Hey, I just remembered, I saw Meaney's car in the back lot this morning! Maybe he did it," Paul announced. Meaney was the only student in the history of Greenville's junior high to reach sixteen before graduating, or more precisely, before even being remotely eligible to graduate from its eighth grade.

"Meaney, that deadhead! He isn't even supposed to be on school property," Jason complained.

Meaney had been suspended from school for the current year for assaulting a fellow student and selling drugs on school property. When Meaney's student buyers had not paid him his asking price or had ceased going back to him for more drugs, he had used brute force to intimidate them into seeing things his way. Hence, the reason Manny had become known as "Meaney." This same brute force was what ultimately had prompted the school administration to take action against Meaney.

One morning, a seventh grader had bolted into the principal's office with blood dripping from his broken nose. The injured student had gushed out everything he knew about Meaney to the principal, except for a few choice details concerning his purchase of drugs from Meaney. That same day, the administration had taken action to suspend Meaney for one full year. The incident had occurred last June, just days before the last day of school. As a result, Meaney was forbidden from returning to school until after Jason's class graduated. If Meaney so much as appeared on school property, that would constitute grounds for expulsion at a hearing before the entire school board.

"Let's check out whether his car is still here," Paul suggested, pulling Jason out of his thoughts. "If not, that's a good sign he's the one."

The three agreed this would be strong evidence that Meaney had been the assailant. Paul, Scott, and Jason left homeroom right after the bell for their first period class. They would be late for science and risk an after-school detention, but they could serve the detention any day that week. It was well worth the risk to find out who the assailant was.

Jason peered down the corridor stretching past his locker. The fire escape was no longer propped open. The three of them wound their way to the school's front entrance and, once outside, jogged around to the back parking lot. Meaney's beat-up Dodge Omni was nowhere in sight.

"He was right there in that space," Paul said, pointing to an empty space near a huge trash bin in the back of the lot.

"Yeah, looks like you were right, Paul," Jason said. "Meaney must have done it. He had no reason to be here other than to injure me on race day. He must have taken off as soon as I bolted down the hall to get away from him."

They began walking back to the front of the school. Suddenly, Scott spotted a Dodge Omni right across the street from the school. Glen Stiller was exiting out of the car's passenger door. He waved goodbye to the driver, whom they could not identify for certain but who looked a lot like Matt Stiller. Crouching down, Jason, Paul, and Scott sprinted behind some bushes lining the path to the front entrance of the school. They found themselves just within earshot of who they now could verify were the twins. Matt, a mere two years older than his average classmate, was fifteen and driving illegally.

"Catch you later, bro. I've got to get this wreck back to Meaney pronto. I'll owe him another fifty bucks if I don't get it back by nine."

"Later, Matt," Glen said and started to cross the street.

"Remember, bro, we saw Meaney enforcing his *business sale,* right?"

Glen turned with a nasty smirk on his face. "Right, bro. Nobody will know nothin'."

Jason turned to Paul and Scott in shock and disgust. Paul signaled Jason to keep quiet until Glen had passed them and entered the school.

As soon as the front entrance door closed, Jason exclaimed, "Those maggots! Trying to make it look like Meaney was beating me up for stiffing him on a drug sale."

"Calm down. Calm down," Paul said. "They won't say a word if we don't report this."

"Don't report this? One of them—and I'd say it had to be Glen from his red bull neck—tried to put me out of commission for this race and probably for the season," Jason protested. "Why shouldn't I report the incident?"

"Jason, you don't want to risk sullying your reputation over this," Paul answered. "Look at it this way—you weren't injured, and you're still going to kick Stiller's butt out there on the course today. At worst, we'll get a detention for being late to first period."

Jason thought things over. He wasn't injured, and Matt and Glen would probably not spread their story around unless they came under suspicion for the attack. Conversely, if Jason did report them, he had a lot to lose if the administration believed the twins' version of events.

"You're right, Paul. It's not worth risking my reputation over those morons. Besides, I've got a race to run, and the last thing I need is a lot of this commotion going on."

"I think that's smart, Jason," Scott opined. "Matt and Glen will be keeping a low profile now, just to be safe. And besides, you weren't injured. Put it behind you. Just concentrate on the race."

The three walked back together into the school and to first period. Mr. Sanders, the science teacher, was in a good mood that day. He admitted the three with only a warning not to be late in the future.

They all sat down. Jason breathed a sigh of relief and shook his head.

What more could happen to shake me up? Focus, Jason reminded himself. *Remember the power of the mind. This is just extra incentive to win today. I'll make Stiller pay for this by showing him up today. And I'll be sure there are plenty of people there to see it.*

At lunch that day, Jason approached the cafeteria monitor and made a request. The monitor nodded, and Jason walked up to the front of the cafeteria.

"I have one brief announcement," Jason stated in a loud voice that quieted the lunchroom. "Our cross-country team is having time trials today, and it looks like we have a great team this year. In fact, there's a good chance the school record is going down today. So, we encourage anyone who can to come out to support the team."

Someone asked for details of the time and place.

Then Glen rose to his feet. "My money's on Matt!"

"Make sure you have enough left over for lunch tomorrow," Jason said, walking back to his seat.

A couple of students caught themselves from laughing aloud, afraid that Glen might hear them. Glen snorted derisively and noisily took his seat, challenging anyone at his table to take him up on his bet. Nobody did.

Jason had just raised the stakes. As the self-appointed team spokesman, he had come close to predicting that he would beat Stiller and set a new course record in the process. A tremendous will to win burned within him.

CHAPTER 16

The bell rang, signaling the end of seventh period. Jason made his way to his locker, picked up his sports bag, and departed the school from the back entrance. Paul and Scott met him over by the athletic locker room facilities.

"Hey, tough guy, you made it through the day. Now, you just have to win this lousy race," Paul kidded.

"You better do good. I could be home watching *Hawaii Five-O* re-runs," Scott piped in.

"Why don't you two get a head start on re-measuring the course," Jason said with a fake punch to Scott's well-nourished paunch.

"Talking serious here for a minute, buddy. I think we should stick around outside just in case your teammate has any tricks up his sleeve," Scott proposed.

"I'll be fine, guys. I don't need any bodyguards," Jason assured them. "I'll see you at the starting area in a few."

Paul and Scott ventured a measured distance away from the locker room, then turned around and began to keep an eye out for trouble as soon as Jason had gone inside. They chatted about Coda, whom they considered the coolest "pet" imaginable based solely on the embellished stories Jason had told them about the cub. They had yet to meet Coda and experience his wild nature in a real-life encounter. Their conversation turned into speculation as to whether their pets could outmatch Coda in a fight.

“My dog could probably take him down,” Paul asserted, referring to his golden retriever.

“Your dog is so stupidly good-natured, he would probably share his food and bed with Coda,” Scott said.

“Stupid? Murray could outsmart that dimwitted mutt of yours,” Paul countered. Scott owned a Siberian husky, German shepherd mix that he had picked out as a puppy from the local pound. The two had grown up together.

The truth was that neither of their dogs was among the brightest of their breeds. However, as with most boy-dog relationships, both boys had grown rather attached to their outdoor companions. Paul and Scott had hunted, swam, and even played a joint game of baseball frisbee with the two dogs roaming the outfield.

“Give me a—” Suddenly, a male scream rang out from the locker room facilities.

Paul and Scott sprinted for the locker room entrance. As they neared the entrance, they could hear a weak, plaintive voice pleading with Matt Stiller, whose mean, husky baritone was unmistakable. They opened the door to find Stiller holding a fully clothed six grader under a steaming hot shower. When Stiller saw them, he unceremoniously dropped the sixth grader onto the tile floor.

“What are you two pansies doing here?” Stiller shouted. “Worried about your boy? I wouldn’t want Jason to have any excuses out there today, now, would I? He’ll get initiated with the steam machine some other time.”

Jason made an effort to totally ignore Stiller and his threat. He pulled his team sweatshirt over his blue and white Laker racing jersey and clamped a lock onto his locker.

Paul and Scott stood uneasily in the doorway, appearing unsure of what to say or do. Jason motioned that everything was okay and then proceeded to walk out of the locker room alongside a sixth-grade runner who considered Jason his running mentor.

"Take a good look at my man, Stiller, because you won't be seeing much of him after the starting line," Paul shouted into the locker room as they left.

It was a good thing for the three that Stiller was not yet fully clothed because it sent him into a fury. Stiller raged obscenities and threats at them until they were out of hearing range.

Jason glanced at his watch. There were thirty minutes to race time. For Jason, the start could not come soon enough.

»«»«»«

Back at his lakefront abode, Sasquot hurried inside to grab his vintage black-and-white camera. Kyle had given Sasquot the afternoon off so that both of them could watch Jason's race. Sasquot treasured photographs of his father as a trophy hunter and avid canoeist, and he hoped that one day, Jason's children would similarly enjoy looking over photographs of their father's showdown against the defending school champion.

A large bang issued from Coda's shed. Sasquot glanced through the window at it. Seeing nothing out of place, he quickly gathered what he needed to spectate the big race.

Sasquot reemerged from the house with the camera and climbed inside the truck. He glanced in the rearview mirror, detecting a blur of movement. He paused and twisted around, his eyes falling upon an old comforter he and Kyle used to cushion furniture transported into town. The bag of fruit slices had fallen over, but nothing else seemed to be out of place. Thinking nothing of it, he headed straight to Kyle's farm, eager to pick him up and catch every minute of Jason's long-anticipated duel.

»«»«»«

I've been too hard on the boy growing up, Kyle thought as he brushed wood dust off his clothing and departed the farmhouse to wait for Sasquot. *He's been a good kid—loyal, eager to learn, hard-working, and, yes, most importantly, loving.*

Kyle had really been touched by Jason's concern over his well-being in the wake of Cynthia's jarring return into their lives. He had always thought of himself as an independent man—hardy and self-sufficient. Kyle's reaction to the devastating news that Cynthia wanted to divorce him and marry another had unleashed emotions that he fought. He had been taught never to show weakness or emotions to others.

Kyle walked toward Sasquot's pickup as it pulled up to the front of the main house, absorbed in his thoughts. He felt excited and anxious at the same time about the race and his son's prospects.

"Do you think my boy can win?" Kyle asked, proud that Jason was even vying for number one on the team.

"Jason trained hard and has a great heart. If he sets his mind to win the race today, he will win," Sasquot affirmed.

The two continued toward Greenville Consolidated School with Kyle silently imagining how sweet it would feel to share the moment of victory with his son.

»«»«»«

"Fifteen minutes to race time!" Jason's coach announced through his megaphone. "Begin proceeding to the starting area for race positions!"

Jason looked out onto the track and soccer field along which the course began and ended. He estimated that at least seventy students, teachers, and parents lined this critical part of the course, a turnout higher than he had ever witnessed.

Surely more must be scattered in the woods and at other points along the course, he thought.

Energized, he began walking toward the starting line along the back straightaway of the track. He presently felt a friendly pat on his back.

"How're you holding up, sport?" Paul asked.

"Focused. Focused on winning," Jason answered, staring straight ahead at the course.

"Man, looks like you're in a trance," Scott observed, joining the pair.

When Jason gave no response, they each wished him good luck and walked out a few hundred yards along the course to the point where it first entered the woods. This was a strategic point, as the leader going into the woods, by being in front during narrow stretches of the forest trail, would be able to dictate the tempo of a good portion of the race.

Jason finished his calisthenics and did several forty-meter sprints in order to get his muscles loose and his blood flowing.

"Wilson! Second position!" Coach roared. "Stiller, first position!"

The lesser talents had all lined up on the starting line. Only Jason and Matt Stiller remained to take their positions. Jason took one last sip of lukewarm water and slapped some ice water onto the back of his head and neck to invigorate himself and keep his body cool.

"Five minutes to starting time!" Coach Sullivan shouted. "All runners, assume and remain in starting positions!" The coach gave a pointed look to both Jason and Stiller.

Jason walked over and assumed his position in the second box. Stiller walked over and likewise assumed his position. Neither so much as glanced at the other. Each bore a stone-cold expression, showing no outward emotion.

Jason scanned the parking lot. He could see Sasquot's Chevy pickup parked toward the back, but he had not yet spotted Sasquot or his dad anywhere along the course.

Spectators began shouting the names of their favorites. Above the other names, chants of "Jason, Jason, Jason" could be heard.

"One minute!" Coach Sullivan cried out.

Everything Sasquot had taught Jason about running flashed through his mind: "Take short breaths from your diaphragm"; "Lean forward to where you run on the toes and front of your feet"; "Lift your knees as you run up hills"; and, above all, "Remember, your mind and spirit command your body." One question burned in Jason's mind: *Do I have the mind and spirit and will to win?*

"Thirty seconds!" The coach raised his starting gun into the air. Jason could feel a gentle breeze—soon to become a mild headwind—blowing in the direction of the starting line. "Runners, take your mark! Get set!"

The gun fired.

The runners burst into motion, striding along at a quick clip. As in the first seconds of each cross-country race he had ever run, Jason felt strong, his form smooth and efficient. The pain and labored breathing had not yet set in. Jason expected these to manifest themselves as he neared the one-mile mark, unless, of course, somebody tried to break out from the pack and take a commanding lead. In that case, he would have to push his body early and keep the runner within a two-hundred-meter striking range, lest the runner add crucial distance to his lead.

The entire field aligned in a cone formation with Jason and Stiller side by side forming its point. Each knew that the leader going into the woods would have a considerable short-term advantage. Jason gradually increased his speed, hoping that Stiller would fade slightly so that he could take the lead into the woods. But Stiller matched Jason stride for stride, not ceding an inch. Only two hundred yards separated the pair from the pines that marked the entrance to the forest trail.

The crowd realized there could be only one leader going into the woods. Shouts of "Come on, Jason!" and "Take the lead, Jason!" filled the air. The atmosphere was electric; Jason could feel a shot of adrenaline surge through his system and a tingling sensation running up and down his neck and upper back.

Suddenly, Stiller accelerated, running at a modified sprint to break away. Jason determinedly shortened his stride and kicked. The surge edged him closer to Stiller. He was closing in, but there were only thirty yards to go.

Should I risk physically bumping into Stiller in order to be first at this point? The thought flashed through Jason's mind.

"Teach Stiller a lesson!" Paul shouted loudly enough for both Jason and Stiller to hear.

Jason decided not to risk the physical confrontation. Strategically, it was not worth the risk of getting tangled up, elbowed, or possibly even shoved into a tree. However, rather than accelerating and maintaining his lead, Stiller slowed and ceded the lead to Jason.

What in the world is he thinking? Jason frowned at Stiller's action. *What is motivating Stiller to let me lead?*

Pleasantly surprised, Jason took advantage of the opportunity and led going into the woods. The forest trail was too narrow for Stiller to pass him for another couple hundred yards. Grateful for the breathing room, Jason intentionally slowed the pace to fully recover from his recent surge. He deftly stepped only on solid ground, avoiding mud, sticks, and rocks. There were no spectators lining this portion of the course. They would have to be standing in the middle of brambles and saplings to watch the action at this point.

Jason rounded the next corner, still in the lead. He was almost a half-mile into the course and felt strong. The next thing Jason knew, he had lost his footing and fallen headlong onto the forest floor. Stiller jumped over him.

"Watch your step, Jason!" Stiller shouted out derisively as he continued on, second by second adding to his lead.

"Shoot!" Jason cried out and struggled to his feet. His feet had been tangled up in a vine, which was strung unnaturally across the trail. *A setup! I was suckered into running into a setup*! Jason realized, emboldening himself more than ever.

Jason felt a fire rage within, propelling him onward at a blistering pace. Stiller had gained about seventy yards through his contrivance, but Jason had already gotten twenty of them back.

Stiller crossed over the stone bridge.

"Five minutes, twenty-eight seconds!" Coach Sullivan cried out as Stiller passed the mile point. Stiller was running a fast race, trying to wrap things up early so as to avoid a mad dash to the finish.

Jason quickened his pace as the woods opened to the mile point bridge, which spanned a tumbling stream descending from the mountains.

"Five minutes, thirty-five seconds!" Coach Sullivan's voice boomed. "Two-point-one-four miles remaining."

The next mile was critical in Jason's mind. This was when the pain really became intense and races were won or lost.

Jason raised his knees and scaled the upgrade at top speed. He correctly lengthened his stride on the backside of the incline to take advantage of his momentum. As Jason gazed ahead, Stiller loomed large before him, a figure only thirty yards ahead.

The two followed the white line marking the course along a two-hundred-year-old stone wall overlooking the forest, and, beyond that, the scenic vista of Moosehead Lake. Recalling

Sasquot's words, Jason focused with single-minded intensity upon narrowing the gap before he and Stiller reentered the woods.

Stiller was running strong. He had not faded or broken stride. Yet with stride, Jason made ground, continuing to surge. Flickering shadows fell upon Stiller's white and blue jersey as he reentered the woods. Standing at the forest entrance, Glen Stiller and one of his muscle-head friends hooted as Matt ran by. Three seconds later, Jason passed the same point.

"Watch your knee, Wilson!" Glen shouted out and sneered, disappointed that his morning gambit had failed.

Jason summoned all his powers of self-control to keep himself from becoming mentally and physically sidetracked from the race. He focused on breathing from his diaphragm in short, shallow breaths in order to maintain his concentration during this critical stage.

The forest trail became increasingly treacherous, with slippery moss covering jutting rocks and roots protruding up from surrounding trees. However, Jason did not slow one bit. He was running with more intensity than he had ever run before, engaging the terrain with every stride. Ahead of him, Stiller's jersey lit up with sunlight as he left the forest and headed for Amazon Hill.

Amazon Hill was infamously steep, and many athletes had succumbed to it over the years, giving up during workouts or races and shamefully walking up its sharply inclined face. In training camp, Greenville High football players carried fellow players up Amazon Hill on their backs in order to build strength and stamina. For several players, it had instead built lasting knee and back injuries.

Jason envisaged the poor football players laboring up the hill carrying teammates as he nimbly bounded up its face. He was an extremely strong hill runner and would certainly make up ground on Stiller here. Stiller panted to the top, Jason merely twelve yards in back of him. Jason could now make out two emblems written in black marker on the back of Stiller's shoes. One read, "Eat my dust!"—the other, "Second place—first loser!"

Stiller's face grimaced with pain as he flew down its backside. Jason patiently held his pace, ceding only eight yards to Stiller. He remained within striking range.

"Eleven minutes even!" the coach shouted out as Stiller passed by. Coach Sullivan sat in a golf cart and drove in a beeline from marker to marker in order to personally give and record the splits of the lead runners at each mile, as well as the two-and-a-half-mile point.

"Eleven minutes, three seconds!" he bellowed as Jason reached the two-mile point.

Jason recalled Coach's first mile readout and quickly calculated he had run a negative second mile split. Despite Amazon Hill, Jason had run the second mile even faster than the first. He felt recharged, spurred on by this auspicious sign that he would finish strong.

Stiller momentarily disappeared behind a fir tree. They had come to the "Fir Tree Slalom," one of the few points in the course that could be referred to as fun. Jason darted around each of the fir trees as quickly and efficiently as possible. When he rounded the last one, he looked up and saw Stiller only ten yards ahead.

They began to tackle the quarter-mile "Monster Hill," named for its tremendous length and difficulty and the fact that it comes very late in the course. Stiller was clearly tiring. Jason could hear his labored breathing and see his reddened arms and neck. This was Jason's moment, his opportunity to forge ahead.

Jason's mind focused on the phrase "will to win!" The phrase echoed and resounded within him. Jason accelerated, closing to within a few feet of Stiller. Now, Jason was confronted with the decision of when to attempt the uphill pass. Coach had taught the team to "take people strong," meaning that no runner should risk a pass unless he could put some distance on the passed person. Otherwise, the passer displayed his weakness, and the original leader would soon reclaim the lead.

Jason kicked, moving at a near sprint up the hill past Stiller. Stiller put every ounce of strength he had left into fighting Jason's pass. For a few seconds, they strode up the hill side by side. Then, suddenly, Stiller lagged behind, unable to keep up the exceptionally strong pace. At the top of the hill, Jason glanced behind him. Stiller was holding on to his chest with one arm, clearly cramping from having gone out too hard.

Jason once again lengthened his stride down the backside of the hill. He had a fifteen-yard lead that was widening by the second.

"Fourteen minutes, forty-five seconds!" Coach Sullivan boomed at the two-and-a-half-mile point. "You're on pace to break the course record!"

The race was progressing even better for Jason than he had visualized in his mental imaging. Jason closed in on a cluster of trees just beyond the soccer field. He now spotted his father standing next to Sasquot right in front of these trees.

"That's my boy!" his father cried out. "Keep it up, son!"

"Heart! Big heart wins the race!" Sasquot shouted out. Jason surged, his mind and spirit commanding his body to dig deep in honor of his family, friends, and schoolmates who had endured Stiller's bullying. He heard camera clicks as he swept by Sasquot and his father. Jason was now thirty yards in front of Stiller and continuing to gain on him. The crowd was going wild, rapturously chanting Jason's name and cheering. A few spectators were so excited, they were enthusiastically jumping up and down.

Suddenly, the crowd's cheering turned into uncontrollable laughter and cries of "Run, Superman, run!" Out of the corner of his eye, Jason could see Stiller running off course in his underwear. Clad only in a racing jersey and Superman boxer shorts, Stiller was screaming for help at the top of his lungs and sprinting straight for the finish line.

What in the world? flashed through Jason's mind.

Stiller was cutting off a good tenth of a mile from the course, running in a beeline that would literally cross the track's infield to reach the finish line.

Jason turned his head, unable to resist the temptation of finding out what was going on. A black streak was chasing Stiller across the soccer field toward the track.

Coda! How on earth did Coda even get here, and what is driving him to chase after Stiller, who's half-naked and screaming in terror?

With the bright blue and red image of a terrified Stiller fresh in his mind, Jason had to concentrate hard to refrain from bursting into laughter. He now began his final sprint, kicking for all he was worth down the final stretch onto the track. Half of the crowd was jeering at Stiller, the other half cheering Jason on.

Jason could not have imagined a more fitting finish to the race. The pain intensified to an almost unbearable level as he pushed his body to the limit in order to shave precious seconds off his time. His will to shatter the record was incredibly strong. Jason thrust his chest across the finish line.

"Seventeen minutes, four seconds! A new course record by twelve seconds!" Coach Sullivan announced. The place erupted in cheers and applause. Students and friends started running over to congratulate Jason, but Jason still had one more thing to do.

"Coda! Coda, come here!" Jason commanded.

Hearing Jason's voice, Coda quickly called off his pursuit of Stiller and happily bounded over to his master.

"Don't be afraid. The only person Coda doesn't like is Superman," Jason announced, looking over at a mortified Matt Stiller. The crowd broke out into another burst of laughter.

"Real smart, Stiller, to kick a real, live bear cub!" a student shouted.

"Yeah, you sure showed it—and all of us—how to be a superhero," another called out to a chorus of joyous jeers.

Stiller, humiliated and utterly defeated, bolted red-faced toward the locker room.

Paul and Scott grabbed Jason and thrust him high above the crowd. "Jason! Jason! Jason!" they all chanted. A new hero had been crowned.

CHAPTER 17

The rest of the week flew by. Jason felt as though he were in an exhilarating dream that whisked him along at a dizzying speed. Everyone was so congratulatory to him after the race and seemed genuinely happy for him. Jason's father had hosted an impromptu barbecue for his friends the evening of the race, serving up his finest barbecued ribs, choice steak cuts, and fresh salmon filets to eager guests. Sasquot had showed Jason pictures of his father and grandfather engaging in various athletic feats and contests, including the ball-stick-game, hurling snowsnakes—a sport similar to the javelin throw—canoe racing, canoe tilting, foot racing, and wrestling. Jason felt incredibly proud when Sasquot informed him that he would add Jason's racing photo to his treasured family album. The photo showed Jason in full stride and classic form heading for the home stretch followed by the barely visible figure of Coda, who had just popped out of the woods.

As if I needed an extra reminder of what happened at the finish! Jason laughed to himself, recalling Coda's surprise appearance in the photo.

Most enthusiastic of all were Jason's classmates, who swarmed around him, asking him over and over again to retell the race finish, relating what he had seen and the way he had felt. Scott made sure to let everyone know how he had infuriated Stiller by boldly predicting Jason's victory before the race. Not unexpectedly, Matt took the remainder of the week off while his brother, Glen, maintained an exceptionally low profile at school.

Jason's father, in a particularly cheery mood, suggested that he, Sasquot, and Jason go fishing that Saturday at his secret fishing hole west of Moosehead Lake. Accessible only by foot, the trout pond drained into the waters of Indian Pond. Jason loved the pond because of its peaceful seclusion and its rich stock of wild brook trout, more commonly referred to as squaretail by Maine fishermen. In addition, a number of hard-fighting small-mouthed bass that he loved to reel in inhabited the pond.

Half an hour before dawn, the three took to the road in his father's pickup. Shortly after passing Big Squaw Mountain, his dad turned onto a gravel road, which they followed through rough, rocky terrain for the next four miles. At long last for a vehicle reduced to eighteen miles per hour, the gravel road ended at a logging "carveout," a small tract of land that had been cleared but not yet replanted by a local logging company.

Fifty feet before the end of the road, his father parked by the edge of the woods. The three assembled their fishing gear and proceeded through the woods along a barely perceptible path toward the pond.

The brisk air, so cool and pristine, invigorated Jason as he made his way behind his father and Sasquot through the thick pines, spruces, and fir trees. The soothing sound of tree crickets filled the air, signaling to the world that the forest teemed with life, from tiny insects to huge bears. As they neared the pond, the forest began to change to bigtooth aspen and silky willow.

Jason spotted movement ahead. Whatever the creature was, they were downwind of it, greatly increasing their chances of coming upon it undetected. Sasquot crouched to the ground and motioned for Jason and his father to do the same. Jason peered through the thinned-out trees lining the pond.

At first, he could not make out anything. Then gradually, he could make out a fully antlered bull moose standing at the opposite end of the pond. The moose nonchalantly dipped its head into the pond to feast upon water lilies and aquatic grasses by the shore. It was at once majestic and ungainly, trotting seven feet above the ground and carrying twelve hundred pounds upon long, spindly legs.

Suddenly, it lifted its head up and peered toward the three of them.

It was unlikely the moose had seen them from across the one-hundred-yard expanse that presently separated the parties. However, being downwind of them and armed with acute senses of hearing and smell, chances were that the moose had heard the snapping of a twig when Jason maneuvered into a more comfortable crouching stance.

Jason was struck by the tremendous size of its antlers. As Sasquot had taught Jason, during the rutting season, bulls would challenge fellow suitors with bellows that echoed through these woodlands. If answered by a challenge from another bull, Sasquot had explained, the rivals would circle each other and stage mock fights that generally settled which was more powerful. When neither ceded dominance, bulls would charge, clashing antlers and attempting to push back the other.

"Just as with humans, Little Hawk, when reason does not prevail, tragic consequences can occur. If in battle, moose horns become interlocked or a moose stumbles, it can result in death," Sasquot had taught him to his dismay. For Jason had learned from an early age from his wise mentor to value all forms of life and to avoid needless suffering and death of any creature.

"Didn't bring your bullhorn, did you?" his father whispered in jest to Sasquot within his earshot.

Jason saw Sasquot smile and shake his head. It took Jason's thoughts back to a brisk evening last October spent at a campsite in Lily Bay State Park along the eastern shore of Moosehead Lake, listening to hunting stories. Earlier that same day, Sasquot and Jason's father had shown how to successfully hunt two ruffed grouse in a forest cove of aspen and birch further east of the lake. Slowly roasting the grouse on sticks over a campfire with his father, Sasquot and Autumn, Sasquot had mesmerized Jason with hunting stories about moose . . .

»«»«»«

"Little Hawk, one day, we will hunt together in the age-old tradition of my tribe. We will make camp along a marsh where large bulls roam and wait patiently until the early hours of the morning. I will teach you how to make long, quavering calls on a birch-bark moose horn. The bull will answer, mistaking it for a mating cow. We will call back and forth with calls resounding through the night until we hear the sound of the bull trampling underbrush and thrashing thickets with its antlers. As soon as its shadowy form becomes visible, you will bring it down with your rifle."

"Wow, that will be so exciting, Sasquot. I hope you'll back me up in case I miss," Jason said enthusiastically.

"Yes, of course, Little Hawk. I will teach you as well as I have taught Autumn the ancient ways. She has already accompanied me on a successful moose hunt. We canoed alongside the shore of Moosehead Lake at dusk last November using an old Penobscot moose-hunting technique. Autumn sounded our birch-bark moose horn at regular intervals, repeating it once answered by a bull. When the bull approached, she used the moose horn to scoop up water and poured it back into the lake. The bull mistook the sound for a cow dripping water from her mouth. It emerged from the forest thickets into the open waters of the lake. Autumn paddled away from the bull to lure it into deeper water. Enraged that the cow was escaping, the bull followed our canoe into deeper water. There I brought it down with my rifle."

Jason had been spellbound by the story and greatly admired the skills which Autumn had exhibited, luring the bull first by the call of the moose horn and then by bailing water with it and deftly backing the canoe away from the pursuing bull.

»«»«»«

Jason was jolted from his memories as Sasquot cupped his hands together and made a loud, tremulous sound, ending in a cough-like "moo-agh." The powerful bull became agitated, ceased its aquatic feeding, and withdrew from the water. Once fully ashore, it issued a bellowing call into the forest.

"That'll do fine, too," Jason's father whispered. "By the way, try not to get us killed," he kidded. As Jason's father had warned Jason, during the mating season, bulls sometimes attacked people and cars and had even been known to charge into trains.

Sasquot raised his index finger, signaling for Jason's father to give him a few moments. He then, once again, cupped his hands together and let out a long, querulous howl, imitating the early morning communal howl of the gray wolf. The bull moved its head back and forth in fright and then lumbered noisily back into the forest in the opposite direction of the predatory hunting call. Moments later, it was out of sight.

"Now we can fish in peace," Sasquot declared with a satisfied grin.

Jason never ceased to be amazed at Sasquot's resourcefulness when confronted with all kinds of challenging situations in the wild. The three now walked down to the edge of the pond. Jason's dad slipped waders on over his jeans to complete his transformation into the consummate sports fisherman. In addition to the waders, he wore fishing boots, a fishing vest, and a well-used fisherman's cap. He held a fly rod in one hand while he rummaged through his tackle box with his other.

"I'd like to fish for bass to start out, Dad," Jason said.

"Okay, then. I'd recommend the plastic frog. Bass expect frogs here among the lily pads, insects, and vegetation, and I've yet to meet a bass that didn't like them." His father smiled.

He handed Jason a traditional rod and reel as opposed to the unique fly-fishing rod, which called upon a totally different set of fishing skills. "I've got a fifteen-pound test line on this pole, son, so you can handle anything this pond has to offer. Here, I like this green frog with the white underbelly. It moves through the water really well, just like a frog swimming along through the lily pads."

Jason attached the artificial lure to his leader and looked out onto the water, becoming familiar with the lay of the pond. The far end of the pond had a bunch of lily pads and appeared to be shallower than their side. On the east side, there was a canal linking the pond with another pond that was smaller but appeared deeper and clearer. Jason knew from experience that there would certainly be fish lurking in that canal waiting for smaller fish to pass by in either direction.

Something caught Jason's eye to his right. It was Sasquot crouching down near the high grass and reeds by the pond shore. Well-camouflaged among the lush grass was a northern leopard frog with dark green splotches lining its back. Sasquot crept up behind the frog and kept as still as possible. Very slowly, he extended one hand toward the frog's backside. Suddenly, the frog leaped diagonally through the air right into Sasquot's other hand, which lay waiting and ready.

"How in the world did you catch it?" Jason asked.

"A leopard frog jumps in zigzags, Little Hawk. Experience is the best teacher," Sasquot answered, showing Jason the frog's head. "I will use the real frog to catch bass. The key is to hook the frog but not to kill it. Bass like to eat live frogs more than dead ones."

Sasquot hooked the frog through its right hind leg and cast it out among the water lilies. The frog swam jerkily along the pond surface in pained, animated spurts. A ripple of water appeared among a cluster of lily pads. A bass was moving in for the kill. Sasquot waited patiently, allowing the frog ample slack to move about at will.

Suddenly, the frog disappeared in a swirl of turbulence. Jason could hear the sound of the water surface break once, now twice, from the violent commotion. Sasquot's line went taut. The fish had swallowed at least part of the frog and was diving for the bottom. Sasquot simply held the rod steady for the next few seconds, giving the fish additional time to swallow the frog and get hooked. Then he pulled the rod back forcefully to drive the hook further into the fish. The fish tugged back with substantial force, bending the pole.

"Looks like a fighter, Sasquot," Jason said, excited by the unfolding battle of fisherman against fish.

"I enjoy a good fight, Little Hawk," Sasquot said good-naturedly. "The most fun in fishing comes from the fight."

Sasquot began to reel in the fish. Every inch was a struggle, as evidenced by Sasquot's bent pole and visibly strained line. Abruptly, the fish leaped into the air—an impressive small-mouthed bass well over a foot in length.

Jason heard the sound of the reel automatically releasing line to the powerful bass as the fishing line became excessively taut. Seconds later, Sasquot resumed his battle with the bass, reeling in the line in order to tire it.

The bass put up a commendable fight, and it took another ten minutes for Sasquot to finally bring the bass ashore. Jason grasped the bass in both hands as soon as it landed on the grass. He knew from painful experience that a fish could, by chance, wring free of the hook once ashore and flop back into the pond. That was always an embarrassing anticlimax to an otherwise triumphant moment. Jason skillfully removed the hook from just inside the bass's mouth and placed it in a large bucket well away from the pond.

"Looks about fifteen inches long, a real nice specimen," Jason's father pronounced. "Let's see if we can't get it some company there in the bucket."

His dad tied the eye of a colorful red, black, and yellow fly to his line that resembled an aquatic insect. His father then waded out a few feet into the pond in his rubber waders. With an expert snap of his wrist, he gently cast the fly upon the water. His father reeled in the fly slowly in the still waters, giving it lifelike movement. As Jason watched the fly skate along the lake surface, it seemed to dance playfully, inviting attention with vivid color and spirited movement. His father did not allow the line to go slack for even a moment, sustaining its magical dance across the lake.

"No luck on the first cast," his father announced matter-of-factly. He tried a second and a third cast.

Jason decided it was time to test his luck. He cast his artificial frog lure out into the pond. Unfortunately, he released his line too late in the cast. It crossed over his dad's line, presenting the danger of tangling the two lines. Jason loosened his line and began to walk toward his father, planning to switch places with him once on shore to correct the situation. However, before he could do so, the frog lure disappeared beneath the pond surface. Jason immediately clicked in the line to prevent any more line from running out.

"Dad, we've crossed lines," Jason said.

"Don't worry. I'll have my line reeled in before there's a problem," his father replied without much concern.

Just then, his dad's line jerked, and a flurry of movement agitated the pond surface.

"Well, I'll be . . . " his father cried out. With crossed lines, Jason and his dad each had a fish on the line struggling to wrest free of their tackle. "Jason, stay right there. I'll cross in front of you to uncross the lines. Just keep your line high enough for me to pass under."

His dad began slowly walking along in the water toward Jason, who stood to his right. Jason held his pole up as high as he could without snapping it. His father was just about to walk underneath his line when Jason's pole plunged down, striking his dad on his right shoulder. Startled, his father lost his balance and fell into the water. His pole abruptly plunged into the pond and began to drift away.

"For crying out loud, Jason. What in the world did you do that for?" Jason's dad sputtered, spitting out pond water.

"I'm sorry, Dad, I just lost control of my pole for a split second after it pulled real hard and . . . "

"Well, be more careful next time for everyone's sake," his dad angrily interrupted.

Jason felt crestfallen. He continued to fail in his father's eyes.

Sasquot lunged into the pond and handed the rod to Jason's dad. The trout had managed to get away, though.

"Great, and I lost the fish, too," his father announced.

"I'm really sorry, Dad. I'll be more careful," Jason promised.

Jason landed that bass and added two brook trout later as well, but he took little relish in these feats. To Jason, his father was the judge of his accomplishments. Even Sasquot's reassurances that

"Everyone makes mistakes" and "Experience is our best teacher" did not fully soothe him or restore his sense of self-worth. His dad seemed mildly happy after landing five brook trout later that morning but conversed very little with Jason.

During the truck ride home, Sasquot told several Penobscot jokes he had learned when he was a child. His father laughed at each one and seemed to be back to his normal mood by the time they reached the house.

Once back on the farm, Sasquot indicated to Jason that he needed help with the sheep. The two walked side by side out to the pasture.

"Jason, your father loves you very much. He has a heart of gold inside that I have seen over many years. However, by his nature, he is hard on himself and on other people. He tries his best to do what is right but sometimes fails. No matter how hard we try, it is human nature that we make mistakes," Sasquot began.

Jason looked up into Sasquot's deep brown eyes. Wisdom and compassion gazed down at him.

"Jason, divorce is a difficult matter. Your father tried very hard to make your mother like it here and to make things work. But things did not work out, and your mother is now gone. I know this is hard for you, too, Little Hawk. As someone who cares about you and your father like my own family, I want to give you two pieces of advice. Number one, talk to your father. Tell him how you feel and ask how he feels. Share your heart and your thoughts with him; let him know how much he means to you. Sharing what is inside with those we love is a key to a happy life," Sasquot said, pausing briefly to gauge Jason's reaction.

Jason nodded. *If just talking about Mom leaving is too emotional for dad, it must be incredibly difficult for him to cope with the separation,* he thought but didn't voice out loud.

"My next advice, Little Hawk, is very important. You need to believe and to understand that deep inside, you are a special person. What makes you special is not what you do but who you are. This is what is important," Sasquot said, patting his chest.

"Thank you, Sasquot, thank you," Jason said, hugging his beloved friend and mentor. Tears flowed from Jason's eyes. "You're my best friend, Sasquot, my best friend."

CHAPTER 18

Over the course of the next two weeks, Coda grew stronger, healthier, and fatter. He began to lose his baby fur and to grow a longer, darker coat in its place in preparation for the brutally cold winter which lay ahead. He also became increasingly attached to the people with whom he interacted on a regular basis, namely Sasquot, Autumn, and Jason. At the same time, Coda grew bolder and more exploratory in his expeditions out into the forest. At times, Coda would simply dart off in any given direction, and it would take the better part of an hour for Jason or Autumn to catch up with him or track him down. Such was the case on the last Saturday in September, when the fall foliage sprayed glorious hues of fiery red, burnt orange, and bright yellow upon the forest and the surrounding environs in a magnificent conflagration of color—a day that Jason, Autumn, and Coda would not soon forget.

Jason had thought long and hard about his talk with Sasquot some weeks ago. Since that time, he had made a conscious effort not to put on chauvinistic airs with Autumn. He now treated her as an equal in every respect and, above all, as a good friend. So, it was no aberration that on this crisp, clear Saturday afternoon, Jason and Autumn frolicked along behind Coda as he rummaged along the forest floor for soft vegetation, tasty acorns, beechnuts, and hazelnuts. As they sauntered through the forest, she and Jason exchanged their fondest Coda stories and their most humorous moments with the bear. Number two for Jason was the beehive incident, while for Autumn, it was the gray squirrel's bold escape over the stunned cub. First on each of their lists was, without a second thought, Coda's stripping Matt Stiller down to his Superman underwear.

Just as they reached the outer perimeter of their usual area of exploration and began to turn back, they noticed that Coda had bounded off yet further into the woods in the opposite direction of Sasquot's home and Moosehead Lake. They both shook their heads but had some time ago resigned themselves to the fact that a bear cub was an inherently inquisitive creature, whose curiosity often had to be entertained or suffered, depending upon one's point of view, for its own good. Exploring in a somewhat supervised environment would stimulate Coda's learning and development in the wild while hopefully, at the same time, keeping him out of any serious danger.

With those thoughts, Jason and Autumn lumbered off after Coda, able to get only within forty feet of him before he continued onward. On this occasion, Coda moved in the same direction, northeastward, rather than bounding off in haphazard directions.

"He must have caught hold of some interesting scent," Jason said.

After traveling for a good twenty minutes in this fashion, Jason, too, could smell something in the air. It was a foul smell, as of spoiled food or putrefying garbage.

"Do you smell that?" he asked Autumn.

"Yeah, what do you make of it?" she asked in return.

"I don't know. I've never been this far out here before. Maybe there's a dump or something around here."

After following Coda for another five or ten minutes, they came to it: a pile of trash, a refuse heap which must have been six feet tall and twenty feet in width. The stench was almost overpowering, even at one hundred feet away.

"This can't be a legal dump," Jason stated, having noted that the refuse heap lay in the center of a grassy clearing in the middle of nowhere, without any road leading up to it.

From this distance, Jason could make out several sets of truck tire tracks leading up to the trash pile. Someone had evidently been dumping food, glass, plastic, cardboard containers, and other assorted garbage onto this heap for some time now.

As far as Coda was concerned, this was a food paradise, a bear's utopia. By the time Jason and Autumn had set their eyes on him, Coda was already sampling three food groups represented in the refuse heap: rotting cabbage from the fruit and vegetable group, half-eaten hamburgers from the meat group, and stale bread from the cereal and grain group. Coda was about to make it four food groups when he abruptly lifted his head into the air.

"Coda! Coda, get out of there!" Jason cried out, frightened at the prospect of the refuse heap's creator suddenly appearing with his gun and putting a quick end to the cub nuisance.

But Coda appeared mesmerized by whomever or whatever was approaching. The cub bounded toward the edge of the woods on the side of the refuse heap opposite to where Jason and Autumn stood. Jason and Autumn each carried only a pocketknife. If Coda was putting himself at risk, there was little either of them could do to stave off any kind of serious attack.

Suddenly, a huge black bear emerged from the forest not more than twenty yards from Coda. It was a massive adult male weighing surely over four hundred pounds—the combined weight of ten Codas. Coda became somewhat wary of the bear as it came into view, freezing his movement. The bear took a few moments to size Coda up and then lumbered toward the refuse heap, largely ignoring the puzzled cub.

Jason and Autumn had backed away further into the forest. Unfortunately for the stench but fortunately for their safety, a steady wind was blowing toward them, such that the boar had not yet smelled their presence. He signaled for Autumn to retreat yet further into the woods to the point where Coda and the adult bear were barely visible. They were now roughly two hundred yards from the refuse heap.

Coda turned toward the bear, who was engrossed in gorging himself upon an easy meal, and then slowly sauntered toward the refuse heap. The adult bear continued to claw through the trash and feed upon the scraps of food lying therein without casting more than a fleeting glance at the cub.

As a rule, black bears were solitary animals. The main exception to this for female black bears, or "sows," was the one-to-two-year nurturing period following the birth of their cubs; for male black bears, or "boars," the major exception was, not surprisingly, their interaction with sows during the mating season. A boar would probably not even recognize his own cubs and might well constitute the greatest danger to them of any creature. Thus, normally smaller bears gave great deference to larger bears and steered clear of their claw-marked territory. Fully-grown boars dominated the black bear hierarchy and deferred to no one, not even to a sow with cubs. If a boar threatened a cub, the sow would risk serious injury, if necessary, to do battle with the male.

Coda was therefore violating traditional principles of black bear deference by remaining so close to an adult boar, particularly one that was feeding. However, the boar seemed not the slightest bit concerned with the cub, single-mindedly immersing himself in a never-ending quest to satiate his appetite. Coda, curious to a fault, playfully approached yet closer to the feasting boar. Failing to elicit any reaction from his newfound friend, Coda poked his head directly into the space separating the boar from the piece of meat upon which it was feeding.

This was a serious mistake. The boar suddenly bared his teeth, revealing long canines that threatened the lives of lesser beasts. Coda recoiled in fear. The boar then slapped the ground with a resounding thud and bellowed, sending tingles up Jason's spine. Coda lunged for the nearest tree. The ferocious male pursued Coda, taking a mighty lunge toward the panicked cub. Just as Coda approached the base of the nearest pine, the boar roared and clawed viciously at Coda. The claw caught some fur on Coda's back, breaking his stride and bringing him to a fateful halt. Desperate, Coda dug his claws into the ground for traction and lunged forward, wresting himself free of the attacking male. Then, in a feat Jason had never before witnessed, Coda leaped twenty-five feet up the tree in tremendously quick, agile lunges.

The mighty bear roared in rage, but the infuriated bear would pursue no further.

Sparing Coda much further alarm, the roused male let out a final snarl before bounding away from the tree and back to the refuse pit to continue feeding. It then blissfully proceeded to gorge itself unperturbed by man or beast.

This provided some welcome breathing room for all members of their trio. Fortunately for Jason and Autumn, Coda had scaled a tree at the opposite side of the clearing. Realizing that climbing a tree did not assure one's safety against a black bear, Jason and Autumn had, nonetheless, likewise ascended a good thirty feet up into the higher branches of a towering oak.

In a sense, all three of them had been treed by this fearsome beast. It was not until two interminably long hours had passed that the boar finally satisfied his appetite and sauntered back into the woods along the same path by which he had come. And it was not until Coda, with his keen sense of smell and acute hearing, had slid down the pine in a controlled fall typical of black bears that Jason and Autumn dared to begin their own descent.

When they had at last jumped down from the lowermost branch, Autumn called out to Coda, "Awasosis! Awasosis!"

As enthusiastic as he had ever been to see his keepers, Coda bounded over to Jason and Autumn. Autumn calmed down the rambunctious cub while Jason examined his injury, carefully ruffling through Coda's fur. Besides the loss of a fair bit of fur, Coda had escaped unscathed from the potentially fatal encounter. Jason breathed an audible sigh of relief.

"Coda, you crazy beast!" Jason shouted, half in anger and half in bemusement. "You won't be satisfied until all three of us are dead!"

Autumn shook her head in disapproval of Coda's reckless behavior. "The only time I've ever felt that scared was when the rattlesnake attacked . . . "

Autumn abruptly stopped mid-sentence, but Jason had already homed in on the word rattlesnake.

"What rattlesnake are you talking about?" he immediately asked.

Autumn reluctantly told him the entire story. Jason reassured her that she had acted bravely and congratulated her on saving Coda's life. He could sense her immediate relief, as she smiled and said with great modesty, "I'm sure you would have done the same thing under the circumstances, Jason."

Deliberately keeping within twenty feet of Coda at all times, Jason and Autumn walked through the woods toward Sasquot's abode, bonded closer through the trauma they had endured together.

CHAPTER 19

That week, Jason's father became engrossed in his work, carving and polishing furniture pieces well into the night. Each day, Jason ate a simple supper alone and retired to bed feeling lonely and neglected. He knew something was wrong, but his courage to confront his dad had evaporated ever since their fishing trip together. Gone was that easy self-confidence Jason had lived, breathed, and felt with every waking moment following his victory over Stiller. In its place was a sense of helplessness, knowing that his father was wrestling with troubling thoughts but unable to summon the strength to approach him regarding them. Jason wanted desperately to comfort his father but above all else feared being rejected by him.

Days passed without further event, the weekend fast approaching.

»«»«»«

That Friday evening, Kyle unwittingly emerged from the shell he had formed to shield his inner feelings from the outside world. Standing by the door of the farmhouse, he was mesmerized by the beauty of the sun setting over Moosehead Lake. As it did to the Greeks thousands of years before, the sun appeared to him a golden chariot dripping fire upon the earth, leaving him to marvel and reflect soberly upon his life.

Am I living life like I should? What kind of father am I? What kind of life am I offering my son?

These thoughts had tormented Kyle ever since he had learned that Cynthia had left them for good. Kyle questioned whether he had the skills, the will, and the strength to raise Jason on his own—to be both mother and father to Jason. Kyle was confident that he could survive in the wilderness on his own but unsure whether he had the skills to raise his own son. This uncertainty struck him with fear and worry. Each day, Kyle dwelled on his inadequacies in caring for Jason, from his quick temper to his periodic inability to express his emotions and communicate with his son.

Kyle resolved to speak with Sasquot as a father seeking the wisdom and understanding of another father. He walked briskly toward the driveway in front of the main house, where Sasquot stood loading up his pickup truck with farm tools and equipment.

"Sasquot, do you have a minute?" Kyle asked in an unassuming but husky voice. Sasquot nodded and looked directly at Kyle.

"Well, I just have a couple of things on my mind." Kyle turned once again toward the sunset. Majestic mountains rose up on all sides of Moosehead Lake, casting slate blue reflections upon the tinted waters.

Sasquot stood beside Kyle, patiently waiting for Kyle to share his thoughts.

"You know, Sasquot, I always thought that being a father would be something instinctual, something automatic. Be a good person; be a good father." Kyle coughed to clear his throat. "I've come to realize how difficult it actually is. I'm . . . afraid that I'm failing to be a good father to Jason."

"How do you think you are failing?" Sasquot asked, trying to draw out Kyle's thoughts.

"I just have trouble knowing what to say to the boy, understanding what his needs are, and meeting them. A lot of times, I'm too hard on him—too rough with his emotions. I don't think before I become angry and criticize him."

"Do you ask Jason for his thoughts?" Sasquot queried.

"I . . . don't usually ask him how he's feeling," Kyle answered honestly. "I fear that I won't understand what he has to say or that I'll say the wrong things and make him feel worse. Sometimes, by saying nothing, I feel like I'm protecting him from me."

"Fear of failure stops communication," Sasquot stated. "Communication is the key to understanding Jason's feelings and meeting his needs."

"Yes, you're right, Sasquot. It's just that if I failed with Cynthia, why should anything be different with Jason? I failed with—"

"Cynthia is a much different person," Sasquot interrupted. "Jason is your flesh, your own blood."

"When we were married, we were supposed to become one flesh and one blood," Kyle said.

"That is true, but Cynthia violated this law of God by choosing not to remain one with you as part of one family. Jason is your son forever," Sasquot explained. "Your son has an extremely good heart. He looks up to his father as a hero. Cynthia is her own hero. She fails to respect her duties to her family. Jason, by contrast, strives to become a man and to help his family grow strong together."

"How can he look up to me?" Kyle asked. "I failed to keep our family together."

"It is not your fault that your family separated, Kyle. Cynthia made the choice to abandon your family. Cynthia placed more value on what she thought was good for her career than on what she knew was good for her family. The Bible says that a person who brings trouble on their own family will inherit the wind."

"But I blame myself for her leaving," Kyle responded, a pained look on his face.

"Let me tell you a story about a boy," Sasquot replied. "This boy met a second boy. Both boys came from the Bear Family and loved each other like close brothers. They swore to always help one another and to share their fortune, whether good or bad. In our tribe, this oath creates a sacred bond. The father of one of these boys was a medicine man. One day, the mother of the other boy became sick—so sick that she came very close to death. The medicine man traveled to her home in the middle of the night to cure her sickness. She recovered and lived a long life.

"Many moons passed. One of the boys became a rich man and moved to a town far away. He founded a business selling goods to people all across the country. The other boy stayed in the town where he was raised to be with his tribe. He lived a simple life and kept few possessions.

"One day, his father, the medicine man, fell very ill. No one in the entire tribe knew what his sickness was or how to cure it. So, his son took the medicine man to a doctor in the city. This doctor said the medicine man urgently needed an operation that cost more money than all of the savings of the medicine man and his entire family combined. The son of the medicine man called his blood brother and told him his father needed money for a surgery in order to survive. To the son's shock, his blood brother said he has his own family and business expenses and responsibilities and could not help him.

"The medicine man grew weaker every day and died the next month. The whole tribe mourned the death of this great medicine man. His son dressed his father in his best clothes, placed his father's prized bow and arrows over him, and wrapped his body in birch bark. The dying wish of his father was for his body to be placed next to the body of his father, also a great medicine man, on Katahdin. His son carried his body alone for three days, resting only at night, to the top of the mountain. There, next to his grandfather's grave, he buried his father with unspeakable grief."

Kyle stared at Sasquot without uttering a word.

"I am the son of the medicine man. My blood brother allowed my father to die," Sasquot stated.

"That's unspeakable what he did," Kyle responded, grimacing at the ugliness of the blood brother's actions. Despite their close friendship over many years, Sasquot had never told Kyle any part of this story. In fact, Sasquot had never shared it with anyone outside of his immediate family.

"It is also unspeakable what Cynthia has done to you and to Jason," Sasquot answered. "But the heart must forgive. I hated my blood brother when my father died. I felt anger at my blood brother and at the whole world for not curing my father. How can this be? I felt that I had failed as his son. Then I realized that I, too, have, at times in my life, wronged my family, my tribesmen, my friends, and strangers. How can they forgive me for the many wrongs I have done to them?"

"But surely you wouldn't have allowed your blood brother's father to die like that," Kyle asserted.

"All sin is wrong, Kyle. God is the rightful Judge of my moral sin," Sasquot responded. "Let me tell you a story from the Bible. Peter asked Jesus how many times he needs to forgive his fellow man—seven times? Jesus told him to forgive his fellow man seventy times seven."

"Sasquot, I've always known you to be a good, honorable man, but I never realized you were a Christian," Kyle observed.

"Kyle, I try to do good deeds for my fellow man, demonstrating to him the love that God shows me. You know how I found faith in God?" he asked. "After the death of the father I loved more than my tongue can express, my heart grieved deeply. I wondered what gave my father strength to smile and provide me love and joy even when he was very weak in the days before his death. One day, when I was looking through my father's belongings, I found a prayer book. In it, my father wrote thanks to God for sending His Son to die for him; he thanked God for blessing him with me and his wife and a tribe whom he loved. He thanked God for each morning and each night. He thanked God for giving him peace during his deepest pain. Lastly, he thanked God for the joy of knowing that if he died, he would be with Him in Heaven. He wrote this while he was in great pain, struggling for his life, and abandoned by my blood brother."

Kyle nodded, listening intently to Sasquot's words.

"I understood in that moment that my father had found great faith and peace from God. I wanted to be like my father, a man with peace in his mind and joy in his heart no matter what happened. So one day, after a church minister answered many questions I had for him, I gave my heart to God, to Jesus Christ, His Son. This changed my heart and my life.

"I then prayed for God to give me the courage to do a very hard thing—to go to my blood brother and tell him face-to-face that I forgave him. When I did this, he wept. He acknowledged his mistake and begged me to be blood brothers once again. I told him God gave me the strength to forgive him and that I loved him. He became a changed man, too, and his heart is now right, focused on the man he is and no longer on his possessions."

Kyle nodded in silence, touched by the story and the power of forgiveness. *Clearly, Sasquot no longer harbors anger against the world for this,* he thought. *Sasquot forgave his blood brother for a most terrible offense. He must truly have experienced a change in his heart in order to have had the strength to forgive such a sin. Perhaps I, too, can summon the courage to forgive Cynthia for what she has done and the strength not to blame myself for her leaving Jason and me.*

Sasquot started talking again. "It is very hard to tell this story. I told it to you because I know how it feels to lose someone you love. I lost two people I love—my father and my blood brother at the same time, but one day I regained my blood brother by forgiving him. Do not be angry at the world; rather, forgive the persons who wrong you," Sasquot instructed.

"How can I receive this strength, this courage to forgive?" Kyle asked.

Sasquot knelt beside Kyle and prayed for God to soften Kyle's heart, to make Himself manifest to Kyle, and to change his heart to a godly heart—one with the power to forgive the most heinous wrongs and filled with the courage to give his life over to Him.

Once he had concluded praying, Sasquot said, "I know you feel pain in your heart. To live a happy life, you need to forgive the person who has hurt you the most."

Kyle felt overwhelmed by everything that Sasquot had said. He placed his head in his hands, deep in thought. *What unbelievable power and strength this old man possesses. If God could give Sasquot the power to forgive a blood brother who had refused to come to his dying father's aid, surely God can give me the power to forgive Cynthia for leaving us.*

"I'll try to forgive her," Kyle said with great emotion. "It was . . . it was so hard to get those divorce papers, Sasquot. I thought—I think—about her every day. How much I love her and care about her, even today. Every day, I feel betrayed and abandoned. I search myself for answers—why she did this, what I did wrong, how I am failing as a father and as a human being."

"Healing is a process," Sasquot explained. "My father taught me it is more important to heal your spirit than to heal your body. He died a happy man. You need to heal inside, talk to your son, ask God how to forgive Cynthia, and learn not to blame yourself for bad things that happen in your life outside of your control."

Kyle sighed with relief that someone seemed to truly understand and care about what he was going through while not blaming him for it.

"Last week, Cynthia called me," Kyle said in a low voice. "She told me that I was hurting Jason by keeping him here and that I don't have the 'requisite parenting skills.' She said . . . that I should not in good conscience continue to raise him." Kyle's voice trembled. "Do you think this is true, Sasquot?"

"Cynthia spoke from a heart of anger. You are a good man, Kyle, a man learning how to become a good father. Jason looks up to you very much. He loves and respects you."

"She won't sue for custody, Sasquot, but said she wants Jason to know that he can go to Exeter if he wants and live with her and . . . her fiancé."

"Jason received her offer long ago. Jason's mind has not changed. He loves living here on your farm near the woods where he can fish, climb mountains, hunt, run in the woods, and live in harmony with nature every day. He wants to live with you here," Sasquot stated.

Kyle looked up at Sasquot and smiled. "I think you're right, Sasquot. I think you're right."

"Jason is concerned about you. Tell him you are okay and that you want him to stay here to be with you as your family."

Kyle nodded.

"Now, I must go home to be with my family. I leave you to be with your son, to give him this most important message," Sasquot said.

"I will, Sasquot, my friend and brother," Kyle said, patting Sasquot on the back. "Thank you . . . for everything."

Kyle went inside, humbled by Sasquot's wisdom. Sasquot, a man without worldly wealth or formal education, understood so many things that most people spend a lifetime struggling to understand. Sasquot accepted what he could not change and forgave those who wronged him. He had a sense of inner peace and fulfillment that Kyle had seldom encountered.

"Jason," Kyle called out. He spotted Jason slouched back in a comfortable, old chair reading a book.

"Hey, Dad," Jason answered with a hopeful smile.

"I see you're reading a book about deer hunting, son. How would you like to hunt one with me when the firearms season opens at the end of the month?"

"I'd love to," Jason answered enthusiastically.

Kyle had taken Jason to hunt pheasant, bobwhite quail, and wild turkey before but never to hunt big game.

"I picked up a new rifle a couple weeks back, a real nice 7mm-08 bolt-action rifle with limited recoil. That would work well on your first big hunt."

"That sounds great! Can it take down a big buck?"

"You better believe it. It can drop a buck from about three hundred yards out. You and I are going to get a trophy buck, son. And if we don't, we still are going to have one good time," Kyle said, messing up Jason's hair in good fun. He cleared his throat. "I also have something more serious to talk to you about, Jason. Your mother has offered to take care of you and to pay for you to go to Exeter for high school next year."

Jason's countenance immediately clouded over. "No way! I'm staying right here with you, Dad. You couldn't pay me enough money to leave Greenville to go to Exeter," Jason responded without the slightest hesitation. "All she cares about is her image, sending a son to Exeter so she can brag about it to her friends. I love it here."

Kyle smiled, touched by his son's spirited response. "Your mother cares about you, son," he said, "but I'm glad for both of us that you want to live here as one family. We can make it through this, Jason. I want you to come to me whenever you need to get things off your chest. I'm not great with words or feelings sometimes, but I just want you to know that."

"Thanks, Dad," Jason said, optimistic and seeming to pick up on Kyle's desire to tear down the invisible barriers that far too often separated the two and kept them emotionally apart.

"How about tossing around the pigskin out back for old times' sake?" Kyle asked expectantly.

Jason nodded and quickly volunteered to dig the football out of the hall closet.

They turned on the floodlights and threw around the football that Jason had gotten as a birthday present two years ago. The father-son team enjoyed a good, long game of running patterns that Friday night.

»«»«»«

Each went to bed feeling a lot more hopeful about the future. Kyle was determined to be a changed man with the inner peace and joy to enjoy living life with Jason to the fullest, and he hoped that the deer hunt would be a major step in that direction. Jason, for his part, was greatly relieved that his dad had talked things over with him and had offered to be there when he needed someone to talk to. For the first time, they both felt a sense of confidence that they could make it through the divorce as one close family.

CHAPTER 20

In a sweeping vista around Moosehead Lake, trees clad themselves in robes of luxurious color. Like a living creature, the forest emerged each day from a cold, shiftless slumber resplendently transformed in the pure light of dawn, bleeding color onto the earth. This was Kyle's favorite time of the year, for never did he feel so alive and invigorated as he did during the fall. Not only did he behold the peerless beauty of Maine's foliage, but he also felt the refreshingly cool, brisk winds, the pristine chill of the early morning air, the first fine crystals of snow landing upon his brow, and the shifting currents of time and season playing themselves out across the land.

In Kyle's readily shared opinion, this was the perfect time of year in which to venture forth into the woods on a deer scouting expedition. So, one crisp, clear Saturday morning, mid-way through the month of October, Kyle set out into the waking wilderness adjoining his farm in search of a coveted trophy buck.

Landing a trophy buck—a male deer with a highly rated set of antlers—represented a meaningful feat to any deer hunter, particularly one as proud and determined as Kyle Wilson. A hunter since childhood, Kyle had long ago mastered the intricacies of the Boone and Crockett Club Point System. This technical system rated buck trophy antlers based upon such factors as the spread between the antler beams, the length and thickness of these beams, and the length of the unbranched tines behind the forward main beam antlers. Kyle could just picture the look on Jason's face when he arrived home from school to see a massive buck sporting a beautiful set of trophy antlers.

In that moment, Jason will understand why Maine is so special, Kyle thought. He hoped and somewhat even expected that Jason would have had the time of his life on this hunt, which would have been Jason's first big game hunting foray. He wanted Jason to experience the exhilaration of the Maine outdoors during the hunting season, a feeling that Kyle would never outgrow.

As Kyle crept through the woods in his quietest pair of leather hunting boots, his mind was flooded with recollections of the surrounding deer habitat: the thicketed ridges upon which the deer bedded and watched for predators, the shallow streams in which they drank, the specific trees and shrubs upon which they fed this time of year, and the thick evergreen cover into which they fled upon the first sign of danger. Kyle knew not only the daily activities of an average Maine white-tailed deer—feeding and watering during the twilight hours, becoming active around midday and midnight, and bedding in secluded safety during most of the day—but by the end of each year, he was also host to an amazing wealth of information about individual deer. Through scouting expeditions and stalking hunts, Kyle would learn the particular feeding, watering, mating, bedding, and roaming habits of a number of these deer, including the area's dominant bucks.

Last year, Kyle had the good fortune of coming across a group of bucks that he was able to follow throughout the late summer and fall, observing the intriguing establishment of an intra-male social hierarchy. He had gone to great lengths to keep from being detected by these bucks. From August through October, he had used powerful binoculars, masked his scent with pine needles and cedar, worn camouflaged hunting jackets, and conscientiously shifted his position to be downwind of the group.

During the summer, the group of five bucks established their hierarchy through body signals, such as the lowering and raising of heads and ears. Kyle did not witness the use of force even once during this period. Then in September, the bucks began to shed their antler velvet, leaving hard, polished antlers. As fall approached and then arrived, Kyle observed the bucks become increasingly aggressive to the point where they would spar with each other. The sparring generally seemed to reinforce the social hierarchy that had been created during the summer.

The most dramatic moment came when the two most dominant bucks of the group, each over six feet in length and close to three hundred pounds, refused to back down to each other. The muscular bucks abruptly lowered their heads and clashed their antlers together, producing loud racking sounds that ricocheted off trees and dissipated into the suddenly quieted forest environs. Though noisy and physical, the duel neither lasted long nor produced injury. After having been pushed back, one buck, whom Kyle named "Smoking Joe," angrily bowed out of the fight in favor of an undefeated "Rocky." As its reward, Rocky got to stake out the immediate area as its mating territory, an advertisement to nearby does that it was the dominant buck and was ready and willing to share its genes with them.

Deer thrived here because the area offered mixed habitat, thereby providing a variety of terrain and conditions which met the deer's changing needs throughout the year. This debunked the popular misconception of deer hiding in unbroken forest many miles away from civilization. The prime deer habitat upon which Kyle, Kyle's father, his grandfather, and his great-grandfather had settled included tracts of mixed growth forest broken by farmland, swamps, and stream corridors, along with rocky ridges and thickets that provided ideal places for deer to bed and reconnoiter.

The sprawling farms of Kyle's grandfather and great-grandfather had been divided and subdivided over the years, such that four separately owned farms now encompassed what had once been sixty-four continuous acres of Wilson farmland. That hefty acreage had marked the peak of the family's hard-earned foothold in the New World toward the end of the nineteenth century.

Throughout these divisions, the hospitable Wilsons had always retained good relations with their newfound neighbors. For each of the last dozen years or so, Kyle's three adjoining frontier families had granted reciprocal deer hunting rights to each other for the fall season. Last year, a team comprised of Kyle and his three neighbors had even collaborated to catch two bucks and a doe in a single drive, where two of them had walked through a small forest tract in the direction of Kyle and another awaiting hunter.

The trick was to choose a tract which provided a predictable avenue of escape for the driven deer. Knowing this, they had cleverly selected a narrow pine thicket bordered by open fields. Faced with the choice of exposing themselves to open fields or staying within the cover of woods, the startled deer had made the fatal mistake of remaining covered. It ran directly past the posters positioned downwind of the deer where Kyle, hidden behind a pine, had brought it down with one shot. He had mounted that fine specimen of a buck in his den.

As Kyle lightly tread through the thawing woods, he observed the fierce gaze of a Northern Goshawk peering down at him from its lofty perch high up in the coniferous canopy. Rare to spot in these parts, he thought it an especially auspicious sign to have sighted the magnificent broad-winged hawk. Even so, he still did not expect to spot deer bounding to and fro in the open.

Kyle had learned to respect the deer's uncanny senses of smell, hearing, and sight long ago. He knew that deer bedded during most daylight hours for a variety of reasons, the most important of which was to place themselves in the safest position from which to detect approaching threats such as himself. As Kyle's father, Stephen, had taught him, a deer lying motionless amid thick forest brush was much less likely to attract the attention of predators than one bounding through the forest. Deer generally bedded in elevated areas of dense cover where approaching predators could be heard, seen, or, most likely, smelled well before they detected the deer's presence. Perhaps the optimal deer bedding area was a ridge, facing downhill with the wind at the deer's back.

Kyle moved toward higher ground, which was more likely to contain deer bedding areas. He followed alongside a deer trail into the ascending pine and fir woods, continuously scanning the surrounding vegetation for signs of deer browsing.

Covering up their signs of feeding is one thing these creatures don't do well. Lacking upper incisors, deer tore buds and twigs off saplings, leaving ragged ends which were easily discernible to the trained hunter's eye.

As Kyle came to a cluster of pine saplings, he noted these telltale signs of deer feeding. In addition, he observed a pile of large, dark-brown pellets clumped together in a shapeless mass on the mossy, frost-covered forest floor. These were deer pellets. Kyle bent down to judge their size and freshness.

Suddenly, a clump of melting snow from the previous week's storm hurtled down upon him. Startled, he jumped away from the sound of the falling snow, only seeing it peripherally. He averted most of the snow but got smacked in the back of the neck with some cold slush, instantly piquing his senses. Kyle sprang to his feet, cleared the slush off his neck, and looked up into the snow-laden branches above.

Looming over him was the culprit, a mother pine which had also produced the saplings Kyle had examined just moments ago. He returned amused and freshly awakened to the few deer droppings that were not covered in snow. A good-sized buck had deposited them within the past several hours.

If this is a regular feeding area for the buck, he's probably not far from here, Kyle thought as he noted the feeding signs and deer droppings on a topographical map strewn with scribbled notations of landmarks and deer activity.

Kyle scanned the bark of an adjoining thicket of birch trees for buck rubs of exposed wood six inches to a foot in length cut by a buck's antlers and marked with its scent. He was especially interested in finding one that was large and well-worn, which would effectively blow the cover of a nearby dominant buck.

As Kyle continued his scouting expedition up into the local highland regions, he followed the trail of a heavy buck, its deep, clipped heart-claw marks trampling vegetation along the way. The one-foot stride mark indicated that the buck was walking along at a leisurely pace unaware of his presence when it had passed through not more than a few hours ago. Fortunately, Kyle was advancing into a steady headwind, so that the buck was unlikely to detect his scent until he was within sight. Moreover, Kyle had covered his hunting jacket and boots in pine needles the day before in order to mask his smell as much as possible.

He now spotted a rub, one measuring a foot in length which had clearly been made and re-made a number of times.

This is probably the same buck that left the droppings that I found on the forest floor, he thought. *And it almost certainly made the claw-mark trail that I've been following.*

Kyle decided to scan the area for additional signs of the buck. He carefully crept forward, peering into his binoculars, keen to the slightest movement. A bright red cardinal flew across Kyle's view, nearly causing him to pull the binoculars away, so edgy were his nerves. However, Kyle saw no signs of the buck as his binoculars completed their first sweeping arc.

Kyle began a second scan.

There! That's a scrape!

Kyle quickly reversed the scanning direction and redirected the binoculars to a position about seventy degrees to his right. In plain view was a three-foot wide circle bereft of leaves and debris: a buck scrape announcing the buck's presence to fellow bucks and does alike. His energy and excitement at a peak, Kyle stealthily made his way toward the scrape. For the first time in this scouting expedition, he broke a sweat.

Ten adrenaline-pumped minutes later, Kyle came to the scrape. Before examining it, he took a look at the branch overhanging the scrape. The branch bore the smell of the buck's deposited scent and had been torn in various places by the buck's antlers.

Given the bucks' bold proclamations of their mating territories during this season, it was truly a deer hunter's paradise.

Kyle once again peered through his binoculars, adjusting their power a number of times as he endeavored to follow the buck's trail as deep into the forest as he possibly could. Then Kyle heard it, the sound he had so eagerly been awaiting, that of brush being strewn aside and trampled at a furious pace not more than 150 feet away. A massive buck, thick-necked and bulging with muscles, emerged into view, thrashing through heavy brush with a huge set of antlers. The antlers, which spread over three feet across, caught some sunlight as the buck raised its head, reflecting magnificently into the surrounding environs.

That is at least a twelve-point buck, Kyle thought as he froze in admiration at the strapping buck.

Despite the unfavorable wind, the buck had at last scented Kyle's presence and emerged snorting in anxiety from its bed amidst the thickets above. In one of those frozen moments of time, the buck turned its head toward Kyle, looking directly into his eyes. The buck had no problem locating Kyle at this exceedingly close 150-foot range despite his hunting jacket's mottled green camouflage patterns.

Flashing its bright white tail to alert other deer of the lurking danger, the buck instantly bounded away. The deer gracefully leaped over brush and disappeared into a cluster of dense evergreens little more than a half-mile from where he had emerged but a minute before. Even with his tremendous size, the buck could leap eight feet, bound almost thirty feet, and attain speeds of thirty-six miles per hour. Unless a hunter was quick to the trigger, an alerted deer was an escaped one.

Kyle stood there transfixed by the majesty and agility of the tremendous specimen he had just beheld. Heart still pounding, he could do nothing but stare with naked eyes into the cluster of evergreens hiding all traces of the buck from his view.

Minutes later, Kyle took out his deer map and painstakingly noted as much information about the buck as he could remember: its color, size, antler features, and other physical attributes, the shape and size of its claw marks, the location and attributes of its rub and scrape, the thicket from which it had emerged, and the cover into which it had fled. Kyle also continued to sketch the buck's main trail from the lowlands to this rugged, hilly terrain.

He decided to approach the thicket from which the buck had emerged. Reaching it and peering through several layers of saplings, brambles, and scrubby vegetation, he noted several buck-sized depressions, numerous sets of tracks leading to and from the thicket, and plenty of cylindrical deer pellets—some fresh and some old. These all pointed to the same conclusion: this was one of the buck's favorite bedding areas, one to which the buck would repeatedly return.

This guy will likely be bedding here, at least for the near future, he thought. *After Jason and I stalk this bed in a couple of weeks, it won't ever be returning here again.*

Kyle briskly hiked the eight miles back home, deep in thought. *I've been successful the last five times out. My trip with Jason will be no exception.*

CHAPTER 21

That Saturday night, Jason, Paul, and Scott waved goodbye to Jason's dad as he pulled out of the Greenville school parking lot. They entered the school, paid the three-dollar admission fee, and walked down to the cafeteria, consciously trying to appear as cool and casual as possible. Jason wore a pair of faded jeans and an untucked button-down shirt over a black t-shirt. To accentuate his size and build, Scott merely sported an open leather jacket over a fairly tight-fitting white t-shirt. To complete the look, Scott had combed back and gelled his hair and wore a pair of cheap shades he had found in some motorcycle accessory catalog. Paul, who liked to consider himself the group leader, led the way, dressed like a model out of a catalog.

Since the race, Jason, Paul, and Scott had risen into the cool group at school, regularly sitting at lunch with the class president, starting junior high quarterback, and son of the Greenville mayor. A palpable layer of student fear of the mean-spirited Stiller twins had been lifted ever since Matt's public humiliation. Now, students could not help but break into knowing smiles or sarcastic snickers whenever the Stiller brothers passed them by in the hallway. As a result, Matt and Glen found themselves more ostracized than ever. Stripped of their power to instill fear, they were reduced to harmless misfits in the eyes of their peers.

The vast majority of Jason's classmates gave him the credit for this and admired his audacity in taking Stiller on in both actions and words. Paul and Scott, for their part, made sure just about everyone at school knew that they had boldly predicted Jason's victory to Matt's face.

They strode into the cafeteria, which had been cleared of tables and chairs for the rock-n'-roll jam; they were warmly greeted by the in-crowd.

"Oh, hey, Jason, I heard about last week's meet against Dover-Foxcroft. Way to go," Brian, the eighth-grade class president, said, extending Jason a soda. "How does the rest of the schedule look?"

Last week, Jason had made a dramatic come-from-behind victory, sprinting in the last two hundred meters to overtake a strong Dover-Foxcroft rival. The team was now five-and-one, and Jason was personally undefeated for the season.

"We shouldn't have any trouble with Monson, but Guilford looks tough. They have a guy, O'Brien, who won the state championship last year."

"You can handle him, champ," Brian said. "Hey, how's that bear—Cody or whatever its name is—holding up?"

"Coda's doing great," Jason answered with a smile. "He's had a couple of close scrapes, though." Jason proceeded to mesmerize Brian and a few other bystanders with his tales of the timber rattlesnake and adult bear attacks.

"Sounds as mischievous as my kid brother," Larry, the mayor's son, said. "But I've got to hand it to him—he really has good taste in clothing."

The group burst into laughter, and Brian gave Larry a solid high-five. "Yeah, you should try reading him some comics. Coda seems to have a thing for Superman," Larry continued, drawing smiles.

Frank, the junior high quarterback, arrived at the scene and instantly joined the group. "Hey, guys, ready for some home-town jamming later tonight?"

"Sounds good," Brian answered. "Hey, Frank, you going to sing for us like last year?" Frank was known for his sarcastic wit and rap-making ability in addition to his athletic prowess. Under his quarterbacking, the team had gone from oh-and-ten to five-and-two so far this season.

Frank began to rap, improvising the words on the spot.

The man of the hour

Feels his power.

He rises to his feet

To feel the beat.

The moves of the night,

They're right, so right.

So come join him

And feel the rhythm.

"Not bad," Brian said, trying hard to assume a serious tone of voice. "You're no Run-D.M.C., but you're making progress every year."

Frank good-naturedly grabbed Brian by the arm and then started for the stage at the back of the cafeteria. "You, my peanut gallery man, are going to provide the background for tonight's rap performance."

Brian pretended to protest but in truth loved the spotlight as much as Frank did. The two approached the deejay, who was warming up with "Thriller" by Michael Jackson. The deejay nodded and set up the microphone.

Moments later, Brian announced to a crowd of nearly seventy Greenville seventh and eighth graders, "On behalf of me and my main man, welcome to the Second Annual Rap Artist Performance Festival, featuring the one and only, the dumb and homely, the quarterback who avoids the sack, Frank the Tank. Let's hear it, my friends! Come on now, make some noise for me and my main man!"

The room came alive with a mixture of shouts, playful whistles, and the chanting of, "Frank the Tank, Frank the Tank"—a nickname Frank had garnered by his goal-line ability to run through defenses to score rushing touchdowns.

Brian began to blow into his hands, making punctuated noises to which Frank could rap. "I'd like to dedicate this song to our good friend, Matt Stiller," Frank cried out to an immediate cacophony of jeers and whistles.

Frank dramatically paced along the stage as his deep voice rang out:

Come hear a story of a man you know:

A man named Stiller from the land below,

Who roamed the school like a wolf hunts prey.

Until one very special day,

A hero came forth from these here streets,

Promising us tremendous feats.

He came right up to Stiller's face

And challenged him to one big race:

A race of glory, a race of fame

To defend his dear friend's challenged name.

The race was close; the race was tight.

Stiller would not go without a fight.

He picked a quarrel with a tiny bear

And ended up in his underwear.

He stood before us, his biggest fan,

A man of steel called Superman.

Hear this story and listen well

To David's triumph that Goliath fell.

"Thank you, thank you very much," Frank intoned in his signature Elvis impersonation. He and Brian were bowing energetically to a receptive crowd, who roared with laughter and applause.

Frank signaled for Jason to join them on stage. Jason eagerly took to the stage, standing beside them. The crowd noise increased in a tremendous crescendo of howling laughter and applause. The students had been whipped into a frenzy.

Taken aback by the whole scene, the teacher monitoring the dance briskly walked up to the microphone and said, "Okay, guys, that's the end of the Rap Artist Festival. Let's all calm down a bit and enjoy the evening."

"No problem, Ms. Hall. Okay, my friends, it's time for some breakdancing," Frank announced. "Come join me on the floor."

Brian requested a song by Run D.M.C. and then proceeded with Frank to the cafeteria dance floor, where they demonstrated what could best be described as a humorous yet energetic version of breakdancing. Brian attempted a headspin that resulted in him grabbing his head in pain and a turtle walk that spun his body around at turtle speed. Meanwhile, Frank amazed the audience with a windmill, followed by an aborted flare power move. The talent bar set low, others soon joined in, attempting handglides, six steps, deadmans, straddles, and UFOs. The participants were clearly having a blast, and just about everyone seemed to be in good spirits.

After about twenty minutes of breakdancing, the deejay announced it was time for the limbo contest.

"How loooow can you goooooo?" the deejay asked in a smooth baritone. "All the way from the West Indies, I bring to you tonight, the Limmmboooooooo. And to get you all in the limbo mood, here's Tina Turner with 'What's Love Got to Do With It?'"

Almost all of the girls and most of the guys lined up. Jason locked eyes with Autumn as he joined the line. He raised his eyebrows as if to ask, "Aren't you going to join in?"

Autumn smiled and shook her head.

Jason smiled back and then took his turn walking up to the limbo bar, held up by two student council representatives. He had to bend backward only a little bit in order to pass beneath it. The bar was set at about four feet high right now so that everyone could survive for the second pass—everyone, that is, except Lenny, the class clown, who did a Michael Jackson moonwalk straight into it.

Now the bar came down to three-and-a-half feet, eliminating a few tall guys and less coordinated classmates. Frank and Scott were among those eliminated, but Jason was still alive. At three feet, fewer than one-third of the girls and only about one-fifth of the guys could make it underneath. Jason, being extremely flexible, was one of them. The bar was lowered a couple inches at a time now, until only two people remained: Jason and Christie.

Christie was a drop-dead gorgeous blonde with soft blue eyes who had just moved into town the past summer. Almost every boy in the eighth grade had a crush on her, whether they would admit it or not. Jason had exchanged a few smiles with her in the past but had managed to convince himself that he did not need to complicate his life with girls at that point.

The deejay ordered the bar be lowered another couple of inches. It now stood at three feet, eight inches, and it was Jason's turn to go.

Christie turned and whispered in Jason's ear, "Good luck, hometown hero."

Jason felt his heart beat harder and faster, as if he had just finished a race. He could not concentrate at all and clumsily bumped his head into the bar. Embarrassed, he turned back to see whether Christie would make it underneath. Christie did a near split to navigate under the bar but, at the last moment, intentionally knocked the bar off with her hand.

Jason stared at her with a puzzled look on his face. In a coy manner, she sauntered up to him and said, "I couldn't bear to beat you. Now, we're both winners."

Jason was stunned. Christie, the prettiest girl he had ever seen in person, was openly flirting with him. He could do nothing but put on a dumb smile. The deejay called them onstage to share the first-place prize.

"Two tickets to see Bruce Springsteen in concert in Portland on December fifteenth," the deejay announced. "Looks like you two could be going together."

Jason blushed. He couldn't look at Christie, who was filling the room with her radiant smile.

"Okay, guys, now we'll slow things down a bit for some romance," the deejay announced. "Any requests?"

"'Stairway to Heaven,'" Christie instantly responded.

"'Stairway to Heaven' it is," the deejay said. "Enjoy."

Christie turned to Jason, and before he knew it, they were slow-dancing on stage in front of his friends and almost seventy of his classmates.

This is like a dream, so unreal and unexpected, he found himself thinking.

Christie had already placed one hand on Jason's shoulder, and she now leaned over and rested her head on his other shoulder as the song played. Everything seemed perfect, until Jason saw Autumn sitting with downcast eyes in a corner by herself. Wearing a cute denim skirt, she sat chin in hand without anyone to dance with or talk to.

No one ever treats her like she's special, like she's anybody, he thought as he danced. Feelings he had not realized that he harbored rose within him.

Without a second thought, Jason excused himself from Christie as "Stairway to Heaven" ended and walked over to the deejay and made a request

"By special request for Autumn, the number one hit from 1983, 'Every Breath You Take' by The Police," the deejay announced.

Jason didn't even glance at his fellow classmates; his eyes were riveted to one person and one person only: Autumn. Jason strode straight across the room to where Autumn was sitting alone in the far corner. "May I have this dance?"

Autumn could only nod her head as she stood. She buried her head against Jason's chest, overwhelmed by the gesture.

Most of the students were too shocked to dance. Christie looked mortified and left for the restroom.

Jason couldn't care less.

Somebody tapped Jason on the shoulder. It was Paul. "Jason, do you realize that you've offended Christie? I mean, you don't get a chance like this every day. She's the best-looking . . . "

"No, she's not," Jason answered, cutting him off. "Autumn is, and I'm dancing with her right now. So, if you'll please excuse me . . . " he said and turned away from Paul.

Looking back at that night in the future, Jason would always be proud. He might not have gained in popularity, but he ultimately won the respect of thoughtful classmates and touched the heart of a person about whom he truly cared.

CHAPTER 22

It was five a.m. the morning of October twenty-eighth, the first day of the deer firearms season for Maine residents. Jason awakened from a strange dream in which the animals of the forest spoke to him and assumed human mannerisms. They continually asked him what his intentions were and why he visited them in the forest.

That's really weird, he thought as he sat up in bed and turned off his alarm.

Jason usually neither paid much attention to his dreams nor tried to interpret them. But ever since last summer, when Sasquot had told him that dreams could have great meaning and reveal a person's otherwise hidden thoughts, fears, and desires, he had made an extra effort to remember his dreams in case actions or events subsequently revealed their meaning.

Jason had all of his clothing draped over his chair ready for bundling. He would dress in several layers of clothing, putting on his waterproof and windproof jacket over a fleece pullover, which in turn would cover a flannel button-down and a long-sleeved cotton t-shirt. To complete his array, he would wear insulated pants; thick wool socks; broken-in leather boots that he had waterproofed; and a thermally insulated hat, scarf, and pair of gloves. Living in Maine, it had not taken Jason long to realize that the key to braving the cold was to wear layered clothing. For now, he put on his cotton t-shirt, flannel shirt, and pants and walked downstairs to breakfast.

"Good morning, son!" Jason's dad called out in the happiest voice Jason had heard in a long time. "I'm making some hot oatmeal and scrambled eggs to fortify us for our big day." His father finished stirring the oatmeal, then pulled back the curtains to reveal a landscape covered in snow. "As you can see, the weather is a bit cold. That will make the going more difficult, but it will also give us some advantages. We'll be able to track the buck's prints more easily in the freshly fallen snow. And since the weather is somewhat colder than usual for this time of year, it's more likely our buck will be active during the morning and afternoon—the warmest part of the day."

"Wow, it looks beautiful out there," Jason said, admiring the layer of soft, pure snow that garlanded every tree in sight.

The snow had been falling slowly but steadily for a few hours now, and two inches had already accumulated. Jason noted that, fortunately, the wind was mild and would not drive most deer to bed during the day. If the weather worsened, however, combining fierce winds with the cold snow, deer would seek thick cover in which to bed and might even move to their winter quarters—thick, sheltered evergreen stands.

"Well, today will certainly be an adventure, son. We have some real Maine weather out there and a very real trophy buck to hunt. He's a keeper, I can tell you that. You'll impress a lot of folks around here by taking him down. He has the best set of antlers I've seen in these parts in the last two years."

"Can we mount the antlers in the den?" Jason asked expectantly.

"Sure, son, we're going to want to showcase them to everyone. Now when you're done with breakfast, I want you to put some more of this pine-masking scent on. Hopefully that, combined with the snow and wind conditions, will make it harder for the deer to pick up our scent."

"What about camouflage, Dad? Do deer get scared off by traditional orange hunting clothes?" Jason asked, taking a look at the bright orange hat, vest, and gloves hanging over a chair by the door.

"No, it appears brown or gray to deer, so it doesn't bother them. So, we'll both wear orange for safety from other hunters, just like when we hunted pheasants. If we use stealth and cover and approach from the right direction to the wind, we'll be golden. And we won't have to get too close, either. If you shoot accurately, your rifle can place three shots within one-and-a-half inches from three hundred yards out. Not bad, huh?"

"Yeah, that sounds real powerful, Dad. Sure I can handle the recoil?" Jason asked, concerned that the rifle would throw him back and misdirect his shot.

"It won't be easy. You'll definitely feel it, but this rifle has more limited recoil than a bunch of other high-powered rifles. I'll get you in close enough so that even a slightly misdirected shot will have a good chance of landing. Just leave it to me to set you up for the perfect shot," Jason's father instructed.

"Okay, no problem," Jason responded with a smile.

"Let's get a move on. Meet me down here in five minutes ready to head out," his dad said, pushing back his breakfast bowl and plate. "I'm bringing some trail mix and granola bars and a full canteen."

Jason nodded and quickly finished his last bite of hot oatmeal. He was looking forward to the hunt and, most of all, to pleasing his father during it. He wanted to perform well so that his dad would be justifiably proud of his hunting prowess.

Minutes later, Jason was ready and waiting by the front door. His dad came down the stairs, carrying Jason's rifle in one hand and a collapsible frame pack stuffed with a compass, deer map, hunting knife, flashlight, canteen, bag of trail mix and granola bars, bullets, matches, extra clothing, two pairs of binoculars, synthetic antlers, and a small first aid kit. He hoisted the so-called "lightweight" frame pack onto his back.

"For safety reasons, mostly, I'm going to carry the rifle, Jason. When it comes time to fire, though, it'll be sitting in your hands. Trust me," his father stated.

"That's fine with me," Jason said, actually relieved not to have to carry a rifle around. No matter how many safety precautions Jason had been taught, he still feared something going awry and could not bear the thought of injuring his dad, himself, or some other hunter with an accidental shot.

They walked out into a frigid winter wonderland. The glow of dawn cast a peach sheen upon the freshly fallen snow, which glistened in the slanted rays of the early morning sunrise. All around them, trees and bushes stood garbed in robes of tinted crystal.

The snow playfully fluttered to the ground in a light breeze that blew toward the southwest. Jason drank a snow crystal that landed on his lips and melted into his mouth.

"Quite a scene, isn't it?" Jason's dad remarked, marveling with his son at the serene beauty of the winter scene that enveloped them and seemed to transport them into another world altogether.

Jason nodded, storing up the magic of the moment in his mind. If this was all they saw the entire day, Jason would be content.

"All right. Follow me. We're going to head up into the highlands, where this buck roams. Keep alert for any broken twigs, trails, or other signs of wildlife along the way," his father instructed.

Minutes later, Jason's dad brushed aside some snow on the path before them, revealing split-heart depressions in the damp dirt below. "This is it, Jason. This is the same trail I followed in my scout of the area a couple weeks back. We're on our way to Lookout Ridge and our quarry," his father stated with unbridled enthusiasm.

Jason smiled. He had anticipated that it would be difficult to find the deer path in the midst of a winter snowfall, but his father apparently knew the area well.

"You always want to walk by the side of the trail as opposed to over it," his dad explained. "Otherwise, not only do you ruin the trail, but you alert creatures passing along the trail of your presence."

As Jason and his father tracked through minor brush five feet off the trail, Jason noted the last splashes of fall color struggling to be seen through the snow cover. Despite the storm, the bright yellow of silver birch and fiery red of sugar maples painted the forest.

No wonder this is Dad's favorite season, Jason thought as he trudged along through the two-inch accumulation.

Abruptly, his father crouched down and signaled for him to look toward a clearing to their left as a red fox lunged through the snow in pursuit of a patchy white snowshoe hare. Alerted to the predator, the hare bounded across the clearing, heading for the safety of brush not more than seventy feet away. Unfortunately for the hare, the fox had stealthily approached too close before being detected, and this hare's desperate bolt would be its last.

The sleek fox speedily closed in on its prey and, now within striking range, reached out and pawed the rabbit, causing the creature to tumble sideways into the snow. The fox instantly sprang on top of the disoriented hare. Within seconds, it clamped down on the hare's neck with its jaws and shook the hare until its neck snapped.

"That's amazing," Jason whispered. "The fox is so vicious."

"That's how it survives, son," his dad whispered back as they watched the fox trot back into the woods carrying the hare by the neck. "Red foxes stalk their prey like cats. They also have an acute sense of hearing that lets them hear woodchucks, mice, and rabbits underground. Once they locate their prey, they dig like crazy into the ground to uncover them."

"Have you ever seen a fox catch a rabbit before?" Jason asked.

"No. Believe me, it's rare to come across a fox in the wild, let alone one stalking prey. On a chicken farm, you're more likely to see one. When we had chickens some years back, fox would come during the night, dig their way into the hen house, and make off with a bunch of chickens. We extended the fence farther into the ground to take care of the problem. Well, since we're already stopped, why don't we take a food break?" his dad suggested, turning his pack toward Jason so that his son could remove the bag of trail mix.

Jason removed his gloves to grip the assorted fruits and nuts. Even exposing his fingers for a brief minute left them feeling raw and half-numb.

"Geez, I didn't realize how cold it was," Jason observed. "My fingers are practically frozen already."

"Yeah, it's a real cold morning, but this is good for the hunt. Deer will rest during the night and feed during the warmer daylight hours."

After his father had shared his canteen with him, the two resumed their hike. As they passed another open field with scattered trees and shrubs, they heard the low, mournful song of the mourning dove calling out "cooh-ah, coo, coo, coo." The attractive sand-colored dove was nestled in a white poplar tree not more than thirty feet away. Its song was easy to imitate, and Jason responded with a plausible rendition of his own.

"Not bad, not bad. You must be learning things from Sasquot."

The two continued their ascent toward Lookout Ridge, the trees becoming more and more uniformly coniferous as they reached higher altitude. They were probably eighteen hundred feet above sea level at this point. The wind died down to near stillness, and the snow lightened, with only scattered crystals flittering down around them.

Seemingly out of nowhere, Jason's father suddenly spotted something and excitedly directed his attention to it.

"That's the buck's rub," Jason's dad explained. "He's marking his territory for less dominant bucks to see. Note how well-worn the wood is here—that means the buck has come back several times to reinforce the rub. It's a good sign he's still around these parts."

"What happens if another buck enters his territory?" Jason asked.

"Generally, that won't happen because the buck will see the rub and detect the buck's scent. But if it does, there can be some clashing of antlers. Usually, one of the bucks backs down, and neither ends up getting hurt," his father responded. "See that clearing up ahead? As soon as we come to it, I'm going to try to attract the buck to our site through some simulated male sparring. Make sure you brace yourself for some fast and furious action because, if it works, the buck will come charging straight for us."

Jason raised his eyebrows and looked at his dad. He looked as happy as a child on a playground.

They crept up to the clearing. His father whispered to him, "What I'm about to do is called rattling. I'm going to simulate the sound of antlers clashing together so that the buck thinks that two rival bucks are on his territory battling to determine dominance or to win the right to breed with some doe. We're coming into the peak of the rutting season, when does come into heat and bucks go crazy trying to mate for all but a few hours of the day. In other words, it's prime time to try this rattling technique."

"Okay. What do I do?" Jason asked.

"You're going to take this rifle, which I'm loading right now, and wait for the buck to come charging into the clearing. When he does, you're going to have a good, close-range shot. What more can you ask for?" his dad asked rhetorically. "If this works, you'll drop a trophy buck on your first deer outing. Not bad for a first timer, right?"

Jason nodded, trying to mask his anxiety as his father placed premium bullets into the barrel. "Now, Jason, I want you to lie on the ground in order to maximize the steadiness of your shot. That's it. Now prop your rifle end up against this rotting log but keep your left hand underneath the fore-end. That'll keep her nice and steady. Aim for the far edge of the clearing. I'm going to crouch down behind that fir tree in the middle of the clearing and smack these synthetic antlers together as loudly as possible. I'll do this for about forty seconds, then quickly rake the antlers apart. I'll also thump the ground, break some twigs, and drag the antlers through some nearby brush and leaves to make it sound like two bucks are really battling here. Now, remember, the buck will come charging in real aggressive—ready to do battle. You've got to be ready and not be scared when he does."

"Okay, I'll be ready," Jason answered, his voice flat and nervous. "Where should I aim?"

"Good question. Assuming the buck is facing you, picture a football wedged between its two front shoulders and aim for the football. The buck's heart and lungs are located between its front shoulders. Even if you miss the heart and lungs, you can still hit its spinal column or its jugular vein or liver. So, you have a greater margin for error. All right, now, you all set?" Jason's dad asked, looking straight at him.

Jason cleared his throat and nodded. "Yeah, I'm set."

Jason felt nauseated. He shivered.

His dad began smacking and rubbing the antlers together, producing sharp, crisp sounds that echoed throughout the nearby forest. For the next thirty to forty seconds, he stomped the ground and dragged the antlers through a pile of leaves as well.

Jason expectantly gazed out into the forest by the far edge of the clearing but saw nothing.

His father waited for a minute, then signaled Jason that he would repeat the rattling. As soon as he had begun to clash the antlers together once again, they heard it—the sound of the dominant buck trampling through the woods irate that two lesser bucks had dared to venture onto its sacred territory. Jason could hear the sound of vegetation being thrashed around and trampled underfoot by the furious buck as it closed in on the clearing. For good measure, his father dragged the antlers through his pile of leaves once again.

Jason found his heart racing faster and harder than he had even realized was possible. Without further warning, the strapping buck crashed through the last set of brush and charged into the clearing, brimming over with testosterone. The buck stood directly in the line of fire before Jason, not more than eighty yards away. Jason aimed the rifle right between the buck's front shoulders, his rifle finger trembling. However, inexplicably, he found he could not fire.

What's wrong with me?, he thought. *Isn't this what I've been waiting for?*

He recalled his dream, and all at once, it made sense to him. Looking out into the clearing, Jason realized why he could not resolve to pull the trigger. The buck was a magnificent creature—a wonderful, innocent creature that reminded him of Untamed

Heart, the horse he had ridden as a boy. He could not kill such a noble animal. Jason lowered the rifle and clicked on the safety.

Meanwhile, Jason's father was pointing toward the buck with great animation and mouthing the words, "Shoot! Shoot!" but to no avail.

Puzzled, the buck made a tight circle by the edge of the clearing and then bounded back into the woods. Soon, it could no longer be seen amidst the dense forest cover.

Jason's dad ran over to him, leaving his pack behind.

"Why in the world didn't you shoot?" he demanded to know. "Did the rifle jam?"

"No," Jason answered. "I—I realized that I thought it would be wrong to kill the deer."

"What do you mean, son?" his father asked in astonishment.

"I mean I didn't feel that I should be taking its life away for sport. It just looked so noble, almost like a horse."

"I can't believe . . . " his father abruptly paused, visibly wrestling with his thoughts. At last, he said in a soft voice, "That's all right, son. That's all right."

"I'm sorry, Dad," Jason responded, shaking his head and looking down at the ground in embarrassment.

"There's nothing to be ashamed of. You followed your conscience—and did what you believed was the moral thing to do. That's what I've been trying to teach you to follow your whole life, so I can hardly fault you for it. I'm still learning myself to practice what I preach."

Jason looked up at his father with relief.

"Come on, son. There's a great college football game on this afternoon that I wouldn't want you to miss: Notre Dame versus Michigan," his dad stated, relieving Jason of the rifle. His father slung the rifle over his shoulder and headed for the fir tree where his dad had left the pack. "So long as we don't kill anything on the way, I think we can make it home for the one o'clock kickoff."

Jason smiled. "That sounds good, Dad, real good. Let's go."

They trudged through the woods back home together, holding entirely different beliefs about the morality of deer hunting, but each respecting the other's opinion and admiring the other's actions.

CHAPTER 23

Having soundly vanquished Matt Stiller and established himself as Greenville's course record-holder, Jason now focused on dominating his conference. As the season progressed, he established himself as one of the top junior high runners in all of Maine.

It was thus not surprising that, on a cold, windy afternoon in early November, spectators from Guilford and Greenville lined Guilford's home cross-country course to see whether Maine's defending junior high champion would stave off the upset from Greenville's hometown hero. As it turned out, it all came down to one furious finish.

Two figures emerged from the final bend, their arms pumping and legs kicking in a sprint that increased in speed and intensity as they each neared the finish. Jason took command of the race, spurting ahead at maximum speed down the final stretch. He held nothing back physically, mentally, or emotionally. All of his energy, focus, and emotions poured into an excruciatingly painful dash to the finish. Jason looked straight ahead, the victory tape stretching across the finish line only ten yards before him. He would win the race within the next two seconds.

Out of Jason's peripheral vision, a blurred form streaked across the line. Jason crossed the line a split-second behind Craig

O'Brien, the defending state champion. Jason gawked at Craig, who stood with his arms at his hips, his chest heaving from the exertion. Jason's stare was a blank one; he was incredulous.

The Greenville spectators sighed in disappointment as the coach announced through his megaphone that Craig O'Brien had won the race. As the race stupor dissipated from Jason's head, his first thought was to feel sorry for himself. He had given this race his all but had not prevailed. He was utterly spent. Then he thought of his teammates still on the course, pushing themselves just as hard as he had in his race.

Jason ran as quickly as he could manage to a spot adjacent to the course about fifty yards in front of the finish line. He shouted in a hoarse voice for Phil, his running mentee, as Phil rounded the final turn.

"Come on, Phil, you can do it! You're on the homestretch!" he shouted as Phil fought exhaustion to finish the race strong. Jason ran to the finish line behind Phil, cheering for him all the way.

Jason felt like a big brother as he handed Phil a cup of water and a towel to wipe the sweat off his face.

"Great effort out there! You took third place, which really helps the team," Jason said.

"How'd you do, Jason? Did you take Craig down the stretch?" Phil asked, still breathing hard.

"I had him going into the finish line. He nipped me by about a foot," Jason said. "Hey, this is a team effort. We still have a good shot at winning this race. Let's cheer for the rest of the guys coming into the home stretch."

Since running was a sport in which individual determination and grit played so important a role, receiving encouragement from teammates and spectators down the final leg often gave runners the huge emotional lift needed to finish the race without letting up. Jason and Phil excitedly cheered their teammates to the finish.

Guilford's number two runner finished fourth, its number three and four runners fifth and eighth, respectively. Stiller, not the same runner since his pre-season defeat, took sixth place, while another teammate took seventh. Each team would receive the number of points that corresponded to the place of each of its top five finishers. The team whose first five runners scored the least number of points would win the meet. Right now, the two teams were in a dead heat, eighteen to eighteen. Four runners had scored for each team. The next runner to finish would determine who won the meet.

"It's tied with one man to go!" the coach cried out. "Come on, Tyler, the race is on the line!"

Tyler trailed Guilford's number five man with thirty yards to go. Both looked totally spent, their arms flailing, their legs kicking up mud.

Jason cried out, "This is the race, Tyler! You've got to pass him for us to win!"

Realizing the race was on the line, Tyler expended 110 percent of what he had left, bolting for the finish line with terrible form but a lion's heart. He took the lead with five yards to go and dove across the finish line in victory. Teammates rushed to congratulate Tyler and, perhaps more importantly, prevent him from flying headlong into the muddy grass. The swarm became a jubilant one, as teammates slapped him on the back.

"You won the race for us!" Jason announced, beaming with pride.

"Thanks, guys," Tyler said, not used to getting much attention for his running exploits.

"I'm taking all of you guys out for pizza," Coach Sullivan announced. "Great race, Tyler! No guts, no glory, eh, boys?"

Jason was elated for his team but also felt lingering disappointment over his first loss of the season. He gathered himself together for what he knew would be the right thing to do.

He walked over to the Guilford team, a team filled with long faces of disappointment. The squad was not eager to see Jason.

"Hey, Craig," Jason said, walking over to Craig. "Great race out there today."

Craig turned from his teammates to talk to Jason. "Thanks, man. Good race yourself. You had a mean kick at the end," he offered.

"Not quite mean enough, but I lost to a worthy opponent," Jason said with sincerity.

"Appreciate that. Good luck at states, Jason."

"You, too."

That evening, the team had a spirited time at the local pizza parlor, accepting the cook's challenge to eat three monster-size pizzas. It was tough, but with the help of Rudy, a 180-pound kid who somehow was able to lumber through cross-country races, the team managed to rise to the occasion. As their reward for finishing the three pizzas, they received one free to take home.

"Everyone take a slice home to commemorate our achievements—both on the field and in the pizza parlor," Jason instructed.

“All right!” the guys shouted out, high-fiving each other.

“Hey, guys. We have state this weekend. Let’s not hold anything back. We showed we could beat one of the top teams in the state today,” Jason said forcefully. “Now we’re the team to beat!”

»«»«»«

Inspired by the tenacity of their tight team victory against Guilford, Greenville took the momentum into that weekend’s state championship meet. With tremendous willpower and dedication to maximizing each runner’s ability for the good of the team, Greenville achieved unprecedented success, returning home with two trophies: a first-place school trophy for the first time in the history of the school’s cross-country program and a first-place individual trophy for Jason, who avenged his loss to Craig with a come-from-behind victory.

Elated at having witnessed the success of Jason and the entire team, Jason’s father and Sasquot attended the post-race ceremonies where the trophies were presented.

The master of ceremonies called out the name of each of the top twenty-five junior high boy runners to come on stage in order to receive a medal, beginning with number twenty-five. Trophies were reserved for the top three finishers.

“We had a very exciting finish this year, with the race coming down to the final sprint. The runner-up in this year’s state championship and defending state champion from last year is Craig O’Brien,” the emcee announced.

Craig walked onstage to retrieve the trophy, politely thanked the emcee, and walked back into the audience. His teammates clapped respectfully, but the applause was subdued. His expectations of repeating as champion had been thwarted by an opponent he had beaten just five days before.

Jason's heart was pounding. It was time for his moment in the sun.

"The winner of this year's junior high cross-country championship meet for the state of Maine and new state champion is Greenville's Jason Wilson!" the emcee announced.

Jason's teammates cheered wildly, clapping, whistling, and attempting to make Jason revel in his amazing victory as much as possible. Jason scanned the audience, gladly finding his dad and Sasquot in the back of the auditorium, applauding his championship run. Amid the welcome clamor, he could hear his father call out, "That's my boy!"

His teammates chanted, "Speech! Speech! Speech!"

Grinning ear to ear, Jason took the podium and obliged his teammates.

"First thing I'd like to say is congratulations to all of my teammates for making us Maine cross-country champions for the first time in our school's history! It's an amazing feat to stand up here with a first-place team trophy and a first-place individual trophy. Next, I'd like to thank Coach Sullivan for inspiring us to push ourselves to the best of our ability and for training us well over the course of the season. We had some ups and some downs—mostly ups—and we ended up on top today because of a huge effort from everyone on our team. Most importantly, I'd like to thank my dad for always supporting me and encouraging me on the race course and my friend and mentor, Sasquot, who taught me not only the mechanics of racing but how to believe in myself no matter what or who I face. Thanks, guys."

Jason was hoisted into the air by his jubilant teammates as he left the podium, trophy in hand. His father and Sasquot joined the swirling throng. It was incredible—one of the moments that would be indelibly etched in Jason's memory for the rest of his life.

CHAPTER 24

As the days shortened and the average temperature dropped to below freezing, Jason observed a marked change in Coda's behavior. Coda's once-insatiable appetite waned, and he appeared increasingly lethargic and less interested in the world around him. Coda now weighed well over fifty pounds and noticeably bulged with fat as he lumbered about lazily in his supervised romps into the surrounding forest.

He had witnessed Coda gorge himself upon hard mast as an apparently preferred fall diet. He followed the cub through glorious autumn woods as he eagerly returned time and again to familiar clusters of oak, beech, and chestnut trees to feast upon fat-rich acorns, beechnuts, and chestnuts. As a supplement to these hard mast foods, Jason noted the cub eating fall-ripening.

"Raspberries, mountain ash berries, and apples are sweeter and tastier than nuts, Little Hawk," Sasquot had stated. "But their energy will not last long enough for Coda's winter sleep. He must feast upon all kinds of nuts whose reserves will last through the entire four or five months of his hibernation."

"Wow, I never realized how much energy is packed into little acorns. No wonder squirrels go crazy storing them before each winter," Jason had responded.

As Jason observed Coda lap up water by the shore of Moosehead Lake, he marveled at Coda's growth and maturation. Sasquot had told Jason that at birth, Coda would have been deaf, blind, and almost completely bald, a tiny bundle of life nine inches long that weighed only eight ounces. He had explained how, born during his mother's hibernation late last January, Coda would have nursed upon his mother's milk throughout her winter sleep.

"To reduce his odor, his mother would have cleaned his fur so adults bears and wolves would not detect him, curled up with his mother until spring," Sasquot had told Jason. "Coda emerged from their den around April probably weighing just four pounds but ready in body and spirit to play, explore, and learn everything possible."

"It's amazing how much he has learned just over the past few months," Jason had said.

"His life depended upon it," Sasquot had stated. "His play is key for him to learn how to explore and interact with nature. Just as with humans, he has learned some things through trial and error."

"Yeah, I do not think he will make the mistake of trying to share a meal with a hungry boar again any time soon."

"I hope you are right, Little Hawk. Our ever-curious pupil has also grown well. He weighs over forty pounds and is healthy, I think, in mind, body, and spirit."

Coda had finished quenching his thirst and lumbered back toward Jason and the shed. Jason could not believe how much water the cub had consumed over the past few days. It was a sign, Sasquot had told him, the cub was preparing for a prolonged sleep in which it would not be able to eat or drink.

"Where will Coda sleep during the winter?" Jason had asked Sasquot just a few days earlier.

"Coda will sleep in a bear nest in the shed," Sasquot had replied.

"What in the world is a bear nest?"

"A bear nest is a pile of leaves, needles, and grass from the forest that Coda will sleep on inside the shed. The nest also will keep Coda dry and warm if any water from ice or snowfall enters the shed during the winter, Little Hawk."

Having learned this, Jason had gathered fall leaves, pine needles, and the softest vegetation he could find in mid-November and built a hollowed-out bear's nest resting one foot above the shed floor. To induce Coda to become familiar with it, Jason had laid some acorns and Coda's much-favored chestnuts within the hollow. Coda seemed to enjoy lying within it, and Jason hoped Coda would choose it as his winter denning site.

Jason's greatest fear was that Coda would repeat his feat of sneaking out of the shed and then disappear into the woods to find an outdoor denning site, never to return. To guard against this, Sasquot had placed an exterior lock on the shed every evening. Absent some furious digging or a daring jump through the shed window, Jason's fear would not be realized.

In doing this, though, Sasquot had reminded Jason of their agreed plan to release Coda into the wild in the spring. "We need to make sure Coda will survive the winter. If Coda has any trouble, we can feed him during the winter or give him some water to drink; but once it is spring, our duty is to set Coda free."

"Can't we keep him just one more year?" Jason had pleaded.

"Jason, I know you have grown attached to Coda. But he is a wild animal who belongs in the wild. If we keep Coda until he becomes an adult bear, Coda will fail to develop the skills he needs to survive."

"But if we keep him for good, Sasquot, we won't have to worry about him surviving in the wild at all."

"Little Hawk, a grown bear is a great animal that needs to roam free. A black bear is a solitary animal that enjoys traveling through the forest. As an adult, Coda will not be happy living in a shed."

He had become as attached to Coda as he was to Max, and he had grown up with his Newfoundland. Coda possessed a mischievous curiosity which opened up a fascinating world of discovery and exploration. More than that, he had a sweetness about him, a concern for the welfare of his masters. Coda had risked certain death by fighting to protect Autumn from a timber rattlesnake, and Coda had periodically brought back dead animals from the woods for his companions to eat. He apparently did not yet realize that his human friends lacked his taste for woodchucks, pine marten, and squirrels.

Coda bounded ahead of Jason in the direction of Sasquot's cabin, breaking Jason out of his thoughts. Jason good-naturedly pursued him. Coda seemingly loved playing this game of chase whereby he streaked ahead and waited for Jason to approach before bounding ahead once again.

When they arrived back at the shed, they ran into Autumn, who was taping up the window to the shed to prevent it from shattering during a winter hailstorm or blizzard.

"Hey, Autumn!" Jason called out. "Coda livened up playing chase on the way back today, but he's been slow and sleepy lately."

Autumn stopped taping the window and walked out to greet them. "Hi, Jason! How's my Coda doing?" she asked the cub, rubbing his handsome fall coat. Coda's summer coat had molted during the fall to be completely replaced by a black, oily coat with longer hairs and a healthy sheen.

Coda licked her hand and affectionately rubbed up against her.

"Sometimes, he's almost as tame as Mitch and Max," Jason observed. As agreed with Sasquot from the outset, Jason had made sure not to allow Coda to interact with his dogs. This stemmed both from concern that this might precipitate a violent confrontation between them and from the converse fear that Coda might relax his guard around the dogs and later in life endanger himself through a misplaced sense of trust in them.

"He's a sweetie," Autumn said, reflecting on how much she would miss Coda during the winter and, most especially, after his release into the wild. "You're right about his slowing down. He hasn't wandered more than a mile from the shed in over a week. I think he's going to fall into his winter sleep pretty soon."

"Do you think he'll make it through the winter?" Jason asked.

"Oh, sure. He looks so healthy, and we can check on him to make sure he's okay over the winter—you know, check that his nest holds up and that this window doesn't break," Autumn reassured. "Last winter, that blizzard blew this window right out, but this tape should do the trick."

"Yeah, you're probably right. I just hope he doesn't somehow sneak out of the shed and that another bear or a pack of wolves doesn't break in during the winter."

"We could put some fencing around the nest after he goes to sleep," Autumn suggested.

"No, that wouldn't stop a full-grown boar from getting to him," Jason said, trying to think of an alternative. "I know—I can have

Paul help install an alarm on the shed. We can punch in the code to disable it when we check up on Coda. If anything or anyone else breaks in, it'll trigger an alarm in your house."

"That's a great idea, Jason," Autumn commended.

»«»«»«

That weekend, Jason, Paul, and Autumn installed an alarm on the shed. In the process, Paul had the opportunity to meet Coda up close and personal. He had thought more highly of Coda and his capabilities ever since the Stiller incident. Upon actually meeting Coda, Paul became absolutely enthralled with the cub, requesting to feed him, walk him, examine his paws and teeth, and even touch his fur. Jason obliged, amused by Paul's fascination with Coda. Paul was impressed with everything about the friendly but intimidating cub, from his large canine teeth to his sharp, curved claws. Clearly, Paul would no longer question the cub's toughness.

Distracted from the task at hand, the three of them consumed three-and-a-half hours installing the alarm. Upon completing the set-up, Jason felt more at ease that Coda would be safe for the winter—so long as he stayed within the confines of the shed.

It turned out that their preparation for Coda's hibernation was well-timed. The following Thursday when Autumn entered the shed to check up on Coda, he was not immediately visible. He was contentedly curled up in a winter stupor within the bear nest that Jason had constructed, protected in an alarmed shed from would-be-predators.

CHAPTER 25

It was the fourth Thursday in November, Thanksgiving Day. Jason's dad and Sasquot had quartered all of the Katahdin sheep within the warmth and shelter of the barn the previous weekend. These hardy sheep had subsisted upon crop residues, including cornstalk and milo stubble, into early November, before turning to turnips and rape, crops which could survive even severe frosts. Housed within the barn for the duration of the infamous Maine winter, the Katahdin rams would enter a period of listless doldrums, doing little else but feeding upon a variety of grains, including winter wheat, rye, barley, and oats. The ewes, on the other hand, would earn their keep throughout the winter. Jason's father would continue to milk the Katahdin ewes during their quartering, taking full advantage of their renowned ability to produce five liters of milk per day.

Jason's dad and Sasquot had likewise led the farm's lone bull and three cows to winter quarters within the barn. For the duration of the winter, they would survive upon a mixture of corn products, including hominy meal, corn silage, corn meal, shelled corn and corn distillers, alfalfa haylage, and soy hulls. The cows, like their ewe counterparts, would continue to produce fresh milk for the Wilson and Adjessategwe families throughout the winter.

Following family tradition, Jason's father would sell most of the excess cow and sheep milk to Greenville Consolidated School and churn the rest into butter.

Jason rose early that morning, eager to spend the day with his father, Sasquot, Autumn, and Zephyr. Celebrating special occasions with Sasquot's family was always pleasant and entertaining. Sasquot's affable manner and fatherly concern for Jason's well-being put him at ease and made him feel welcome and secure.

As Jason dressed and got ready for breakfast, he realized just how much he looked forward to spending this day of thanksgiving and family celebration with Sasquot. For Jason felt as though he had earned some of Sasquot's respect over the course of the past few months—respect which Jason coveted more than trophies and accolades. He sensed that he had matured inwardly ever since that fateful August encounter with a roused mother bear and that this was more significant than his summiting Mount Katahdin or even winning Maine's junior high cross-country championship.

Since that defining moment, Jason had learned that hunting exploits meant less than exploits of the human spirit. He had become more passionate about defending the dignity of a human being than he would ever be about hunting an elusive trophy buck. He had resisted strong peer pressure and temptations in refusing to sacrifice principle for popularity and social acceptance, risking even his physical safety to denounce Stiller's ugly bigotry toward Native Americans. He had passed up the opportunity to impress his classmates at the dance in order to be a true friend to Autumn and to demonstrate to them the importance of tolerant inclusion. Jason had become more sensitive to Autumn's feelings, learning that consideration and kindness were more manly than chauvinism and blustery bravado.

Alongside Autumn, he had also learned responsibility, caring for Coda in much the same way as a parent cared for a child. He had taught the cub to become more self-sufficient while at the same time steering him clear of danger—to the extent that was humanly possible with such an intensely curious and fun-loving creature. And perhaps most importantly, Jason had been there when his father needed him most. He had shared his father's joys and sorrows over the past few months more closely than ever before, and he had established a friendship with his father that he hoped would deepen as they came to better know and appreciate each other.

For all these reasons, Jason felt that he had taken some major steps to becoming the man Sasquot hoped he would become. Today, he would give thanks for the friendship and kinship of his father and Sasquot's family.

Jason walked into the kitchen, where his dad was busy dipping white bread into beaten eggs.

"Hungry for some French toast, son?" his father asked. "I'm planning to head out to Sasquot's place around one, and we probably won't eat until about four o'clock."

"French toast sounds good, topped with that maple syrup from the Thompsons," Jason answered.

Their neighbors' full-scale maple syrup farm produced maple syrup, maple sugar candies, and maple fudge. The syrup and maple sugar were freshest in the early spring, when the sap ran, and the

Thompsons' wood-fired evaporators heated up sweet sap until only sugar remained. However, the light amber syrup tasted great at any time of year, and the Thompsons generously provided an ample, year-round supply of maple syrup to his father each spring.

"Wouldn't think of making French toast without the Thompsons' maple syrup," Jason's dad responded, placing four pieces of bread in a frying pan. "Looking forward to getting some real snow soon? They say there's a big snowstorm heading this way."

"Yeah, with Coda asleep for the winter in Sasquot's shed, I'm looking forward to some winter weather," Jason answered.

"I had a feeling that's what you would say," his father said with a knowing grin. "So, I guess you won't mind breaking in our new snowmobile this weekend."

"New snowmobile! Are you serious?" Jason asked excitedly.

"It's parked in our garage right now," his dad answered.

"Can I see it?" Jason asked, getting up from the table.

"Sure, but relax and wait 'til after breakfast. It's not going anywhere."

As soon as Jason had scarfed down his two pieces of French toast, he announced, "All right, I'm ready to go."

His dad led him to a brand new Arctic Cat, a sleek, black snowmobile with double-wishbone suspension, liquid twin cylinders, and a ninety-horsepower engine producing 420 cubic centimeters of displacement.

"Wow! This is awesome!" Jason exclaimed, sitting down upon the comfortable, black vinyl seat. Jason quickly noted that the speedometer went to seventy miles per hour. "This thing can really move, Dad. Just check out the speedometer."

"I know how fast it can go, and I know how fast you're allowed to go," his dad answered sternly. "You won't be exceeding twenty-five miles per hour in open terrain and fifteen on trails."

"Okay, okay," Jason responded. "I'm just saying it's cool to know how powerful its engine is."

"It *is* pretty cool," his father said, his tone softening. "And it's a two-seater." His dad proceeded to show him a number of its features, from its hydraulic disc brakes and rpm sensing drive to its state-of-the art adjustable torsion springs and slide-rail rear suspension.

Forty minutes later, the two re-entered the house, discussing when to take their first duo ride on the Arctic Cat.

"I'll take you out this Saturday," Jason's dad said. "We'll have plenty of snow by then if the forecast holds up."

Jason nodded, as happy as a kid in a candy shop.

At a quarter to one, they began heading over in his father's pickup to Sasquot's house. The sky was an ominous gray, the air cold and chilly, without even a breeze. There was a palpable sense of expectancy in the air. According to all of the weather reports streaming in, this was the calm before the storm—and quite a storm was forecast: twelve to eighteen inches of snow and winds gusting up to thirty miles per hour, producing potential five-foot snowdrifts. Jason looked forward to the storm, welcoming the opportunity the snow would provide to try out their new snowmobile.

The weather still holding, Jason and his father arrived at the Adjessategwe's home a couple of minutes before one, bearing rice pudding, a bottle of wine, and a jug of Maine apple cider. Sasquot greeted them heartily at the door and ushered them inside.

"Our friends have arrived," Sasquot announced as they entered into the main room. Autumn and Zephyr each emerged from the kitchen and warmly embraced their two guests of honor.

"We just finished basting the turkey," Autumn said. "It's a big one—a sixteen pounder."

"And we have a few surprise dishes besides turkey," Sasquot announced. "You will enjoy it, Little Hawk."

"Thank you, Sasquot. I'm sure I will. I've never been disappointed with your family's cooking."

"You are a gracious guest and a good liar, my young friend. Please, take a seat by the fire, my friends," Sasquot replied, offering them seats by the stone fireplace, where a lively fire burned.

As soon as they had sat down and made themselves comfortable, Sasquot offered them his family's tea. Jason savored the flavorful mixture of medicinal herbs, plant roots, and tree bark, ingredients that were a family secret which Sasquot had learned to brew together from his father. Sasquot had explained to Jason that various kinds of tea could treat a wide variety of ailments, with tea made from chestnut leaves relieving coughs and nasal congestion, tea from the bark of wild cherry treating diarrhea and lung ailments, tea from balsam fir relieving chest pains, and tea from wintergreen leaves treating rheumatism.

And so, when offered the family tea, Jason eagerly accepted the offer. Drinking the tea always gave Jason a feeling of bodily cleansing and purification.

"Do you know the story of the first Thanksgiving, Little Hawk?" Sasquot asked, as Jason sat by the fireplace enjoying his tea.

"I know that the Pilgrims and Native Americans shared their harvest and celebrated being friends," Jason answered.

"This is true, Little Hawk, but let me tell you more of the story of the first Thanksgiving," Sasquot said, pausing to clear his throat. "The fall before the first Thanksgiving, the Pilgrims landed at Cape Cod on the *Mayflower.* They sent a party ashore to find food and a place where they could build shelter. Some pilgrims saw baskets of corn on the ground and ate them right away, not realizing that the corn was a tribal gift for dead buried underneath. These Pilgrims had walked on the graveyard of Nauset Indians and taken food belonging to them.

"The Nauset Indians were also angry that not many moons before, the English had kidnapped some members of their tribe. The English had tricked Nausets into boarding their ship by pretending to trade beaver furs with them. Once aboard, they were taken against their will back home to England as proof of their successful voyage to America. Even worse, having used them as evidence, the English then sold some Nausets into slavery in Spain.

"Understandably angry and distrustful of the Pilgrims, the Nauset Indians shot arrows at them. The frightened Pilgrims fired guns back at the Nausets. Thanks be to God, no one was injured in this exchange. However, the Pilgrims feared for their lives and fled to the *Mayflower.* A storm blew their ship across the bay to Plymouth Harbor. That winter, the Pilgrims landed at Plymouth. There they built shelters on land that had belonged to the Patuxet tribe up to a few years before that. That entire tribe had been killed by a plague brought by settlers from the Old World."

"That's terrible, Sasquot. How did one disease kill a whole tribe?" Jason questioned.

"A new disease can kill a whole people, young friend. Indians did not have immunity to diseases that people brought to the New World. The bodies of my people did not have the ability to fight new disease brought by the English, French, and Spanish. Smallpox was a new disease to the Patuxet Indians that killed them before their bodies could learn how to fight it. Many tribes are no longer in America today because of disease brought by explorers and colonizers," Sasquot explained somberly. "But let me continue with the story of Thanksgiving, which has a happy ending . . . The shelters built by the Pilgrims did not protect them well from winter. Most of them died during their first winter in New England from cold, sickness, and lack of food. Pilgrims searched for friendly Native Americans but did not find any. Then one day that spring, a Native American walked straight into the Pilgrim village, unafraid. The Pilgrims were frightened. The man greeted the Pilgrims and introduced himself as Samoset, an Abenaki brave from Maine."

"You're an Abenaki, too, right, Sasquot?" Jason asked.

"Yes, Little Hawk. My people are the last tribe of Abenaki Confederacy alive today who live on the land of our forefathers and teach our Abenaki traditions to our children. The culture of my people is sacred to me, Little Hawk."

Jason nodded solemnly, listening intently to every word.

"Let me tell you the rest of the story, eager friend. Samoset learned English from fishermen fishing off of the Maine coast. Samoset stayed that night at Plymouth and became befriended by the Pilgrims. Then Samoset left Plymouth to find a friend who could speak better English. He returned with the last survivor of the Patuxet tribe named Tisquantum—who was also known as Squanto. Years before, an English captain had kidnapped Squanto and sold him as a slave in Spain. Spanish monks had freed him and tried to teach him the ways of Spanish people, but Squanto had instead sailed to England and asked to return to his people. The English took Squanto to Newfoundland to help them understand the language of the native people. Squanto then returned to Plymouth only to find his family and all of his tribe dead from disease."

"That's terrible, Sasquot, all of his people dying like that."

"Yes, very tragic, Little Hawk. But do you think Squanto harbored hate in his heart for people from the Old World?"

"I would have. I mean, Europeans kidnapped him, sold him into slavery, and brought the disease that killed his family and loved ones," Jason reasoned.

"Squanto found the strength to forgive. He did not let anger weigh down his spirit, Little Hawk. Squanto settled with Wampanoag neighbors at Pokanoket and lived with their great chief, Massasoit. Squanto traveled with Samoset to Plymouth and greeted the Pilgrims with good English. He told the Pilgrims that Massasoit, the leader of the Wampanoag, wished to speak with them. The governor of Plymouth and Grand Sachem Massasoit made a peace treaty and alliance to help the other if their peoples came under attack. Squanto taught the Pilgrims how to grow food and survive in the New World. He taught them how to tap maple trees for sap, how to use plants to treat illness, how to plant Indian corn, and how to use fish to fertilize. Without Squanto, the Pilgrims would not have had a good harvest and would not have survived a second winter.

"At harvest time, the grateful Pilgrims invited the Wampanoag to Plymouth in order to share in their harvest. Massasoit arrived at Plymouth with ninety braves and feasted for three days. Wampanoag braves killed five deer as a gift for the Pilgrim governor. The Pilgrims and Wampanoag played games, ran races, marched, beat drums, and taught each other how to fire bows and arrows and muskets. A harvest feast became a great festival, marking the first Thanksgiving in October of that year."

"That's a different time than when we celebrate it," Jason observed.

"Yes, Little Hawk. Thanksgiving was celebrated in October of 1621 by the Pilgrims and the Wampanoag people. The Pilgrims and the Native Americans never celebrated Thanksgiving together again after that."

Jason's father piped in. "Thanksgiving didn't become a holiday until many years later, Jason. The Continental Congress suggested a day of thanksgiving during the Revolutionary War, and George Washington declared a Thanksgiving holiday on the last Thursday in November to celebrate our new Constitution." Jason had learned a lot of American history from his father, who was a great admirer of the resourcefulness and resilience of the American people in the days of the Founding Fathers. "But Thomas Jefferson ended the holiday, calling it a *kingly practice*. Some presidents declared one-time Thanksgiving holidays, son, but Abraham Lincoln was the first president to proclaim Thanksgiving a national holiday, prompted by a series of editorials written by Sarah Josepha Hale.

Thanksgiving was the last Thursday in November until World War Two, when FDR changed it to the fourth Thursday in November."

"Another reason to consider Lincoln our best president ever," Jason stated. "What kinds of food did the Pilgrims and Native Americans eat at that first Thanksgiving?"

"The Pilgrims and the Wampanoag feasted on many foods, Little Hawk: venison, wild turkeys, geese, ducks and swans, Indian corn and squash, wild raspberries and strawberries, chestnuts and walnuts, and animals from the sea—cod, clams, lobsters, and mussels," Sasquot recounted.

"What about traditional Thanksgiving Day food, like cranberry sauce, sweet potatoes, and pumpkin pie?" Jason asked.

"Pilgrims and the Wampanoag ate no ham, sweet potatoes, corn on the cob, cranberry sauce, or pumpkin pie, Little Hawk," Sasquot answered.

"But we have all of that today," Autumn chimed in. "Mother and I have homemade cranberry sauce and pumpkin pie made fresh from the garden pumpkins we picked last month."

"Sounds delicious. I can't wait to eat," Jason said.

"We must wait a couple more hours, Jason. Dinner will not be ready until about four o'clock," Zephyr stated.

"That's okay, Mrs. Adjessategwe," Jason replied, turning toward Sasquot's classic black-and-white television, which had weathered fifteen years and four presidential administrations. "But can we watch some of the Cowboys game in the meantime?"

"Sure, Little Hawk," Sasquot answered, turning on the television to the traditional Thanksgiving Day football game featuring America's team, the Dallas Cowboys.

The attention of each man in the room was now riveted upon a flickering, fifteen-inch screen. The ascending roar of an expectant Texas Stadium crowd seemed to pour in from all around them. There were under two minutes remaining in the first half with the scored tied seven to seven, and the Cowboys were trying to mount a touchdown drive to close out the first half.

"On third down and five, Danny White hands off to Dorsett. Dorsett charges up the middle, breaks one tackle, and another tackle. He's out in the open! The Lions' defensive back closes in. Dorsett stiff-arms him . . . and is finally taken down from behind at the Lions' twenty-yard line!" the announcer called out excitedly. Dallas' star running back, Tony Dorsett, had just rushed through the heart of the Lions' defense, breaking three tackles and gaining twenty-four yards.

"He's my favorite player and the best player I've ever seen," Jason said of the Dallas superstar.

"Dorsett is a very good player, Little Hawk, but he cannot compare with the greatest football legend."

"Who do you mean?" Jason asked without a clue about whom Sasquot spoke.

"The best football player of the century was Jim Thorpe," Sasquot stated, reminiscing about his childhood days. "During the Great Depression, I was born. When I was a child, one day, I noticed my father looking troubled. So, I asked him why he was so troubled. He told me that the hero whom he most admired was now digging ditches to make money. I asked him who this hero was. My father told me that the hero was Wa-Tho-Huk, a Native American name that means 'Bright Path.' He was from the Sac and Fox tribes but had some French and Irish blood, too. To most people, he was known as Jim Thorpe."

"Why did Grandpa admire him so much?" Autumn asked.

"Young Dove, Grandpa admired Wa-Tho-Huk because he made native people proud for many reasons. At the 1912 Olympic games, he won the pentathlon and decathlon, setting a world record in the decathlon. The king of Sweden was very impressed and gave Wa-Tho-Huk a bust of the king and proclaimed him the greatest athlete in the world. Wa-Tho-Huk played football and baseball as a professional and as an amateur and won three world football championships. He played football for a college that trained and educated Native Americans. He scored more than fifty touchdowns and kicked many field goals for a coach who became a legend named 'Pop' Warner."

"You mean like Pop Warner Football?" Jason asked, impressed.

"Like Pop Warner Football, young friend. Wa-Tho-Huk also played basketball, lacrosse, hockey, and tennis; competed in archery; boxed; and swam. The press named him the best football player and best athlete of the first half of this century. He had great stamina and a strong mind and body. Let me tell you one example. In one football game, Wa-Tho-Huk once rushed ninety-two yards for a touchdown. The play was called back on a penalty. The next play, he rushed ninety-seven yards for a touchdown."

"Wow!" Jason exclaimed, shaking his head in disbelief.

"But Wa-Tho-Huk was more than just an athlete, my friends. Wa-Tho-Huk cared about his people. He spoke to students about Native Americans and helped them to get roles in films. And very importantly, he helped the government to give money to tribes without first giving money to the Bureau of Indian Affairs. This helped more money to go directly to tribes. He was the hero of my father."

"Sounds like he was a really good person and an amazing athlete," Jason said.

"He was a good person who deserved good treatment," Sasquot replied. "But an official stripped Wa-Tho-Huk of two gold medals because he had played baseball semi-professionally before the Olympics. The official did not have the right to take away his Olympic medals. The Olympic Committee did not return these gold medals until three year ago, many years after Wa-Tho-Huk died."

"Why did it take so long?" Jason asked innocently.

"Little Hawk, there has been a lot of prejudice against Native Americans. In the Olympics, Wa-Tho-Huk beat a person named Avery Brundage in the pentathlon and the decathlon. Brundage hated Native Americans, black people, and Jewish people. He did not allow Jesse Owens to ever run again after the Olympics. He prevented Jewish runners from competing in the 1936 Berlin Olympics, and he did not allow medals to be returned to Wa-Tho-Huk before he died."

"I hate Avery Brundage!" Autumn interjected in anger.

"That is exactly what a person like Brundage wants, my daughter," Sasquot said. "We need to rise above hate and dignify our people by not hating our enemies. We must remember unjust acts against our people and teach them as part of history—both the good and the bad that happened to our people. But in our hearts, we must learn to forgive the people who have wronged us. This will give us peace in our hearts and make us deserving of God's forgiveness."

"Yes, Father," Autumn said, mulling over his words.

They all now turned back to watching the game. The half-time report showed a replay of Dorsett scoring on a run from fourteen yards out just before the end of the second quarter. This would really have impressed Jason a few minutes before. In light of Sasquot's recent discussion of Jim Thorpe's career, though, it understandably had less of an effect.

Nearly two hours later, while the men were still absorbed with Thanksgiving Day football and Autumn was accordingly just about to go stir-crazy, Zephyr announced that dinner was ready to be served. Jason sat down to the savoriest Thanksgiving meal he had ever had. Besides the traditional turkey, Zephyr served stuffing, cranberry sauce, and cornbread—all homemade and delicious—along with zucchini, squash, and eggplant picked fresh from their garden earlier that fall.

Jason and Autumn drank apple cider, while each of the adults partook of his father's bottle of full-bodied, red Merlot. For dessert, Zephyr and Autumn brought out an enticing selection of fresh pumpkin pie, rice pudding that Jason's father had made, and hot apple pie with a thin, tasty crust spiced with cinnamon throughout. Jason could not help but sample each of these delectable desserts. By the end of the evening, he had gained a good two pounds which he would have to burn off to return to his optimal race weight for the start of the spring track season.

The dinner conversation was lively and fast-moving, with Sasquot and Jason's father each recounting stories about growing up in the North Woods of Maine. Listening to these stories evoked in Jason a soothing sense of belonging and rootedness to the area, a feeling that he was a living part of his family's history. These entertaining stories, full of humorous anecdotes, gradually gave way to parental affirmations of pride in Jason's and Autumn's personal growth and development over the course of the past year and, in particular, over the past few months.

"We have grown still closer," Sasquot said with sincerity and affection at the end of the evening. "Like one family, we have shared the joys and sorrows of life together."

It was as if Sasquot spoke for all of them. Each felt a warm kinship to one another.

"If only this moment in time could be frozen forever," Jason mused.

CHAPTER 26

Jason purred along on the Arctic Cat, navigating through the main forest trail east of Moosehead Lake. The fierce winter storm that had been predicted for Friday had slowed and intensified south of Quebec. Though this ultimately was expected to bring yet more snow and stronger winds to north-central Maine once the storm arrived later that Saturday, only a light snowfall was predicted for the next few hours. Taking advantage of the first few inches of snow on the ground, Jason's father had taken him on a training run earlier that morning in order to teach him the basic skills necessary to operate the snowmobile. He had caught on quickly, enough so that his father had agreed to allow Jason to make a brief solo excursion into the woods while he helped the Thompsons repair their sugarhouse in advance of the storm.

Traveling through the woods on this amazing machine, Jason felt as though he were sailing on top of the snow with the wind whisking by as waves of snow particles sprayed up against the vehicle. Snow-laden pines and firs provided a scenic backdrop for the excursion. True to its reputation for easy handling, the Arctic Cat allowed Jason to turn and shift gears without experiencing any jerkiness whatsoever.

As Jason crested a gradual slope, he spotted a narrower trail to his right. The trail climbed into the foothills where he and his father had tracked the trophy buck a little more than a month ago. Before turning over the snowmobile to Jason for his first solo, his father had admonished him not to stray off the main trail for safety reasons. Jason was confident he could handle the snowmobile and was curious to see how well the snowmobile could ascend the hills. Besides, he might just get lucky enough to catch a glimpse of that magnificent buck.

Jason steered the snowmobile onto the new trail. The vehicle turned and accelerated smoothly. Jason deftly navigated the snowmobile through the forest, hugging the trail as it approached the highlands. He eyed the speedometer: fifteen miles per hour.

He gave the snowmobile more gas. It sped ahead at a brisk eighteen, then twenty-one miles per hour. Jason felt exhilarated as the Arctic Cat hummed along effortlessly, skirting the forest brush not more than two feet away on either side of the vehicle.

A sharp bend appeared up ahead. Jason steered the vehicle to the left while maintaining full speed.

"Oh no!" he suddenly cried out. A fallen tree blocked his path just ahead. There was no time to brake before he would crash into the tree.

Jason instinctively swerved the vehicle off the path and into the woods. The vehicle collided into forest saplings, bending and snapping them as it careened out of control into the forest. The snowmobile lurched back and forth as Jason struggled to bring the vehicle back under control. Before Jason even saw what was coming, the snowmobile smashed into a snow-covered block of granite and violently spun in a 360-degree turn. The impact flung Jason headlong into the trunk of a tree, knocking him out cold.

CHAPTER 27

Late that morning, Kyle returned home from the Thompsons, having spent the better part of the morning helping repair the siding on their rustic sugarhouse. Brushing the snow off his coat, Kyle entered the main house and called out that he was home. No answer. Kyle checked the answering machine. No messages. Surprised and increasingly concerned, Kyle peered into the garage to see if the snowmobile was parked there. No sign of the snowmobile.

Kyle looked out into the winter storm that was brewing. The snow was falling at about half-an-inch per hour, and the temperature had dropped noticeably from what it had been earlier that morning. The wind had picked up to between five and ten miles per hour, lowering both the wind-chill-factored temperature and visibility.

Kyle's mind raced through thoughts of what could be keeping Jason out there so long: *He might have gotten carried away and gone out farther than expected; he might have stopped by to see Sasquot—* Kyle's thoughts came to a momentarily panicked halt. *Jason had only two hours' worth of gas in the snowmobile. If he had driven it continually, it would have run out of fuel by now. And Jason always leaves a message on the answering machine when he visits Sasquot.*

Kyle immediately picked up the phone and dialed Sasquot's number. "Hello, Zephyr. It's Kyle. Jason isn't over there, is he?"

"No, Mr. Wilson. We have not seen him since our Thanksgiving feast," Zephyr answered, confirming Kyle's fears.

"And I haven't seen him for hours. Is Sasquot there?"

"Yes, Mr. Wilson, but he's out back right now, chopping wood for our fire."

"Can you let him know it's real important? Jason went out on our snowmobile hours ago and has not returned."

"Oh my! Yes, one minute . . . I will get my husband right away."

Within thirty seconds, Sasquot was on the phone. "Kyle, is Jason missing?" Sasquot asked with great concern.

"I am afraid so. He went out in our snowmobile almost three hours ago and has not come back. It had only two hours' worth of gas, and he doesn't know how to drive it very well. I'm afraid he might have crashed or run out of fuel or gotten lost. God knows what happened to him out there, but the storm is only getting worse."

"Yes, this *is* a serious situation," Sasquot said, thinking aloud. "We must find him fast. We need to take the dogs out to search for him."

"Yes, Sasquot, we have to find him right away. Can you meet me here as soon as possible to help search for him?"

"Of course. I'll be there right away."

"Thanks. Meanwhile, I'll begin searching along the main trail for him."

"The storm has become fierce, Kyle. We will need to bring rescue gear."

"I'll bring emergency rescue gear and medical supplies. You should bring snowshoes. I'll wear cross-country skis. We need speed out there, Sasquot. Time is precious," Kyle warned.

"I'll find you on the main trail soon."

"Thanks, Sasquot."

Kyle threw on a winter parka that was thermally insulated to thirty below zero, a ski mask, thermally insulated gloves, and down snow-pants. Sitting on the front step of the main house, he hurriedly buckled up his ski boots and slipped on his cross-country skis. Kyle slung the collapsible frame-pack that he had used for the deer hunt over his back after quickly stuffing it with standard search and rescue materials, including a compass, switchblade, flashlight, matches, snowshoes, a flannel shirt, canteen, flares, thermally insulated blanket, and a first aid kit. Minutes before, he had filled up a thermos with steaming hot coffee and placed granola bars in the pack as well.

Kyle wanted to be prepared for the worst. His darkest nightmare would be to find Jason injured and freezing to death and not have on hand the supplies needed to assist him.

He now whistled for the dogs. Max and Mitch eagerly bounded up the basement stairs and trotted through the living room and onto the front porch. Kyle closed the door and dexterously hopped off the porch in his skis. He dug his ski poles into the snow and slid forward.

Kyle glided over the snow quickly and with exceptional prowess. His head throbbed with anxiety, and beads of sweat dampened his ski mask. Adrenaline surged through his body, spurring him onward at a furious pace.

Jason is my only son—my only child kept echoing in the recesses of Kyle's mind. Kyle could not bear the thought of living without him.

A wave of guilt suddenly swept through Kyle, making him sick to his stomach. *How could I have let Jason drive the snowmobile himself in a snowstorm? What kind of father would let his son do that?*

Frightened by the loss of his son, Kyle looked out into the bitter storm searching for answers. For the first time, he questioned whether he would return with his son.

As rugged as any of the Wilson pioneers before him, Kyle had never allowed himself to entertain such fear. He did not know how to react or whether he could even control the cascade of emotions that was flowing through and overwhelming him. Kyle found himself clasping his hands together, begging God for Jason's life.

"Kyle!" a voice cried out.

Kyle turned toward the voice.

"Kyle, are you okay?" Sasquot called out, trudging toward Kyle on snowshoes.

Kyle just nodded.

"Kyle, you look sick. Here, drink this." Sasquot took out a thermos.

Kyle unsteadily grasped the thermos and drank. Like a miracle remedy, the tea flowed through Kyle's body, reviving his whole system and calming his troubled mind.

"We'll find Jason. Don't worry," Sasquot assured him. "We'll follow the tracks of the snowmobile."

The snowmobile tracks were still visible but becoming less discernible by the minute.

"Come on!" Sasquot gestured, leading Kyle and the dogs further into the woods along the trail. "Even if we cannot see the tracks, the dogs will be able to smell Jason's scent," Sasquot said, attempting to instill some hope in his lifelong friend.

With their heads bowed to shield them from the headwind, Kyle and Sasquot followed the snowmobile tracks as far as the naked eye would take them. But standing not more than a mile from the crossing with the buck trail, neither of them could make out even the faintest trace of the path the Arctic Cat had taken that morning.

Kyle and Sasquot instinctively turned toward the dogs—their best hope to pick up Jason's trail. Mitch and Max forged ahead, sniffing along the winter tundra before them. Urging them onward, Kyle and Sasquot followed several yards behind. Not more than a minute later, the dogs seemed to lose all interest in the trail. They abruptly stopped and turned back to return to their agitated master, who quickly caught up with them alongside Sasquot. The dogs shook the snow off their fur and, tongues panting, looked up at Kyle to see what he would do next.

"Go! Go find Jason!" Kyle said, pushing Max from behind. Max stutter-stepped forward a few steps, only to turn back to Kyle, without a clue as to what he was supposed to do.

Then, without warning, Mitch barked and darted off into the woods. Kyle excitedly followed close behind on his skis.

A dense cluster of evergreens lay ahead. As Kyle approached the cluster close on Mitch's heels, he eyed a bird scurrying along the ground beneath the blue-green branches of a white spruce. The bird was foraging for needles and evergreen buds along the forest floor. As Mitch abruptly converged upon the startled spruce grouse, which was notoriously easy to capture, the bird clucked in fear. Mitch was about to pounce upon the poor chicken-like bird when Kyle's commanding voice thundered, "Mitch, get over here! You stupid dog!"

Kyle's voice arrested Mitch in his tracks, and with his head lowered in disappointment from the rebuke, Mitch trotted back toward Kyle and the main trail. "What in the world is the matter with these dogs?" Kyle asked aloud.

"Conditions are too extreme for even the dogs to detect Jason's trail," Sasquot answered, standing close behind. "There is only one hope to find Jason's trail."

"What's that?" Kyle demanded gruffly.

"We need to awaken Coda from his winter slumber. Coda's keen smell can locate Jason miles away."

"Will that work? Will Coda be able to wake up and find Jason?" Kyle asked with unmasked skepticism.

"This is our best hope. A search team of people could take days to find Jason," Sasquot answered truthfully.

It was at that point Kyle realized just how desperate the situation had become: His son's life lies in the hands of a bear cub not even a year old—a cub that he helped save from likely starvation.

Kyle gritted his teeth and nodded.

Moving as quickly as possible in near white-out conditions, Kyle and Sasquot continued along the main trail until they reached the dirt road that led to Sasquot's home and shed.

Sasquot lifted the latch and thrust open the door to the shed, triggering the alarm meant to detect wolves and other predatory intruders who would otherwise feast upon an unsuspecting cub. Utterly ignoring the alarm, Sasquot trudged over in his snowshoes to Coda's nest. Coda lay within the hollowed den, gradually waking from his stupor because of the alarm and the smell of Sasquot close at hand. Sasquot spoke soothing words to Coda in Abenaki and reached into his den. Grasping Coda by his armpits, Sasquot brought Coda out into the open. The dazed cub whimpered and slowly opened his warm brown eyes, progressively awakening from his deep winter sleep. Sasquot continued to speak to the cub and placed the cub upon the floor, stroking his fur to invigorate him. Within a couple of minutes, Coda's eyes were fully opened. The cub yawned and attempted a few awkward steps forward.

"I can't believe this," Kyle muttered in exasperation. "We're relying upon this half-awake cub to locate my son?"

"Kyle, Coda knows Jason's scent. The reason why people almost never encounter bears in the woods is because they smell people miles away. Coda is our best hope to find Jason and may be our only hope."

"Okay, okay, but let's get moving. We can't wait all day for Coda to wake up."

Sasquot rubbed Coda's fur more vigorously and offered the cub some plant roots that lay on the shed floor. Coda began to pep back to life and nibbled at the roots.

"Come on! Let's get out there," Kyle urged.

"Leave the dogs in the shed," Sasquot instructed. "Coda fears the dogs."

"Okay, whatever's best to find Jason."

They locked the reluctant dogs in the shed and soon were back on the dirt road, with Coda trailing behind. Coda, who had never been out in so much snow, found it strange that the snow sank beneath his padded paws. As Coda nosed his way toward a rotting log by the side of the road, he unwittingly stepped into a snow drift and abruptly vanished from view. Moments later, an enthralled cub emerged from the drift and promptly proceeded to dive back into the snow drift.

Kyle was not amused in the least.

"Coda! Come here, Coda!" Sasquot called out. "Come here, now!"

To Kyle's surprise, Coda responded to Sasquot's commands and attempted to negotiate his way toward them as quickly as he could. Watching Coda sink unevenly into the snow as he approached them, Kyle and Sasquot soon realized that Coda would not be able to keep up with men on their skis and snowshoes. Sasquot doubled back and scooped up the eager cub, carrying Coda upon his shoulder as he deftly traversed the snow in snowshoes. Their breath crystallizing before them, Kyle and Sasquot pressed on at a brisk pace toward the main trail.

It was now 2:30 in the afternoon. Nightfall would come within three hours. Darkness and the accompanying plummet in temperature would make continuation of the search nearly impossible and endanger the lives of all involved.

CHAPTER 28

Jason's eyes flickered open and shut as he struggled to regain consciousness. Through tremendous force of will, Jason managed to open his eyes and raise his head. Groggily assessing his surroundings, Jason realized that he was lying beneath a sheltering pine in the midst of a furious snowstorm. Gradually, as if piecing together a dream, Jason recalled the sequence of events that had led to the crash: the carefree snowmobile ride on the main trail, his decision to turn onto the side trail and climb up into the hills, the unexpected obstruction that had forced him into the woods, and the snowmobile's wild careening into a snow-covered rock.

A stabbing pain from a nasty gash on Jason's forehead shot through his system, causing him to clench his teeth to keep from passing out. Jason gingerly placed his right hand upon his forehead and felt the blood that had congealed over the gash. Looking up into the pine tree above him, it was only too easy to deduce its origin. A blotch of frozen blood covered some bark just two feet above the tree's base.

Jason winced as a gust of wind whipped particles of ice across his face. "Man, I sure did pick a bad time to have an accident out here," he said to no one in particular.

His heart racing in fear, Jason attempted to assess the full extent of his injuries. He had sensation in all of his limbs and could move without much pain.

The most important thing at this point is to keep warm. He looked over the clothes he wore: a down ski-jacket and ski pants and a pair of thermally insulated gloves. A blood-stained wool hat lay by his feet. Jason's feet were covered with thick wool socks and ankle-high leather boots. These clothes had been designed for New England winters, but clothes alone were insufficient to withstand the negative wind chill this snowstorm had brought.

He braced his gloves against the frozen pine needles below as he struggled to get to his feet. Blood flowed back into his toes, an uncomfortable but reassuring sensation. So far, he had avoided suffering any frostbite.

Sasquot had instructed Jason years ago to build a fire if he were ever lost or injured in the woods and could not readily hope to make his way back home. Most importantly, Sasquot had taught Jason how to start such a fire without a match or even a pocketknife.

A dull pain throbbing against his skull, Jason proceeded to gather the dead evergreen twigs which lay close to the base of the pine into a pile. These would make good tinder for the fire, but the most flammable substance around lay not more than ten yards away. Braving the pelting of pea-sized hail, Jason slowly made his way to a birch tree and began to peel thin sheaths of bark off the tree. The sky was so dark and ominous that Jason could not tell if the afternoon had already passed into the evening. Fortunately for Jason, it was still afternoon, and the most severe nighttime conditions had not yet set in. Jason peeled away enough birchbark to transform a spark into a lively fire. He also collected some small branches that the fierce wind had torn off a nearby oak.

Now came the hard part, obtaining the means to start the fire. Jason had no matches and had not brought his Swiss army knife along with him. Although Sasquot had taught Jason how to construct a fire-lighting bow and drill, the task was long and laborious and entailed finding the right types and sizes of wood in order to construct a drill, fireboard, and bow. In this weather, Jason could very well freeze to death before completing the task. If only he could find two pieces of flint, quartz, or iron pyrite, he could rub them together and generate a spark from the resulting friction.

Quartz was especially abundant in the environs of Moosehead Lake. Digging through frozen tundra to uncover the rocks would be the difficult task. Jason aggressively dug into the snow using a sharp, thick piece of branch as an improvised shovel and pick. Fifteen minutes and a good sweat later, Jason uncovered two fist-size pieces of quartz.

Jason now arranged the oak branches beneath his pile of evergreen twigs and placed strands of birchbark he had separated from broader sheaths upon the pile. He then placed the few unfrozen pine needles he could find on top of the birchbark to provide additional tinder. This done, Jason vigorously rubbed the pieces of quartz together until, moments later, several sparks appeared. One of the sparks caught a strand of birchbark and set it on fire. Jason sighed in relief. He had put together a real woodsman's fire and bought himself a couple hours of sorely needed warmth—a couple hours of survival.

CHAPTER 29

Sasquot placed Coda down upon the ground as soon as they had re-entered the main trail. Coda's acute sense of smell normally would have been able to detect Jason's presence at this distance, slightly over two miles away. However, with winds of twenty plus miles per hour and alternating snow and ice pouring down from the sky at a furious pace, the poor cub could not detect scents beyond probably a four-hundred-yard radius. Moreover, icy particles whipped across the surface of the deepening snowdrifts into Coda's face, creating virtual white-out conditions for the bear. And given the tempestuous winds, no cries for help or other sounds could be discerned at any meaningful distance.

"Coda cannot find Jason. The weather is too fierce," Sasquot intoned with a terrible air of finality and somberness in his voice.

"Jason!" Kyle screamed at the top of his lungs. "Jason! Jason!"

The muffled shouts barely penetrated into the forest.

Kyle halted in the snow, his wild eyes locking with Sasquot's impenetrably deep eyes for one intense moment before glazing over.

Arms outstretched, Sasquot gazed up into the dark gray sky. He began to plead in the beautiful language of the Abenaki for God to spare Jason's life. He prayed with the same passion with which he had implored the Great Spirit to save his father's life hours before he had passed away. Having concluded his private plea, Sasquot motioned for Kyle to bow his head as Sasquot knelt upon one knee and prayed aloud in English for God to protect Jason's life.

"Dear Father, You are Lord and Creator of the entire earth and have power over all things. You have power over life and death. You alone have the power to save Jason's life. We pray to You to save the life of Jason, a boy who is precious to us. Jason has a good heart but has not yet committed his life to You. Please save him so he may know You, Lord. My eyes have seen many things. My heart and soul are content. This beloved boy has just begun to open his young eyes to the world that You, God, created for us to inhabit in peace and harmony with man and nature. Take my life in place of his, for I am happy. I have lived a full life and shared many joys and shared many sorrows with family, friends, and strangers. I have learned many lessons. You taught me and taught them to others. Have mercy upon Jason, that he, too, may learn Your great lessons and live a fulfilling life, sharing joys of life with others," Sasquot prayed. "God, hear my voice and grant Jason mercy!"

Suddenly, a terrifying blue streak of lightning flashed across the horizon, illuminating the sky for a few brief but precious moments. The illumination revealed gray clouds of smoke arising from the forest to the northeast.

"There!" Sasquot cried out to Kyle, pointing to the billows of smoke.

Kyle immediately sprang into action, digging his ski poles hard into the snow and pushing off in the direction in which Sasquot had pointed. Sasquot followed at once but trailed behind Kyle, who skied at a blistering pace, even through an ascent into the highlands.

As he watched Kyle furiously navigate an uphill bend, working his arms and legs to maximize speed, Sasquot's soul felt a sense of peace—he knew that he was witnessing the unshakable bonds of a father's love for his son.

»«»«»«

Jason felt as if he were waking from a dream the moment his father emerged on skis from the forest sapling and around the granite rock. He experienced a sense of relief and elation far more powerful than he had ever felt before. Leaping to his feet, Jason embraced his overwhelmed dad before he had even come to a halt.

"It's a miracle! It's a miracle!" Jason's father cried out as tears of joy streamed down his face.

Jason was speechless, so struck was he by the moment.

»«»«»«

Sasquot caught up to his jubilant friends minutes later, having traversed the icy trail on his snowshoes while carrying a startled cub in his arms. Sasquot, too, felt like a father who had found his long-lost son. He fell to his knees and thanked the Great Spirit and God of all people for sparing Jason's life. Then, rising to his feet and shaking with emotion, he embraced the son he never had.

To their tremendous relief, Jason had not sustained any serious injuries. The gash on Jason's forehead would require some cleaning and probably some stitching at the local hospital in the morning or as soon as roads were passable. However, other than that, Jason was healthy and free from injury. In fact, Jason was feeling sufficiently well that, after affectionately patting Coda on the head, he insisted on carrying Coda all the way back to Sasquot's cabin, where they all would lodge for the night. All of them except for Coda, that is, who would return to his winter sleep within the warmth and comfort of his bear's nest.

Before they headed home, Kyle wrapped his son in the thermally insulated blanket and gave him lukewarm coffee and a granola bar before allowing Sasquot to hoist Coda upon Jason's back. As evening descended over the Maine forest, the three men and a cub steadily made their way back through the storm to Sasquot's home.

God had wrested Jason away from the clutches of death and breathed new life into him. Soon, He would endow Jason with a new spirit. Of that, Sasquot was sure.

CHAPTER 30

During the course of the many long winter nights that followed, Jason reflected upon the miracle of continued life that had been bestowed upon him. He owed so much to his father and Sasquot, for they had risked their health and safety to rescue him from the tenacious grip of one of Maine's fiercest blizzards in recent memory. And after learning from his father of Sasquot's prayer and the true miracle of his rescue, Jason felt enormously grateful and indebted to the merciful God Who had smiled down upon him amidst this harrowing experience. Why he had been spared from the otherwise-fatal consequences of his youthful indiscretion, Jason did not know, but he did know the unbelievable courage and selflessness that characterized the most important people in his life.

At times, Jason would lay awake at night contemplating the long odds of his surviving that night alone and shudder at the sobering realization that he would likely have perished within hours of his actual rescue. Humbled, he would eventually fall asleep praying silently that his rescue would serve as inspiration for him to sacrifice for causes, principles, and, above all, people he held dear. He felt compelled to do something heroic, something to make himself worthy, if this were possible, of what his father and lifelong friend had done for him.

One such restless night, Jason's father knocked at his door.

Jason greeted him, thanking his dad once again for being there for him when it mattered most.

"You know, son, that's why I came, to let you know that I'm not the one you have to thank. You know, Sasquot told me, not long ago, a powerful story about forgiveness."

Jason's dad proceeded to relate the remarkable story of how Sasquot had received the strength and inspiration to forgive his blood brother for his father's death. "Son, I took Sasquot's words to heart, but I did not act upon them. Neither did I challenge myself to trust in God, that He would care and look after me. But after that amazing act of mercy, where God showed me where my son was, who otherwise would have died alone frozen to death in the wilderness . . . Wow, that was powerful. That brought me to realize that I, the doubting Thomas, had seen the nails in His hand and the wound in His side."

"What do you mean, Dad?" Jason asked, his heart beating hard, his brow suddenly sweaty.

"I mean, son, that I realized at that moment—at that very moment when that bolt of lightning streaked across the sky and I saw billows of smoke rising into the air—that there was a God and that not only was there a God, but that this God so loved my boy that He would answer a prayer from a wise, old man to save him."

Jason was quiet for a moment, and then he said, "When I looked at you just now and heard your words, I felt in my heart that there is a God."

"Will you pray with me, son?" his father asked, holding out his hand. Together, they prayed. His dad led his son through that same life-altering experience.

»«»«»«

One day not long thereafter, Jason approached Sasquot and, with profound gratitude, asked what he could do to thank and repay him both for helping to save his life and for leading him and his father, through Sasquot's words and example, to Christ.

Sasquot answered, "My heart flows with joy for you, Jason—for a young man who is like a son to me. But there is no need to repay me, my son. Instead, what I ask you to do, Jason, is to do good to others—to family, friends, neighbors, and strangers. Repay each good turn with kindness to your fellow man and each bad turn with forgiveness. Teach others the lessons you have struggled hard to learn about life. Teach first by example, my son."

Jason was struck by the selflessness of these words, words that mirrored Sasquot's actions during that fateful blizzard and on numerous other occasions.

By gradually appreciating and digesting on a deeper level these sage words of wisdom and the meaning of the events that had transpired on and since that fated day, Jason grew in stature and maturity that winter.

As the chill of winter loosened its hold upon the soil and the woodland lakes and streams shed their icy coats and bubbled back to life, Jason's thoughts turned toward Coda. Soon, Coda would awaken from his winter slumber and, after gradually shaking off the remnants of his stupor, would be ready to venture forth on his own into the virtually unbounded world that awaited him. Jason harbored a deep affection for the playful cub that had simultaneously enriched and complicated his life over the course of the past year. For all of Coda's mischievous curiosity, Jason wanted nothing else but to have the privilege to continue to be with him while he developed into a king of the Maine forest, an adult black bear. At the same time, Jason was aware that Sasquot desired to set the cub free that spring, as he had reminded Jason on more than one occasion. It was the manner of Coda's release that came as such a shock to Jason.

One clear and mild Saturday morning in mid-April, Sasquot told Jason the time had come for Coda to be released into the wild.

"It would be painful for you to release Coda, Little Hawk. I will perform my duty to release our bear brother into the forest."

"It's my duty, too, Sasquot," Jason immediately retorted. "There's no way I'm not going to be there when Coda is released into the wild."

Sasquot warned, "The release will be a very difficult thing, Jason. I will instruct Autumn to stay home. Coda now needs to learn the most important lesson for his survival."

At Jason's insistence, Sasquot relented and reluctantly agreed to allow Jason to accompany him that memorable morning. Now, for the last time, Sasquot and Jason summoned Coda from the shed and led him onto a forest trail. A mere two weeks ago, Coda had arisen from his winter lair as disheveled in appearance as the make-shift bear's nest from which he had emerged.

They witnessed the gaunt and ravenously hungry cub feast upon virtually every living thing that crossed his path. Coda unceremoniously caught nearly every land-borne creature that dared to move about in his presence, from grasshoppers and earthworms to frogs and salamanders.

Jason found it amazing that previously buried, burrowed, and deep-water frogs and salamanders abounded in these parts of Maine each April. Jason had been astounded when Sasquot had explained last spring that certain species of Maine's frogs, such as wood frogs and spring peepers, actually froze solid during the winter but survived using special bodily processes. His mentor had described the thousands upon thousands of amphibious creatures that emerged from their winter hideaways and, under the cover of darkness, hopped or crawled their way through the woods and over Greenville's mud-washed roads to breeding ponds and streams. Those who now had the misfortune to be discovered in transit by Coda in the soft orange light of dawn were quickly converted into breakfast courses via well-timed paw swipes.

Consuming food at a blistering pace surpassing even that of his fall feeding frenzy, Coda presently regained the bulk of the muscle and fat which his remarkably efficient body had slowly burned for fuel during the past four months of hibernation. Healthy and revitalized in body and spirit, Coda now energetically bounded into the woods ahead of Sasquot and Jason.

As the two followed Coda's trail, they approached a lowland area, where they soon caught up to the mesmerized cub. Sitting on his haunches, Coda peered intently into a thicket of shrubs, reeds, and willows adjacent to a brackish swamp. What had riveted the attention of the young cub were the high-pitched calls of scores of miniature spring peepers, which blended together in a spirited yet soothing chorus which signaled the advent of their breeding season. Hidden among the fresh green leaves of the shrubs overhanging the swamp, these tiniest of Maine's frogs were so difficult to detect that even a hungry and brazen cub refrained from pursuing them.

Directing Jason's attention to a nearby swamp spruce, Sasquot pointed out the unique pendulum nest of the northern parula, a colorful blue, green, and yellow-tinted warbler. Woven from wispy strands of a rich lichen known as old man's beard that draped down from the spruce, the spherical nest hung suspended like a ball-drop earring from one of the tree's highest branches.

Assuming the lead, Sasquot now led them beneath a forest canopy overflowing with the voices of wildlife from on high, voices ranging from the melodious singing of the hermit thrush to the noisy chattering of the red squirrel. In contrast to the colors of Maine's fall, which seemed to burn brightly together in a brilliant conflagration of hues, the colors of Maine's spring were soft and delicate, melting with and into the passing landscape as they receded from view. The patches of pure morning sunlight that filtered through to the forest floor served as subtle spotlights, illuminating clusters of fragrant white honeysuckle, pink lady's slipper, and orange tiger lilies as the party meandered their way through the low-lying forest.

Suddenly breaking out into a flood of sunlight, they followed Sasquot into a meadow dotted with wild daisies and black-eyed Susans that appeared to bask happily in the warming radiance of sunshine that flowed in all directions around them. Abruptly signaling for Jason to stop, Sasquot walked briskly to the opposite end of the forest clearing roughly two hundred feet away. Unsure whether to stay with Jason or follow his older master across the meadow, Coda tentatively stepped out into the middle of the meadow.

Sasquot knelt down in the tall grass by the far end of the clearing. Although Jason could not see what Sasquot was doing, he could discern that Sasquot's attention was focused upon manipulating something upon the ground. Soon, Sasquot rose to his feet, gazing at Coda. Sasquot's gaze was stern and rigid, lacking its usual warmth and compassion. It did not once waver from the curious cub, who wondered what new game his masters were about to play.

Clapping his hands together, Sasquot commanded Coda to come to him. Coda enthusiastically shuffled over toward Sasquot, eager to play a game or embark upon some sort of adventure. Coda was not more than a several yards away from Sasquot when the glint of silver caught Jason's eye. Just as Jason opened his mouth to ask Sasquot what silver object lay before him, he heard a loud squeal of pain and then the plaintive cries of the young cub as he struggled with a metal contraption. Jason could now see that Coda's right paw was caught in a steel trap, one that Sasquot himself had set.

"Coda! Coda!" Jason shouted, distraught, as he ran toward the distressed yearling. But before Jason had even come to the middle of the meadow, Sasquot had pulled out a rifle from the hollow of a tree by the edge of the clearing and taken deliberate aim.

Jason froze, screaming in horror, "No, Sasquot! Noooooo!"

The sound of the shot reverberated through the forest, piercing its tranquility and eerily silencing its startled creatures. Jason closed his shocked eyes in disbelief and anger. Flickering open, they witnessed Sasquot bend down toward the trap and release Coda. Sasquot kicked the rump of the poor cub and shouted menacingly at him. Horribly agitated and frightened, Coda cast one last glance at Jason over his shoulder. Coda's face bore a disturbingly human-like expression of betrayal. Then as if pursued by a deadly predator, Coda scurried into the depths of the forest without looking back.

"What have you done?" an incredulous Jason demanded of Sasquot.

"I have done what had to be done," Sasquot intoned in a deep and somber voice. Then peering directly into Jason's eyes, Sasquot explained, "The cub is not injured, only scared, Little Hawk. I set the trap at its lowest force, and it only caught Coda's paw. I fired a warning shot into the ground near Coda to frighten him."

"But why, Sasquot, why?"

"I had a duty to teach Coda not to trust humans, Little Hawk," Sasquot answered. "Otherwise, Coda would soon die in the wild from a bear hunter or trapper. Man is the last major predator of black bears in Maine. Fear of man needs to be taught for a bear to live a normal life. That is the way of the wild, my son."

Jason stood in place, motionless, his body turned in the direction in which his beloved companion had fled.

"Come, Little Hawk, I will walk with you back to your home," Sasquot gently offered.

Sasquot led Jason through the woods toward Jason's home, further explaining his actions. "It is a sacred duty for me to teach Coda, my bear brother, how to survive on his own. If Coda depends on people for his survival, he will lose his survival skills. Men would trap him, shoot him, or lure him to danger. It is more merciful to release Coda than to keep him, my friend."

"But, Sasquot, if we had just kept Coda, he wouldn't have needed to fear man and learn all of these survival skills," Jason argued.

"Bears were created to roam the forest, not to be pets of man, Jason. God gave black bears senses and instinct so that they can survive in the forest, but a young cub needs to learn many skills for it to grow into an adult bear. Like other creatures of the forest, Coda needs to explore the world on his own to teach himself these skills, Little Hawk. I would be a death sentence to teach a yearling to depend on man for its survival."

Jason said nothing. He knew deep down that Sasquot was right, but it was simply too difficult to admit this with the pained expression on the cub's face so fresh in his mind. In silence, they proceeded the rest of the way to Jason's home.

CHAPTER 31

That spring, Jason made a point to integrate Autumn into the school social scene and to help her make friends. He sat with Autumn at lunch, introduced her to his friends and acquaintances, and convinced her to attend school-sponsored dances and movie nights. As Autumn grew more self-confident and relaxed, she actually began to look forward to going to school each day. Jason was pleased that most of his peers were finally judging Autumn based on who she was rather than on the color of her skin or her family's cultural identity. And Jason felt that through these deeds, in some small way, he was paying Sasquot back for all he had done.

Jason also rekindled his interest in history. For the first time in his young academic career, he read unassigned history books outside of class that compelled his interest. He could not read enough books on Penobscot Indians, colonial relations with Native Americans, and Maine's storied history in the years leading up to the Civil War. The primary lessons that Jason took from these readings were the importance of respecting cultural differences and that one should be guided by kinship and charity toward one's fellow man. Jason did, however, believe that there were certain universal values, morals, and human rights that should be protected in all societies regardless of cultural differences; among these, he saw freedom, equality, and respect for human life as universally sacred values. Otherwise, Jason reasoned, the United States would have tolerated the greatest shame upon the nation, the dehumanizing system of slavery.

The more Jason read, the more fascinated he became with these historical themes. He became excited reading about the great strides which societies had made in expanding the right to participate in society as equals to women and religious, ethnic, and racial minorities. He hoped to become a historian or a history professor one day and to teach others to embrace diversity and respect other cultures, including Native American tribes.

Notwithstanding Jason's love with history, he continued to devote substantial time to running. By the time the spring season rolled around, Jason was in peak condition, having trained on the indoor track as well as having skied cross-country throughout the winter. As the co-captain of the outdoor track team, he was especially looking forward to scoring plenty of points for the team and to leading it to victory in its opening meet against Guilford.

It was not to be. Two days before the season opener, Jason rolled his ankle badly while running over a drainage grating. He was forced to rest his sprained ankle for the next ten days, icing and compressing it with bandages each day until the inflammation had subsided enough to gingerly run on it again. As a result, Jason missed the season's first three meets and lost valuable training time, despite swimming and lifting upper body weights to stay in reasonable shape during his lay-up. In the meantime, while Jason convalesced from his injury, rival Craig O'Brien dominated the season opener and spurted to an unblemished three-and-oh record in the mile.

One month later, Greenville struggled and barely qualified for the state championship meet. Less than five weeks following Jason's pre-season injury, the day of reckoning arrived: Maine's junior high outdoor track championship meet.

»«»«»«

Jason looked over Coach Sullivan's posting of race-day entries in the locker room and was crestfallen to see that he was neither entered in the mile nor the distance medley relay. Instead, he was slated for the eight-hundred-meter race, an event he knew he did not have the foot-speed to win.

Jason quickly dressed and jogged out of the locker room onto the track, searching for his coach. Looking toward the stands, he inadvertently locked eyes with Autumn, who smiled and waved from the stands, sitting alongside his father and Sasquot. His dad waved for him to come over.

Jason reluctantly strode over to his entourage, embarrassed to tell them that he would not be running the crown jewel race of the day—the mile.

"Hey, Jason, how're you holding up?" his father asked.

"Okay . . . Not good, actually. I'm not entered in the mile or the DMR. Coach probably doesn't think I'm up to it after my lay-up," Jason answered with obvious disappointment.

"You're strong as a horse. Go out there and tell him your old man wants to see you run the mile. I don't care if it's in the open or the DMR," his dad prodded.

The actual distance for either event was sixteen hundred meters, seventeen meters short of a mile. But nearly everyone on his team seemed to refer in casual track parlance to the sixteen-hundred-meter event as the famed—almost legendary—mile race.

"Yeah, I've actually been looking for Coach," Jason said, scanning the infield.

"He's over there," Sasquot said, pointing to the far end of the infield.

"All right, I'm off," Jason announced.

"Keep your spirits high regardless, Little Hawk. Remember to first focus your mind and strengthen your spirit; your body will then follow," Sasquot stated.

Jason nodded and darted from the stands, across the track, and into the infield. He tapped Coach Sullivan on the arm to get his attention. "Coach, you've got to enter me in the mile. I can take O'Brien."

Coach Sullivan looked skeptical. "You're only a few weeks off your injury, Jason."

"Almost five weeks," Jason corrected.

"I mean your recovery from it," the coach said firmly. "You were off your feet a good week-and-a-half. I'm just not sure you're up to it. But," the coach said, waving his index finger emphatically, "since this is the last meet of the year and you've trained really hard, I'm going to put you in as the DMR anchor."

Jason was elated. The anchor leg was sixteen hundred meters. Although Jason would not be going head-to-head against O'Brien in the mile, he would be running anchor against him in the premier leg of the distance medley relay.

»«»«»«

Shaking his arms and hopping up and down in place, Jason waited impatiently for the DMR handoff. Jason's teammate, Keith, sprinted down the front straightaway, completing the third leg of the relay. Jason represented the fourth and final leg.

Come on, Keith. Come on, Jason's mind urged. Craig had already received Guilford's final hand-off and was fluidly striding around the first curve, putting more distance between him and Jason every second—seconds which seemed to stretch out into an eternity.

By the time Jason felt the cool aluminum baton against his left hand, O'Brien had run half-way down the back-straightaway. Jason began to accelerate, but Keith pressed down too forcefully on the handoff. The baton slipped through Jason's hand, tumbling onto the track. As the baton tumbled end over end along the rubberized track, fortunately remaining within Greenville's lane, the moment seemed surreal. Without pausing to think, Jason reached down and grabbed the baton as it bounced along. With sweat forming on his forehead, Jason sped along the opening curve looking strong.

Craig was almost ninety meters ahead, but Jason, having beaten Craig in the previous year's cross-country championship, had the psychological edge. Willing his body to perform beyond what it had been trained to do during that injury-shortened season, Jason steadily gained on his running nemesis. Each lap Jason found himself fifteen to twenty meters closer to his target.

The crowd was beginning to get into the race, shouting, cheering, and rising to its feet as Craig rounded the final curve and strode onto the homestretch. Jason was now within five meters of his rival. Jason could hear Craig's labored breaths and see the panicked look on his face as Craig looked back over his shoulder at a person whom he had never counted on being in the race—a person who was intent on pulling out an upset, no matter how painful.

Jason could feel electricity and adrenaline flow through his system as his body received the green light for the final sprint. But his body had already been pushed to the limit and could not muster the energy to make the final pass. Coasting down the final stretch, Craig won by a comfortable margin. Jason lumbered across the finish line three-and-a-half seconds later.

Jason was crestfallen, avoiding eye contact with his teammates as he circled slowly around the infield, catching his breath. His coach had been correct in one crucial respect. Though his sixteen-hundred-meter time had ended up significantly faster than Craig's, Jason had not recovered sufficiently to summon the requisite strength for the decisive final sprint.

Then, Jason remembered what Sasquot had told him the day before his first cross-country meet in sixth grade: "Keep in mind that it is easy to be a gracious winner, Jason. It is much harder to be a gracious loser. Always congratulate the winner. You learn more from one loss than from many victories."

Jason walked over to Craig and congratulated him, just as he had after losing a heartbreaker in their initial head-to-head meet in cross-country. Craig patted Jason on the back and graciously accepted Jason's congratulations.

"Good effort, Jason. You sure kept me honest on that final straightaway. I didn't figure I'd need a sprint to win. Best of luck next fall at our first high school meet." There was genuine respect in Craig's voice.

"Thanks, Craig, looking forward to it. I guess we both push each other out there when we race." Jason felt a little bit better. He took some solace in knowing he had given the race his best shot.

Jason's dad, who had come down into the infield, walked over and put his arm over Jason's shoulder. "That was amazing, son. Your poise in picking up the baton and moving up every lap to almost catch O'Brien at the end was really something."

Jason nodded with a faint smile.

Bounding in a beeline toward them, Coach Sullivan came over from the scorer's table. "Jason!" he called out. "Jason, the DMR points moved us into third place! That's Greenville's highest finish ever at state. Way to go, sport! That took a lot of heart."

Then, and only then, did it dawn upon Jason that his performance had made a real contribution to his team. In an instant, Jason was beaming with satisfaction.

Later that afternoon, Kyle hosted a post-season barbecue celebration for the entire Greenville track team—friends and family included. With classes having ended the previous Friday, Jason's classmates were looking forward to graduating and in a festive mood.

As Jason hovered around the grill, expectantly eyeing the first set of tender steak filets, his dad asked, "So, Jason, you planning to stick around next year to give O'Brien a rematch?"

Jason looked up at his father, surprised that he had even asked him that question.

"I mean, you're not thinking of going off to Exeter, are you?" his dad asked.

"Of course not, Dad. I want to be here in Greenville for high school. I can't think of anywhere else I'd rather grow up."

"I'm really happy to hear that from you, son," he said, relieved at Jason's ready expression of appreciation for their way of life in the environs of north-central Maine. "This is God's country out here—my favorite place in the world."

After everyone had enjoyed a savory dinner of barbecued ribs, Sasquot discreetly beckoned to Jason. Intrigued, Jason followed Sasquot to a shaded area by the farm-house, out of ear-shot of everyone else.

"Jason, you are a strong and good person who learned much this year. Such a person can become an important leader," Sasquot said, removing a small box from his pocket. Looking directly at Jason, he continued, "This year, you learned how to defend what you believe in. You brought honor in sport to both family and friends. You learned to be humble and gracious to both friend and foe. You showed kindness and respect to loved ones. You honored your duty to help raise Coda and agreed to let him go free. You used courage and skill to survive great danger in the snowstorm. And with your humble spirit, you have found your faith in God. In the words of my people, 'You have learned to become a man.'"

Jason was speechless, so struck was he by Sasquot's words of praise.

"It is my honor to give you this," Sasquot said, opening a delicately carved birch-wood box depicting a fully-grown black bear sow and her cub. "This is a bear claw necklace. These bear claws come from Coda's mother. During the fall, I promised I would give them to you once you displayed great courage."

His hands trembling from the import of Sasquot's words, Jason clasped the leather-strung necklace bearing a pair of black bear claws and alternating red and green triangular beads. He understood that such a necklace connoted high rank in the Penobscot Tribe, an honor exceeding anything he felt that he deserved.

"You are truly brave and wise beyond your years, Jason. I feel like a second father to you," Sasquot stated, placing the necklace around Jason's neck. "Wear it with pride and honor for you and your family. Remember the kinship of nature and brotherhood of bear and man. I pray that it will remind you of God's great Spirit and protect you from harm as it has done for members of my family and tribe for generations." Sasquot warmly embraced Jason, as a father would a son.

"This is an unbelievable honor, Sasquot . . . I can't find enough words to thank you. I will try my best to live up to everything this necklace stands for," Jason vowed.

As Jason stroked the thick, black fur of one of the bear claws, memories of the fateful chase on that cool September night swept back into his mind. He remembered the sow's bellowing roar that sent tingles up and down his spine and his fear of death as he lay face down on the ground awaiting the final blow that never came. Intermingled with these memories, Jason felt an odd sensation of fear pass over him.

"You okay, Jason?" Sasquot asked, having witnessed Jason's face turn stone-cold with memories of that fatal confrontation and something more than Jason could explain—a sense of fear—not of the past, but of the future.

"Yeah . . . yeah, I'm all right," Jason answered, snapping back to the present.

"Enjoy this evening, my son. To celebrate with friends and family is a great joy for each of us."

»«»«»«

Jason quickly shook off his strange premonition and lightened up, mingling with his coach, teammates, and friends. Everyone was fascinated by the bear-claw necklace and the story behind it.

After allowing Paul and Scott to each feel the sharpness of the claws, Jason discussed summer plans with them. Besides returning to Camp Deerpoint, where they hoped to play new and more mischievous pranks upon their sister camp, Paul and Scott had plans to white water raft at Magic Falls on the East Branch of the Kennebec River. Located on a stretch of river between a hydroelectric dam and the Forks, Magic Falls was classified as Class IV and V whitewater and featured waves up to eight feet high cascading down from upstream dam releases.

Jason planned to work most of the summer helping his dad out with the farm and learning more about carpentry, but he would have almost all of his weekends free for such trips. The three planned additional weekend excursions to sea kayak, whale-watch for humpbacks at Bar Harbor, and fish in the Yellow Perch Derby at Big Wood Lake in Jackman. Of course, when all three of them were back in town, they would rock climb in Baxter State Park; swim, canoe, and fish in Moosehead Lake; and hike and explore the mountains to the northeast and northwest.

Ever since Sasquot had placed the bear-claw necklace over his neck, Jason had felt a sense of foreboding. Before the sun rose again, the sound of wailing would pierce the quiet of the pre-dawn hour.

CHAPTER 32

Jason awakened abruptly at his father's anguished cry. Before his dad, with trembling hands still clasping the phone, had even told him, Jason knew. Sasquot had passed away in his sleep.

Running out to the pickup, Jason and his father hurriedly climbed in and sped to the humble cabin on the lake. Jason cupped his hands around his face and sobbed quietly the whole way there, while his dad stared in numbed silence at the road ahead. Arriving at the house, they walked somberly up the front steps and knocked on the door. Zephyr came out wearing the saddest black dress Jason had ever seen. Jason and his father each embraced her. Jason cried openly.

Gradually, Jason composed himself and asked where Autumn was.

"Autumn is still in the bedroom," Zephyr said softly.

Swallowing hard and casting his eyes downward, Jason slowly followed Zephyr and his father into the bedroom. They stood before the bed. Jason forced himself to look upward. Sasquot lay on the bed, his eyelids shut, looking eerily peaceful and content. There were no signs of tension or pain upon his face.

Jason turned toward Autumn. Her head lay buried upon Sasquot's right hand, which she kept stroking and holding, as if he would somehow take notice of her and awake.

Jason knelt down by the bed and prayed. "Lord, may Sasquot never want for anything in Your kingdom. May he walk with You forever in paradise. He was such a good man, a man of faith and extraordinary heart who loved others as himself."

Jason's dad looked away from the lifeless body of his lifelong friend and abruptly walked out of the room. He sat down on the porch and wept.

It was Zephyr who, during the course of the next hour, had the strength to bring them together and prepare a meal of fellowship and unity in spirit. Sitting down silently, they shared cold roast beef and buttered bread.

"He told me," Zephyr began, shattering the silence. "He told me of his dream that he must die."

Jason gazed up into Zephyr's eyes. His mind absorbed every nuance of what she said.

Sasquot had dreamed that he was looking down from the summit of Mount Katahdin upon the land of the Penobscots. Alongside him stood his father, grandfather, and great-grandfather arrayed in the most striking tribal garments and headdresses Sasquot had ever seen. Beautifully cut broadcloth coats hung loosely from them, embroidered with intricate white beadwork, porcupine quills, royal blue paint, ribbon, and moose-hair. Beaded headbands decorated with eagle, hawk, and great blue heron feathers fastened stiffly upright sat majestically upon their heads. A pure, white luminescence caused Sasquot to cup his hands over his eyes and squint whenever he cast his eyes upon them. They did not speak but rather beckoned him to look out upon the land that stretched before them.

Clouds and sky, clothed in alternating periods of darkness and light, rushed by as Sasquot witnessed an unbroken wilderness transform before him. As he gazed down at the wilderness, vast stretches of forest became carved and broken into fire-lit Native American camps, then kerosene-lit trading posts and colonial settlements, and finally, electrically lit towns and cities. The sense of wonder and enchantment Sasquot had initially experienced gave way to one of sadness. Sun, moon, and stars streaked by him faster and faster as he witnessed the near-destruction of his people from pestilence and war. Battles over land and money were fought in generation after generation of people inhabiting the land.

Then Sasquot saw his own life play out before him: from his humble birth in a shed by Moosehead Lake to his final celebration with family and friends. He relived his father's proud presentation of a bald eagle headdress for his courage in the hunt, his father patiently teaching him how to restore health to his people without expectation of remuneration or reward, and the first time he set eyes upon lovely Zephyr bathing in the cool waters of Moosehead Lake at sunrise. He felt the nauseating pain of his blood brother's betrayal and the infuriating helplessness of watching his father weaken and die before him. He experienced the wonder of reading the words of thanks and selflessness in his father's prayer journal and felt again the yearning it gave him to seek the God of Whom his father wrote. He enjoyed the freedom that came after summoning the power to forgive his blood brother for abandoning his dying father. He heard his own calm whispering in the ear of a wild horse that Stephen would later name Untamed Heart. He felt the bond of kinship formed from hunting deer for the first time with Kyle in the woods adjoining Stephen's farm. His surged with the incredible pride and joy of helping to deliver Autumn. He suffered the hurt and anger he had felt upon Autumn telling him she had been ridiculed by her peers as an *Injun* and *casino Indian*. He experienced the pride and honor of teaching Autumn the Abenaki language and Penobscot culture. He sensed a familial bond with Kyle and Jason growing stronger every day, culminating in his commemoration of Jason's maturation into a young man with his bestowing of the bear-claw necklace. He relived the unspeakable relief of finding the son he never had and feared he would never see again. His being flowed with a wave of compassion in discovering Coda trapped helpless in the woods, then of grief when the fallen sow's spirit was released into ceremonial flames, and lastly of sadness when his bear brother learned to fear man with his paw clutched by a steel trap.

These feelings and events had poured over Sasquot's being. He had felt and experienced them as acutely as if they were occurring for the first time. Compassion, joy, sadness, grief, anger, pride, honor, forgiveness, humility, love, and courage had flowed through him powerfully as he relived the most important events and re-experienced the most poignant moments of his life.

After witnessing this, Sasquot's father had turned to Sasquot and told him that he had served as an example to their people and their neighbors and that it was now time to join his fathers and forefathers at this sacred place.

"He foresaw his own death in his dream!" Jason blurted out, disturbed by the thought.

"He was told to join them on Mount Katahdin; when, he did not know," Zephyr explained. "He said death could come at any moment, but he did not fear it. He said he will always be watching us from above."

Autumn nodded silently and slowly cleared her throat. "That is why we must bury him atop Mount Katahdin."

"Yes," Zephyr answered softly. "We must honor the sacred traditions of our family."

"I will make him the most beautiful casket I have ever created," Jason's father vowed. "And then I will carry him, with you and everyone who loved Sasquot most, to his final resting place on Mount Katahdin."

EPILOGUE

Jason slowly made his way toward the summit, gazing into a bright morning sun. The sounds and smells of spring invigorated him and made him feel pure and fresh.

It was the first anniversary of Sasquot's death and almost one year since Zephyr, Autumn, and Jason's entire family, including his mother, had carried Sasquot's casket to its majestic burial place on Mount Katahdin. Jason's father had paid tribute to Sasquot's memory by heeding the most important lesson Sasquot had taught him. He forgave the person who had wronged him most dearly in his life. Like Sasquot's blood brother, his mother had been moved by this powerful gesture, prompting her to join them in honoring Sasquot. Together, they had carried Sasquot's casket up the mountain, fulfilling his wish to lay side by side with his beloved ancestors atop a mountain still held sacred by his tribe.

Now, Jason was returning to pay his personal respects.

As Jason neared the site where Sasquot and his forefathers lay, he heard a roar that instantly arrested him.

The sound was haunting. Jason squinted in the direction of the burial grounds. A black bear stood on its hind legs, its eyes flashing and teeth gleaming in sunlight.

Though a couple hundred feet away, Jason cowered to his knees in fear.

The bear looked at Jason and suddenly quieted.

"Coda?" Jason looked into the bear's soft, liquid brown eyes. He saw a tiny cub lumbering through the woods with a boy.

"Coda!" he cried out.

But the bear had disappeared. Jason cupped his hands over his eyes, straining for any sign of the bear. Overpowered by sunlight, he shielded his eyes and ascended in a surge of adrenaline.

Arriving at the burial ground, he scanned the site. There was no trace of Coda or of any other bear. That is, until Jason looked down upon Sasquot's grave.

Imprinted into the ground atop his grave was the claw mark of a bear.

ACKNOWLEDGMENTS

The overall inspiration for *The Year of the Bear* came from my twin sons, Alex and Gregory, even before they knew it or became part of this universe. I wrote it thinking that it would be a novel that each of them would cherish. Thus, it was an especially memorable and rewarding moment when they became old enough to read it for themselves. As soon as they finished reading *The Year of the Bear* with paired enthusiasm, they told me how much they had enjoyed it and strongly encouraged me to publish it. I needed no further inspiration to make *The Year of the Bear* a reality.

The spark for *The Year of the Bear* was kindled by a love of nature and fascination with New England's wilderness, culture, and history instilled in me by numerous influences from my Connecticut upbringing. These include my parents and siblings—my mother, Jean; my late father, Jim; my younger sister, Shane; and my younger brother, Chad Lanzo—as well as close friends, including Larry Small, Andrew Sawyer, Erik Soderberg, and Jason Healy, classmates, and cross-country teammates and coaches with whom I explored and traversed our local parks, trails, and historic sites. Notable childhood mentors included inspirational church and youth group leaders, such as Pastor Stanley Allaby; Mr. Moody; and Erik's father, who helped lead Boy's Brigade hiking trips; as well as third grade teacher, Maureen Bortolot, and fourth grade teacher, Phillip Desser, who further instilled a love of history, nature, reading, and writing within me. Mr. Desser also produced our fourth-grade rendition of *Oliver Twist* in which I "co-starred" as Oliver on alternate evenings alongside childhood friend, Daniel Rosman.

I am especially grateful to the hospitable people of Bangor, Acadia National Park, Ogunquit Beach, and Moosehead Lake, who introduced me to breathtaking landscapes and species, including prodigious, fully-antlered bull moose grazing contentedly before a conflagration of autumn red and gold. Witnessing the spectacular peak of Mount Katahdin overlooking the placid waters of Moosehead Lake was an equally awesome experience, which is shared with readers through the eyes of Jason, Autumn, Kyle, and Sasquot in *The Year of the Bear.*

I am enormously grateful for the thoughtful and friendly assistance of Dr. Samuel Lowry, the founder, CEO, and president of Ambassador International, and his talented team, including COO and Digital Producer, Anna Riebe Raats; Marketing Specialist and Editor, Daphne Self; Senior Editor, Katie Cruice Smith; Publicity Director, Susanna R. Maurer; In-house Designer, Christopher Jackson; Office Manager, Bethany McDaris; and *The Year of the Bear* Cover Designer Hannah Linder for each of their invaluable contributions in the publishing, editing, design, marketing, distribution, and production of *The Year of the Bear.*

Furthermore, I would like to thank the numerous publishers and editors in the poetry community who have graciously announced the publication of *The Year of the Bear,* including *WestWard Quarterly: The Magazine of Family Reading* and its publisher, Dr. Richard Leonard, and Editor Shirley Anne Leonard; *Poetry Pea* and its founder and editor, Patricia McGuire; *The Penwood Review* and its editor, Lori Cameron; and *Time of Singing: A Journal of Christian Poetry* and its editor, Lora Homan Zill. I would also like to thank haiku poetry mentor, Scott Mason, and editors who have offered to review *The Year of the Bear* from nearby or afar, including Australia's Paul Grover, longtime editor of *Studio, a Journal of Christians Writing.*

Though too voluminous to thank individually, besides my wife, Marianna the other family members already mentioned and the encouraging members of my poetry reading group, I would like to especially thank my cousin, Sue Fazzini, a nun whose ministries to improve the lives of prisoners and the downtrodden have inspired and enriched my writing; my highly successful but unassuming Christian friend, Darwin Olympia; my insightful college roommate and friend, Al DiVenuti; my neighbors, Brenda and Tom Corbin, whose gracious astronomy lessons inspired my poem, "The Astronomer Next Door," published in *WestWard Quarterly;* and my beloved friend, Greg Pacific, Sr., a man of great compassion, dignity, and respect for others, whom I am privileged to have known as a quasi-godfather for so many years.

To God I give the most thanks for His bountiful blessings upon this novel, my upcoming novella, and the hundreds of poems I have had the privilege to publish during this pandemic. His inspiration has been the defining factor in these literary works, providing me the voice with which to engage and uplift readers across the globe.

RESOURCES

"Acadia." National Park Service online. Accessed February 13, 2022. https://www.nps.gov/acad/learn/historyculture/wabanaki.htm.

"American Indian History is the Most Searched Topic." Indians.org. Accessed January 12, 2022. http://indians.org.

Appalachian Mountain Club online. Accessed January 13, 2022. https://www.outdoors.org.

"Fish & Wildlife." New Jersey Department of Environmental Protection. Accessed April 15, 2022. https://www.njfishandwildlife.com.

"Home." Bear Smart Durango online. Accessed March 27, 2022. http://bearsmartdurango.org.

"Home." Get Bear Smart Society online. Accessed April 27, 2022. http://www.bearsmart.com.

"Katahdin." The Maine Highlands. Accessed February 27, 2022. https://themainehighlands.com/story/mount-katahdin.

"North American Bear Center, The. American Bear Center online. Accessed May 5, 2022. https://bear.org.

"Pleasant Point Tribal Government." Passamaquoddy at Sipayik. Accessed April 20, 2022. http://www.wabanaki.com.

"The Trek." The Trek online. Accessed March 12, 2002. https://thetrek.co.

Brittanica. S.v. "Penobscot." Accessed March 13, 2022. https://www.britannica.com/topic/Penobscot-people.

Gannett, Henry (1905). *The Origin of Certain Place Names in the United States*. Government. Print. Off. 1905.

Hoag, Ronald Wesley. "The Mark on the Wilderness: Thoreau's Contact with Ktaadn." *Texas Studies in Literature and Language.*, Vol. 24, No. 1, 1982.

Morris, Edmund. *The Rise of Theodore Roosevelt.* New York: Coward, McCann & Geoghegan, 1979.

New World Encyclopedia. S.v. "Penobscot." Accessed May 2, 2022. https://www.newworldencyclopedia.org/entry/Penobscot.

Whitaker, Jr., John O. (1997). *National Audubon Field Guide to North American Mammals.*, New York: Alfred A. Knopf, Inc., p. 703.

Wildlife Informer. "Black Bear Population By State (Recent Reports). Wildlife Informer online. Accessed March 12, 2022. https://wildlifeinformer.com.

ABOUT THE AUTHOR

Douglas J. Lanzo is an award-winning and featured poet and novelist published in over fifty literary publications in the U.S., Canada, England, Wales, Austria, Mauritius, India, Japan, Australia, and the Caribbean. These include over 250 poems published in forty-six literary journals and five poetry anthologies, among them Vita Brevis Press' best-selling *Brought to Sight & Swept Away* and *Nothing Divine Dies* anthologies. *The Year of the Bear* represents his debut novel, which will be followed by his romance suspense novella, *I Have Lived,* scheduled for release by Ambassador International in 2023. Douglas resides in Chevy Chase, Maryland, with his wife and thirteen-year-old identical twin sons and fellow internationally published poets, enjoying nature, tennis, traveling, biking, fishing, and chess. Douglas' author website, featuring hundreds of poems that he and his twin sons have published internationally, is available free of charge at www.douglaslanzo.com, together with pre-order signup for his upcoming novella, links to his Instagram account and resources for active and aspiring writers.

For more information about
Douglas J. Lanzo
and
The Year of the Bear
please visit:

www.douglaslanzo.com

Ambassador International's mission is to magnify the Lord Jesus Christ and promote His Gospel through the written word.

We believe through the publication of Christian literature, Jesus Christ and His Word will be exalted, believers will be strengthened in their walk with Him, and the lost will be directed to Jesus Christ as the only way of salvation.

For more information about
AMBASSADOR INTERNATIONAL
please visit:

www.ambassador-international.com

Thank you for reading, and please consider leaving us a review on Amazon, Goodreads, or our websites.

More from Ambassador International

Willow Rysen has been Miss Popular ever since starting high school. But when she is forced to partner with a nerd, Christian Blythe, for a science project that debates the Bible versus science, her world is turned upside down. Will she find that the grace of God can overcome her past failures or will she allow the lure of the world's ideologies to keep her tight in its grasp?

Fred Thorne must shoulder the full care and protection of his sisters after a fire leaves them homeless and friendless. He sets out to follow the last advice given to him by his great-aunt: Take the girls to Menevace, to the refuge home. But the road to Menevace is fraught with bandits, famine, and unknown dangers. Can the Thornes find a place of rest and safety? Will their journey ever end?

Abandoned as infants, Tovi and her twin brother were raised by an eclectic tribe of warm, kind people in a treehouse village in the valley. After her brother's sudden disappearance Tovi questions her life and her faith in an invisible King. Ignoring her best friend Silas' advice, she decides to search for her brother in the kingdom on top of the mountain. Amidst the glamour of the kingdom above the cloud Tovi is torn between her own dark desires and unanswered questions.

CPSIA information can be obtained
at www.ICGtesting.com
Printed in the USA
HW081504011122
098LV00026B/269